DANGEROUS WEB #2

DARK

Aleatha Romig

New York Times, Wall Street Journal, and USA Today
bestselling author of the Consequences, Infidelity, Web of Sin,
Tangled Web, and Web of Desire series

COPYRIGHT AND LICENSE INFORMATION

persons, living or dead, events, or locales is entirely
coincidental.

DARK – BOOK #2 DANGEROUS WEB

"Maybe you have to know the darkness before you can appreciate the light." ~ **Madeleine L'Engle**

Darkness has fallen upon the Sparrow world.

What seemed secure was breached, and what was assumed unattainable is possible.

In this dangerous underground world, we Sparrows took our power by force. As dusk gave way to dark, we Sparrows are once again determined to use any means necessary to recover what is ours, secure our stronghold, and defeat those who appear unconquerable.

The gauntlet has been thrown.

We will not retreat.

Darkness be damned. It is time for triumph.

I am Reid Murray.

For my wife and my brothers-in-arms, nothing, not even darkness, will stop the Sparrows from victory.

From New York Times bestselling author Aleatha Romig comes a brand-new dark romantic suspense trilogy, Dangerous Web. DARK, book #2, is set in the dangerous world of the Sparrow Webs. You do not need to read Web of Sin, Tangled Web, or Web of Desire to get caught up in this dangerous and intriguing new romantic suspense saga, Dangerous Web.

DARK is book two of the *DANGEROUS WEB* trilogy that began in *DUSK* and concludes in *DAWN*.

Have you been Aleatha'd?

NOTE FROM ALEATHA

Thank you for reading the Sparrow Webs. You're about to read DARK, book #2 of the final trilogy, *Dangerous Web*.

If this is your first trilogy of the Sparrow Webs, please know that there are other amazing stories in this same world ready for you to binge today.

Web of Sin
(Sterling and Araneae's story)

SECRETS (Free everywhere)

LIES
PROMISES

Tangled Web
(*Kader/Mason and Laurel's story*)

TWISTED
OBSESSED
BOUND

and

Web of Desire: (Patrick and Madeline's story)

SPARK
FLAME
ASHES

For a complete list of my books, please go to "Books by Aleatha" following DARK. Thank you again for falling in love with the Sparrow Web world. Enjoy.

~Aleatha

DANGEROUS WEB #2

DARK

Aleatha Romig

Dark
Book #2 of the DANGEROUS WEB trilogy in
SPARROW WEBS

PROLOGUE

Lorna

The conclusion of DUSK, book #1 Dangerous Web

*L*ater that night as I settled into bed next to my husband, I turned to Reid. "I wish you knew more about what happened to us."

His deep voice overpowered the distant ringing within my ears. "Has anything come back? Do you remember anything else?"

I shook my head. "It feels like the information is close, yet I can't find it." I let out a long sigh. "You know, it's like when you lose something, yet you're sure it's right there."

Reid gently encouraged me to lay my head on his broad shoulder as he wrapped his arms around me. "I have you back." He kissed my hair.

While he was gentle, I winced at the pressure on my tender scalp.

"Sweetheart, I'm sorry."

"No, don't be." I turned my gaze to his and as my eyes adjusted to the dimness, I took in his handsome features—his loving gaze, the flawlessness of his mahogany complexion, his high cheekbones, and his strong chin. I ran my finger over his lush lips, imagining them on mine or other more sensitive places. As my insides twisted, I said, "I'll take your affection, no matter how much it hurts."

Reid's brows knitted together. "I never want you to hurt, not from me or anyone else. Whoever did this to you will pay. I promise, you're safe and they'll never hurt you again."

Sighing, I settled into the crook of his strong arm. "I don't care if they pay. I would like to know they can't do this to anyone else."

"I love you, Lorna. I didn't need to lose you to know that."

A smile crept across my face as I hugged his arm. "I love you too. I feel" —I searched for words— "...safe, secure, loved..." When our gazes met, I confessed, "When we're together, I feel like I'm somebody."

"You, Lorna Murray, are definitely somebody."

I ran my fingers over his forearm, feeling the warmth of his dark skin under my fingertips and relishing in our familiar differences. The sounds of our breathing filled our bedroom. His breaths became spaced and rhythmic, alerting me to the fact that he'd fallen asleep. Knowing my husband, I doubted that he slept much when I was gone.

Savoring the security of his embrace as well as the fresh

scent of his recently showered skin, I cuddled toward his side and listened to the beat of his heart, reminding myself of my safety as I drifted into a fretful sleep.

All at once, I woke with a start.

"What is it?" Reid asked, leaning over me.

With his close proximity, the white orbs surrounding his dark eyes were all I could see in our lightless bedroom. Before I could respond, gently and reassuringly, his lush firm lips came to mine.

"Sweetheart, you're fine. You're here."

A moan came from my throat as I pushed closer, returning his kiss.

His large hands roamed down my lower back and over my behind.

Heat flooded my twisting core as I reached for his cheeks, holding his lips to mine as my tongue sought entrance, ready to dance with his.

My desire waned as a wince replaced my moan when his weight came over my ribs and bruised hip bones. My pulse quickened and breathing stalled as perspiration dotted my forehead.

Before I could analyze what had happened, Reid pulled away.

His stare penetrated mine. "No, Lorna, I won't hurt you."

"You aren't," I said, not being fully truthful. "You're loving me."

Holding his toned and hard torso above me, Reid teased a strand of my hair away from my face as he scanned my bruises. "I do and will forever love you. You are still the most beautiful woman in this world. I fucking want to show you that by bringing the head of whoever did this to your feet."

My lips curled upward. "I don't want anyone but you."

"Then I want to show you by making love all night long...but not until you're ready."

"I'm ready. I just need to be on top."

His head shook as a small grin graced his lips. "Sweetheart, I want you on top, under me, with me. Please, for now, humor me. Let me just hold you in my arms and you can tell me what caused you to wake."

I knew he was right, yet I yearned to be with him, connected in a way only we can be.

With a sigh, I settled back onto his shoulder and thought about what had awakened me. "I-I had a dream or nightmare." My body shivered. "It seemed real."

He gently rolled until his front was to my back as he held me safe in his embrace. "You're here and safe."

"It's so weird. It's like I have dreams or memories and I don't know which."

"Tell me."

"It'll sound crazy," I admitted.

"Your crazy hasn't scared me away yet. I don't think it will now"

"It's probably nothing. I was talking with Araneae today, and for some reason the subject of my mother came up."

Reid sat up, turning me back toward him. "Your mother?"

"Yeah, I know it's stupid. I mean, I haven't seen or heard from her—"

"What about your mother?"

"I was just telling Araneae why I'm hesitant to take pain pills."

"In your dream?"

"No. In the dream, my mom is...well, she was with me." My nose scrunched. "She's old, older than her years. Very thin. I guess sex and drugs weren't the best plan for a healthy life."

Reid was staring at me. "Tell me more. Did she talk to you?"

"Reid, it wasn't real. It's all the drugs they gave me, playing tricks on me. Laurel said it could happen. I'll talk more to her about it tomorrow." I scoffed. "You know, I never realized how convenient it was to have a live-in shrink."

"She's not exactly..." He kissed my forehead. "Okay, but if something comes to you."

I stared up at our ceiling, wondering how totally crazy it would sound to say the words aloud. I rolled toward my husband. "Do you promise not to laugh?"

"Laugh, no. Smile, maybe."

"Don't tell Mason. He'll think I'm certifiable. And besides, the subject always upsets him."

"Of your mother?" Reid asked.

"Well, yes, but mostly of Missy."

"Your sister? What about Missy?"

"In my dream, my mother was talking, barely. Her voice was odd, like an old woman who had smoked too many cigarettes, and her laugh sounded closer to that of a witch. She was...I think she was dying." I took a deep breath and tried to push the dream's images away, those of the nearly skeletal woman with faded red hair that could be mine in time. "Anyway, in my dream, she spoke and said it was important for me to know that they forced her to tell."

"Who forced her? To tell what?" Reid asked.

I shrugged. "I don't know. She said *they* know so I needed to know."

Reid reached for my hand. "You're shaking."

"I-I..." I squeezed his hand and cuddled toward his warmth. "It's so strange. The whole thing felt real, but I know it wasn't."

"What did she want you to know?"

"First, she apologized for all the mistakes she'd made." I leaned away, still holding his hand and caught Reid's gaze. "See, like Laurel said, my mind is on some crazy-ass drugs. The only thing Nancy Pierce was ever sorry about was having three kids to take care of."

"Is that what she wanted you to know?"

"Not really." I lay back, pulling our linked hands over me. "Here's the really crazy part: she said she'd lied."

"About?"

"If it were real, the list would be long. In my dream, she said Missy was never kidnapped."

My husband's body tensed beside me. "What?"

I nodded. "Yes, I told you...crazy."

"What happened to your sister if she wasn't kidnapped?" His voice deepened as he lifted his head to see me better. "Oh God, she didn't...your mother didn't...hurt her, did she?"

"No. She said he offered her money so she agreed to sell her."

"What the fuck? Your mother sold your sister?"

"In my dream," I reminded him. "And here's the kicker. It wasn't, like, to a sicko as we'd feared. My mom said she sold Missy to her biological father."

Reid's eyes opened wide.

I laid my head back on the pillow. "I told you, it's nuts. Even Nancy wasn't that big of a bitch to sell her own daughter." I let out a long sigh and rolled toward my husband. "Thank you for listening. I feel better just saying it. Now, I hear how absurd it is. I mean, if that were true, that would mean that Mace's and my sister wasn't taken into the Sparrow or McFadden sex rings. She grew up with her biological father." I shrugged. "Hell, Mace and I don't know the identity of the men who donated sperm to make us much less the one who contributed to her DNA." After a yawn, I scoffed and kissed Reid's cheek. "Good night. I'm going to try to sleep."

As slumber began to overtake me, I heard Reid mutter, "Well, fuck."

REID

Three days before the end of Dusk

My surroundings disappeared.

The remote landscape, drenching rain, or lightning and thunder no longer registered as I stared at the inconceivable sight of my unconscious wife lying upon the back seat of Mason's truck. I reached for the edge of the open door, my grip intensifying and stomach rolling as I took her in, really looked at her. Lorna Murray was the strongest and most beautiful woman I had ever encountered, and yet in this moment, as my circulation slowed and my skin cooled from the sight before me, I felt an overwhelming sense of failure. I'd failed to keep her safe. I'd failed to keep her from harm.

I found solace in her survival, yet where would she go from here? How could she move past this horrible injustice?

Lorna's pulse was faint and slow. Her beautiful alabaster skin marred by evidence of the last few days—the trauma she'd endured and the misery she'd suffered.

With each passing second, every thought, even those of failure, was obscured by a darkness like I'd never known. It clouded my being and infiltrated my flesh. It seeped into my bloodstream and saturated my hardening heart.

This emotion wasn't directed toward Lorna, never to her.

The dark that flooded my mind brought on thoughts I'd never before entertained.

While I'd known disappointment, grieved the loss of loved ones, and battled personal demons, I'd avoided one pure emotion for most of my life.

Until this moment, I'd never known hatred.

Pure, unadulterated loathing.

It slithered through my circulation like a snake, leaving behind drops of its venom in every cell. As I stood under the drenching rain, I felt its presence taking hold, setting roots, and growing ounce by ounce. All-consuming, the hatred fueled a potential for devastation without measure.

My boots splashed in the mud as I fought for literal footing. My muscles spasmed with the desire to hold and comfort Lorna, while at the same time harboring the need to lash out at a world that would allow this to occur.

I'd heard that love is light. Knowing the life Lorna and I had made, I agreed.

In contrast, hate was without light.

It was dark.

And while hate and loathing were new to me, I recognized them without question. This moment in time would mark the instant when, like the sky above, my light became obscured by dark. There would be before and after—everything affected by this point in time.

I recalled instances when I should have known this emotion, yet I hadn't.

As a soldier in war, I'd walked with my platoon into scattered villages, knowing that danger lurked in the most innocent of places. A child's backpack filled with explosives had the potential to take out an entire block. An old woman in a doorframe could be the enticement to death, or worse, captivity and torture. Yet I didn't hate our enemy. I'd understood that the differences between us and them weren't personal. It was war, two opposing sanctions with a long history that time had brought to a head.

As a black man growing up in Chicago, I'd learned at a young age that life wasn't the same for everyone. It didn't matter that some may see a level playing field. It didn't exist.

I'd been born into what many would consider a good upper-middle-class neighborhood. My father was an attorney, given his chance by the US Army. He'd joined the service young and scored exceptionally high on their multitude of tests. Physically and intellectually blessed, the military saw his asset in academic endeavors.

He was encouraged to enter the JAG Corps—the Judge Advocate General's Corps, a branch of the military concerned with military justice. While spending three years in a civilian law school—he was accepted at Loyola, University of Chicago —he met my mother. After graduation, his service was to the military.

When his obligation to the military was complete, they married. Two years later I was born. In hindsight, I realized my father was older than many other dads, yet I was too young then to notice.

Three years later, my father, as a retired lieutenant colonel, volunteered for deployment, taking on a new commission and deployment to the Gulf War buildup, code-named Operation Desert Shield. History would say the war was short—five months. If you asked my mother, it was a lifetime—my father's.

He was one of the less than three hundred US servicemen and -women who didn't return.

While I experienced growing up without a father, I never hated the military. On the contrary, joining the service was my testament to him.

Eventually, my mother, grandmother, and I moved from the neighborhood where I was born to a comfortable, albeit less affluent one. My mother refused to let our circumstances bring us down. Her hard work and dedication along with my grandmother's oversight made me the man I am today. Our life wasn't without challenge, but I was mostly unaware of it. Without a doubt, I never went without when it came to love and support.

I was keenly aware that no matter what I did, I lived with a set of rules not applicable to everyone. Judgment based on the color of my skin was outside my ability to control.

That knowledge made me conscious and weary of the consequences. Sometimes, I admit to being angered, yet through it all, I didn't hate. As my grandmother taught me, hate was a senseless emotion to waste on people who didn't deserve my energy. She and my mother taught me to focus on what I could accomplish, to see and be the light.

Tonight, with the rain falling down, quickly accumulating beneath our boots and creating rivers over what had been hardened packed dirt, the light was gone.

Darkness won.

I now knew hate—to my core.

As Laurel removed objects from her first-aid kit and injected something into Lorna's arm, my heart hardened. As my finger skirted over my wife's bruised and battered face, the organ that had recently beat in my chest metaphorically stilled. As I scanned her body, covered in more contusions and lacerations, my once-functioning heart cracked, its shards shattering as I asked my sister-in-law the question I wasn't certain I could handle being answered.

My eyelids blinked away the rain and my nostrils flared as I worked to keep my rage from the woman tending my wife. "Was she...?" I forced the words. "Was she sexually assaulted?"

Laurel's blue eyes met mine. "Reid, I can't answer that without a rape kit." Lorna's shirt was now raised as Laurel applied an antibiotic lotion to the multitude of bites. We both turned our attention to the panties Lorna was still wearing.

"Do you want to see if she's injured?" she asked.

Exteriorly, there was no blood on the material.

I shook my head. "Fucking...I can't."

"Do you want me to?"

Inhaling, I nodded and turned away toward the blowing storm. The precipitation pelted my face and skin as punishment for my failure to protect the woman I loved.

My gaze went out to the vast landscape. I couldn't continue to watch Laurel as she cared for Lorna. It wasn't that I hadn't seen my wife naked a million times. It was that if I turned and saw visible signs—any sign at all—that not only had my wife been battered almost beyond recognition but also raped, I knew that I would never escape the dark. I would be captive in it forever.

It wasn't that I'd love Lorna any less if Laurel's answer was affirmative. That never even occurred to me. It was that the red currently shading my vision in waves of crimson would be nothing compared to the blood I'd spill for her.

Laurel's hand came to my arm. "You may turn back."

When I did, Lorna appeared as she had seconds earlier, except that now her shirt was again over her breasts and torso. I didn't speak but instead turned to Laurel. I swallowed as emotions mixed with rain blurred my vision.

"I can't be one hundred percent certain without a kit," she said, "but while Lorna has bruising on her hips, I don't see obvious trauma in her perineum."

I gulped large breaths as if I'd just breached the surface of the water after descending into a deep underwater dive. "I-I would still love her."

Laurel nodded. "I know that. You're a good man."

Would she believe that if she knew my thoughts of revenge?

"Lorna's going to need that," Laurel went on. "She and Araneae both. I hope and pray that with all they'll face and deal with going forward, rape isn't one of them." Her lips curled upward into a grin that forgot to tell her eyes she was smiling. "No matter what they face, they won't do it alone. From the first time I met Lorna, when we were kids, I knew she possessed the strength to survive whatever life threw her way. She already has overcome so much. She isn't alone. You'll help. We all will."

I swallowed, trying to push away too many emotions.

How could a cold heart also have feelings?

"She's alive," I said as a reassurance to myself. "That's what matters."

"Yes, and she's going to stay that way. After I get her comfortable, we need to get her back to the ranch. I have some medications back there, and I know Seth also does. There's a regular mini-hospital setup by the bunkhouse. You wouldn't believe the injuries that can happen on a ranch— from broken bones to snake bites. We'll get Lorna on an IV with what she needs and call the doctor back."

I nodded.

Laurel turned to me. "We can also have the rape kit done if you want."

My thoughts were all over the place.

I wanted to know for certain, and at the same time, I didn't want to know.

The one thought that prevailed was untainted hatred for whoever did this to my wife.

I couldn't answer Laurel's question—if you *want*.

Was it a matter of want?

The moment the kidnappers took Lorna, their death sentence was sealed. Due to the additional evidence of her injuries, creative techniques of painful torture would precede their death, one that would eventually be their relief.

I watched for a moment as Laurel continued her work. When she looked up at me with her hair and clothes now as drenched as mine, I asked, "If it were you..." I tilted my chin toward the back seat of the truck. "If you were there, the one injured, would you want the kit done? Would you want to know?"

As rain dripped from her long hair, Laurel's lips formed a straight line and her blue eyes blinked against the rain. "I can't make that decision for you or Lorna. We could wait until she wakes, but by then there's a chance it would be too late."

"I'm not asking you to decide for Lorna. I'm asking what you would want. Would you want to know?"

She took a deep breath, the fabric of her dress pulling the wet fibers tight. "Even knowing what I know about the invasiveness of the kit, *I* would want to know."

"When we get back," I said, making my decision, "ask the doctor to do it but not to give me or you the results. I want them sealed, and when Lorna is better, if she, like Araneae, doesn't remember and wants to know, we'll have her answer."

Laurel nodded.

"The result will not fucking make a difference in how I feel about her. I don't want her to ever question that. But if she wonders, she should be able to get the answer."

"We can do that," Laurel said. "When do you think she'll be ready for that answer?"

I looked again at the beautiful, battered woman I loved more than life itself. "I don't know. Will she be like Araneae and not remember, or will she wake with all the horrible memories of how she ended up like this?"

"I guess," Laurel said, "we won't know until she wakes. We'll all take this a day at a time."

I watched Laurel gather more items from her kit. "Will it be much longer before we can head back to the ranch?"

"Not too much longer." Laurel looked past me to the capos' car. "What's happening with Mason?"

I turned, knowing immediately what Laurel meant. Tension rippled off of him as he stood with his arms crossed over his chest, his neck stiff, staring into the back seat. It was then that I remembered the other woman found with Lorna.

"Maybe it's about the other woman," I said.

Trudging through the mud, I stepped closer to my friend. "Is she..." I bent down and looked at the other woman. Placing my fingers on her cold neck, I did as I had done in search of Lorna's pulse.

This time there was none.

Not only was this woman dead, but with her emaciated appearance, it seemed as if she were a skeleton who death had finally claimed.

"Fucking dead," Mason replied.

The dome light in the car illuminated the woman's gaunt features; indented dark circles caused her eyes to appear sunken and her thin skin looked translucent. It took me a moment to see beyond her obvious gaunt exterior to the woman as a whole. I turned to Mason. "Why does she look familiar?"

"Because she looks like Lorna." His gaze met mine. "She's our mother."

REID

"Your mother?" I repeated. Turning back to the woman, I again scanned her withered form. "Nancy Pierce?" Of course I knew the name of my wife's mother. "That's her? Are you sure?"

With a grunt and a huff, Mason walked away from the capos and the car, toward the night.

I followed a step behind, finally reaching for his shoulder. Rain squished from the fabric of his shirt as I gripped, stopping and turning him back. "Where are you going?"

His green gaze shot through the veil of rain. "I can't look at her anymore."

"Listen, I don't have a fucking idea what to do with the bombshell that she could be the long-lost Nancy Pierce, but right now, I don't give a fuck. You need to get your shit together. Lorna needs to get back to the ranch and get some real medicine and care."

Mason inhaled and nodded. "You're right." His jaw, covered in a few days of scruff, clenched as his eyes searched through the rain toward the car. "We're leaving Nancy to rot."

"What?"

"We'll fucking leave her out here where they found her. You saw her. Hell..." He looked down at the accumulating water. "The rain will carry her away, and wildlife will take care of the rest."

"Wait? You want to leave her? That's your mother."

"She's the woman who gave birth to me, but that doesn't make her a mother. What is a fucking mother?" He pointed toward the car, his volume raising. "That woman was a selfish cunt who never gave two shits about Lorna, Miss..." He took a breath. "About any of us."

"I get that, man. I do. I've listened to Lorna over the years. I know the woman wasn't exactly mother of the year."

"More like *Mommie Dearest*."

I took a few steps to collect my kaleidoscope of thoughts. "How did she get here?" When Mason didn't answer, I went on, "How did she end up with Lorna? Did the kidnappers have her? The Order?" I added.

Mason's voice rose above the increased rumbling of thunder. "I don't fucking care."

"Right now, I believe you. Lorna has been found. My wife and your sister is alive. That's all that matters."

He lifted his chin. "I'll have Christian take her...no, I'll do it."

As Mason started to walk back toward the cars, I seized his arm. In the millisecond that my grip touched his wet forearm, my brother-in-law froze. His green stare sent daggers my direction as he looked between my grasp and my eyes.

Inhaling and shaking the rain from my face, I released him.

While Mason had come a long way with showing his tattoo-covered scars, he drew the line at sight. Touching any of his uncovered skin was reserved solely for one woman. She was currently tending to my wife. I lifted my hands. "Sorry." Before Mason could begin walking again, I spoke, "What if it's not her?"

"It's been almost twenty years, but I'm not mistaken." He looked up into the falling rain and back. "You know how little kids are supposed to find solace in their mom's face? Look in her eyes for comfort and all that shit? Well, to me, seeing her was the opposite. Seeing her meant the beginning of a nightmare, because when she showed up, it was rarely alone. I know in my bones that woman is Nancy Pierce."

"Or...she could be someone who was chosen for her similarities to make you think it's her," I offered. "The Order has replaced bodies before." It was Mason's body they'd replaced with a burnt corpse, but that was old news.

Mason exhaled as his teeth clenched.

"Just hear me out," I said above the increased howling of the wind and the pelting rain. "If this is the Order we're dealing with, couldn't it be possible that they're fucking with you?"

Lightning zigzagged through the sky as seconds later thunder crashed in a rolling long rumble. The lightning and thunder were getting closer together, meaning the strikes were getting closer.

Mason pointed toward his truck. "I don't want to tell *her* that Nancy showed up dead."

"Lorna or Laurel?"

"Lorna," he answered. "I saw Lorna before I laid the blanket on her. The last thing my sister needs is to deal with more shit than she's already been given. What is the sense in telling her a ghost showed up dead?"

My neck straightened as the sky again filled with light. "The choice to tell Lorna about anything isn't yours. Stop treating her like she's eleven."

"I'm not."

I could go down the *I'm her husband* road, but another thought occurred to me. "If it is the Order, what do you believe they expect you to do with the body?"

Mason paused, wiping the rain from his forehead, smoothing back his shoulder-length hair, and shaking the moisture from his palm. "There's no going back in the Order. It's not like when we served. The Order is black and white, succeed or fail. There's no gray, no in between. If you go down on a mission, you're dead. It doesn't matter because you were already."

"So, they expect you to leave her?"

"I'm not fucking programmed by—"

"The capos are taking the body back to the ranch," I interrupted. "I know I'm not thinking straight, but any damn clue to get me to whomever hurt Lorna is one clue I refuse to leave to raging rivers or wildlife. And the last fucking thing we need is to have a body found on your property, prompting Montana authorities to start asking questions."

"The chances she's ever found—"

"Are zero if we take her. If we leave her, the authorities could get an anonymous call."

Mason's neck and shoulders tightened.

"We're taking her," I repeated, "Once we get her back to the ranch, I'll run her DNA. First, we'll verify her identity. No matter who she is, this will give Laurel and me a chance to examine her, figure out her COD, and see if she holds any clues to who had Lorna.

"I sound like a prick, but let's use that corpse to get whatever information we can. Then, if she is your mother and you still want to feed her to the horses, I don't care, but," I added, "no decision is final until Lorna gets a say."

Mason shook his head. "Pigs eat bodies, not horses."

I didn't respond.

"I can agree to that under one condition." He waited for a response, but I remained silent. "I'm not treating Lorna like a kid," he said, "but someone fucked her up. You agree that we don't tell Lorna until she can handle it.

"Fuck, we can keep Nancy on ice. I don't give a shit. But with my sister, we don't know how she'll even wake or what she'll remember."

"Ice." I looked at him side-eyed. "We agree there will be no disposing of the body until Lorna is involved. She's an adult. If that's Nancy Pierce, Lorna was her child too. My wife deserves as much of a say as you."

Lightning again streaked across the sky as simultaneously, thunder shook the ground.

"Mason. Reid," Laurel yelled from the truck. "I'm done. We need to go."

"Deal?" I asked.

"Yeah," Mason conceded. He laid his hand on my shoulder, slapping the drenched material. "You were over there with Laurel. How is Lorna?"

"Alive. That's all that matters. Unconscious and injured. Laurel is going to call for the doctor once we have cell service again. She said Seth has a mini-clinic back at the ranch."

"Yeah, it's a nice setup."

We began walking toward the car and truck.

Christian and Romero were still standing in the rain.

"You can put her in the trunk or leave her in the back seat," Mason said to the capos. "Take her to the main house. We need to do an ID."

"I thought you said—" Romero began before wisely deciding to stop his verbal thought. "Yes, Mr. Pierce."

Christian stepped closer. "If you're serious about the options, a two-hour trip would be better if she were in the trunk. I have blankets and plastic back there."

For just such an occasion, I thought.

Good capos were always prepared.

It was kind of like the Boy Scout motto for killers.

"I honestly," Mason began, looking again into the back seat, "don't give a shit if you drag her with tow chains. Just get her back there. We need to get Mrs. Murray back for medical treatment ASAP."

"We'll meet you there after we do a little wrapping," Romero said.

"No dragging," I said to both men as Mason walked away, hoping they recognized Mason's poor attempt at sarcasm or dark humor.

The capos nodded.

As we approached the truck, Mason asked, "Are you...good?"

"Fuck no. But my wife is alive. For that, I'm thankful and ready to pay a debt."

"A debt?"

"Every second she was missing, I offered to trade my soul for that news."

"No, man, I know what it's like to lose your humanity—"

My steps stopped. "I know what Sparrow said. We're getting Lorna whatever help and attention she needs. We'll get her back to Chicago, and then..."

"We will kill the sons of bitches that took her and Araneae," Mason finished. "We can do that without giving in to the dark. I'm telling you it's a shitty place. Once you give in, it's fucking hard to come back. Take it from me."

My head shook. "Spare me the details. I have a wife to avenge, with or without you."

"You couldn't get rid of me if you tried."

When we reached the truck, Laurel was in the front seat and Lorna was wrapped in the blanket, lying across the back seat. Near her head was a second smaller blanket. "Is it okay if I move her?" I asked.

"Yes," Laurel replied, peering over the front seat. "You can lift her head to your lap. Put the other blanket under her head. I want to keep her as warm as possible."

I did as Laurel instructed, sliding onto the seat and gently lifting Lorna's head. She didn't utter a sound as I covered my drenched jean-clad leg with the second blanket and cautiously lowered her head.

Laurel smiled as Mason started the engine. "That's great," she said. "Now you can monitor her breathing and pulse as we drive."

"What if she wakes?"

"I gave her something to help her sleep. It's best for healing."

As the sky continued to fill with flashes of lightning, rain fell, winds blew, and thunder roared. For the first time in days, I had a small sense of purpose and power. My wife was alive. I had her beautiful body beneath my protective grasp. It was more than that; the poisonous venom that had settled in my veins was no longer foreign. In the short amount of time it had been present, it had taken up residence, giving me focus.

My wife would heal.

My wife would live.

Others would die...a slow and torturous death.

The feeling of impotence that accompanied the kidnapping was gone. In its place, dark reigned, and while other people could accompany me on this quest, as I gently stroked Lorna's tangled red locks, I vowed that I would prevail or die trying.

REID

Four days later

I stared up at the ceiling, my vision accustomed to the dimness of our bedroom. The red numbers glowing from the bedside stand read a little after two. That would be two in the morning. Beyond the blinds, through the windows, and above the Chicago light pollution, the sky was dark.

For the last two hours I held my wife close to my chest. Her petite body melded perfectly to mine, her soft ass pushing against my semi-erection that with her proximity refused to disappear. Its presence didn't matter—as far as I was concerned, sex was off the table for the foreseeable future. It wasn't that I didn't want her or that she hadn't expressed desire for us to be as one—I did and so had she.

The reason for our current state of abstinence was my concern for her comfort.

I refused to cause her any more pain.

Lorna's recent nightmare vied with my myriad of thoughts. She imagined her mother, describing her as she was —is. It was that revelation that had my mind in knots. I should talk to Mason, but I refused to leave her side as long as she slept. Slumber had been difficult for her since she woke from her ordeal. While she claimed her memories were nonexistent, the dream she described told me that they were very near the surface. And then there were the signs she didn't know she was exhibiting.

I watched her as she startled at the sound of a wake-up alarm or a timer in the kitchen. I saw the way she jumped when a knock came to our door or hesitated before entering a dark room.

With my arms surrounding Lorna, I was her shield, her protection from future danger. If that would allow her to rest, I would stay by her side for hours on end.

The familiarity of our bedroom, the one we'd shared for nearly a decade, combined with the way her breathing came in steady breaths could lull me into a false sense of ordinary as if this were any other night, and with simply closing my eyes, I could join her in peaceful slumber. It was as if I could forget that her world had been annihilated and her sense of safety demolished.

I couldn't.

I wouldn't.

While there were minutes I'd fallen asleep, each time I

woke to Lorna's gasps or cries, and I berated myself for letting her down. Again.

My plans for revenge were growing. Such as a flickering spark, as I stared into the night, my thoughts added fuel to my need to destroy. At Lorna's side was my only connection to humanity, the piece I'd clung to since we found her on Mason's land. It was a small slice because when I was out of her presence, the dark thoughts inside of me flourished, festering beneath my skin.

Another check of the clock let me know only fifteen minutes had passed.

Similar to Araneae Sparrow, Lorna's memories of the last two weeks were gone to her conscious mind.

Not gone, Laurel explained.

The recollections were masked, hidden away in an unmarked location within her brain. According to Laurel, erasing memories completely was rare. Instead, they were stored in a difficult-to-access location covered by either a true traumatic occurrence or a chemically induced cloak. The formula that Laurel had been working to recreate strived for the result she saw in Araneae and Lorna. Whatever drug was given to Mason many years ago had succeeded in concealing all of his memories. It worked until the right trigger removed the veil and brought back the memories.

Each time Lorna moved or made a noise in her sleep, my pulse raced, ready to comfort her from a nightmare or soothe her back to slumber.

I worried: what other memories like those of Nancy Pierce would come to her while she was asleep?

Laurel explained that the unconscious mind was unhindered by conscious thoughts. Though I longed to ease myself out of our warm cocoon to further my plans to avenge my wife and check on programs running a floor below, I wouldn't. My desire to be with Lorna was the only reason that those things could wait. As I'd said, she was my only tether to the light.

My thoughts raced in circles, similar to cars on a racetrack. Spinning and spinning, yet never going anywhere. I blinked my eyes, taking only a moment to savor my wife's body against mine.

I woke with a start, sitting upward and trying to orient my thoughts. No longer moving on the track, my thoughts were in a spiral. Darkness still shadowed our room. The clock now read 5:37.

Lorna. My hand went to the empty space on the bed beside me.

Missing.

My heart pounded against my chest.

"Lorna," I called as I threw back the covers. My pulse continued the race as my thoughts sped out of control. "Lorna." My volume rose.

How was she gone?

Did someone take her?

I tried to reassure myself that no one could access the tower.

My circulation echoed in my ears until the sound of running water came into range, urging me toward the attached bathroom. Without hesitation, I reached for the handle and pushed the door inward.

A warm fog of steam hung in the air.

How long had she been in the shower?

Lorna hadn't noticed my entrance or heard the door as she stood unmoving under the falling spray. Her naked body revealed a canvas of grotesque art—evidence of her abuse. Yet as I looked upon her, I saw beyond her bruises, cuts, and insect bites. My dick hardened beneath my boxer briefs as her curves glistened a shade of pink in the hot water.

As I stepped closer, more than the falling water could be heard. Lorna's soft cries came into range. I now saw the way she trembled, her eyes closed as tears added to the shower's spray.

Without further thought, I reached for the handle on the shower door and pulled it open.

All at once, Lorna spun toward me, her green eyes opening in surprise. Her hands came upward to cover herself before she sighed. "Reid."

Even my name was laced with her sadness.

Still wearing the underwear I'd worn to bed, I stepped inside the stall, closing the door behind me. The sweet scents of soap and shampoo filled my senses. "I'm here, sweetheart."

More tears flowed down her cheeks as she nodded and took a step toward me. Pushing herself close, her small breasts flattened against my chest. She fit perfectly under my chin as I again wrapped my arms around her and water continued to fall.

"Shh," I soothed. "How long have you been awake? Why didn't you wake me?"

Her forehead fell against my chest as she shook her head. In my grasp, her body trembled as more tears combined with the shower on my skin. I turned us away, shielding her with my body from the hot spray.

Gently, I ran my large hands over her back, down her spine, and over her tight round ass. "Did you have another dream?"

When she didn't answer, I tenderly palmed her cheeks and lifted her face upward. Her gaze flickered to mine before her eyes again closed. Bending, I brought my lips to hers. Like Viagra, as our lips connected and her soft, naked body molded to me, my circulation redirected, hardening my dick.

She looked down, seeing my confined erection before glancing up and grinning. "You're supposed to take those off before you get in the shower."

"I'm supposed to be with my wife when she needs me."

Her nostrils flared as she took a ragged breath. "I need you, Reid."

My head shook as another part of my body replied in the affirmative.

Slipping from my grasp, Lorna knelt before me upon the wet tile and reached for the waistband of my boxer briefs.

"Lorna."

She didn't speak as she pulled the silk boxers down over my hips and down my thighs until my dick sprang free and my boxers were nothing more than a wet pile of fabric on the shower's floor. Her green eyes, veiled with lashes, peered upward as her two small hands took me in her grasp, running her grip up and down over my stretching skin.

Her touch was electricity to my nervous system. Synapses sparked like rapid gunfire throughout my body, one after another. My dick grew painfully hard as her tongue lapped my pre-come-covered tip.

I reached out to the tiled wall as words of rebuke came to mind. They were there, telling her no, telling her that she needed rest, but the words couldn't or wouldn't roll from my tongue.

My breathing labored as her lips parted, and she took me into her warm mouth.

"Fuck, Lorna."

Deeper and deeper she took my length. Her lips were firm, her mouth warm, and her tongue tantalizing. Her fingers of one hand wrapped around my base, pumping me, while the other reached for my balls.

"Oh fu-c-k." I elongated the word. It had been so long since we'd been together. She was at the ranch without me and then...

A pop filled the stall as I took a step back. "Stop."

LORNA

The hole in my chest, the one that I couldn't identify but was similar to the hole in my memories, ached as I tried to make sense of what was happening and why Reid had told me to stop. My thoughts had been consumed with pleasing and tasting my husband as my core tightened and moistened. And like the flip of a light switch, that was now gone. Everything was gone.

When I looked up, my husband was offering me his hand.

It wasn't his hand I wanted.

It was the massive cock that seconds before I'd had between my lips. I wanted it for more than sexual pleasure, though I knew my husband was capable. It was the closeness that I longed for. When I'd awakened in his arms, I yearned to turn to him and find bliss in our unity.

Reid wasn't always present when I woke. Often, he was

down on 2, doing what he did. But when he was present, it was an unspoken invitation. Sometimes he'd wake me. Other times, I'd wake him. However, since I woke from whatever happened, he'd made it clear that sex was off the table.

When I entered the bathroom, his reasoning was as crystal clear as my reflection.

Who would want to make love to a woman as truly disfigured as me?

Who would want to fuck someone so damaged?

"Lorna," Reid offered with his hand still extended.

Instead of placing my hand in his palm, I acted like the child I'd never been allowed to be. I sat upon the wet shower floor, scooting back to the wall and drawing my knees to my chest. Wallowing in his rejection, I surrounded my legs with my arms and laid my chin on my knees.

"Lorna, come on," Reid said. "Let's get you out of here."

"Fuck you, Reid."

I refused to look up, yet I felt his reaction. I saw it in the way his steps staggered in the swirling water. Though I wondered how I had any left, more tears came, prickling my sore eyes. There must be a bottomless pit somewhere inside me. Not a pit. There was a black hole where memories disappeared and emotions bubbled like a witch's cauldron.

Reid took a step toward me as I pulled my legs closer to my chest. It was as he reached for the shower's handle to turn off the water that I spoke again, "Leave the water on and get the fuck out. I'm not done."

Bending his knees, my husband crouched by my legs. His still-erect cock bounced before me. When I still didn't look up, Reid took my chin and lifted it until our gazes met. If he was trying for compassion, he failed. His cold, emotionless words were simply a directive. "Your shower is done. You're getting out."

If daggers could be sent through eyes, I was sending them. "Fuck you."

"Oh, sweetheart" —his tone deepened— "I want that so fucking bad it hurts."

I blinked, releasing the tears on my lashes as I shook my head still in his grasp. "Obviously not."

Reid released my chin. As his legs straightened, his muscular thighs flexed. With his eyes fixed on me, he reached for his length, wrapping his long fingers around his erection. I sucked in a breath as he moved his hand up and down, pleasuring himself, doing what I had wanted to do.

His tenor deepened as his volume rose, his intonation slowing. "You don't think I want you, sweetheart?"

I couldn't take my eyes off his hand, the way it moved and how his large cock twitched as it grew unbelievably larger. Under the spray of the shower and his manipulation, veins came to life beneath his stretched, velvety skin.

Reid's hand moved faster. "I want inside your tight cunt more than I want anything else."

My tongue darted to my lips as droplets of come glistened from the slit at the tip.

"But I won't hurt you." His hand continued its movement. "You want to make me come. Fine. I'll come and then we can be done."

"Fuck you. Get out. You don't want me. If you can get yourself off, so can I."

His hand stopped.

Once again, I laid my forehead upon my knees. "If you wanted me, you wouldn't have stopped me from—"

My body rose as he grasped my arm, pulling me to my feet until I was sandwiched between the wall and him. The water continued streaming toward us from the side. Still grasping my arms, this mountain of man pinned me in place. While his cock prodded my stomach, it was his handsome face that had my attention. Emotions swirled in his dark eyes that I couldn't fully identify. There was lust and desire but also hurt and even anger.

The shower spray glistened on his skin as the muscles on the sides of his face tightened underneath his morning beard growth.

"You don't understand," he said through gritted teeth.

Though my arms ached in his hold, I held his stare. "No. You're wrong. I understand. I get it. I'm ugly. You can't stand to look at me, and you sure as hell don't want me."

He thrust his hard cock against me. "Does it feel like I don't want you?"

"So you're punishing me? You're keeping sex from me because of what happened? Do you blame me for being taken?"

His answer came quick and loud, echoing through the shower stall. "No. I blame *me*."

The hole in my chest ached. "Reid, it's not—"

He pressed himself against me. "When you were there" — he tilted his chin toward the shower floor— "it felt so fucking good. I started to forget..."

"That's what I want. I want to forget."

His head shook. "I can't. And it makes me so goddamned mad. Lorna, I'm so fucking angry that someone took you, touched you, hurt you...I can't control it and if I let loose..."

Bending my pinned arm, I found his captive cock wedged between us. I moved my hand over the smooth skin. "Make me forget, Reid. Fuck me. Fuck me with all that anger. Or make love to me. Consume me so that all of my thoughts are filled with you, and for a time I will stop thinking about what I can't remember."

His wide chest moved with deep breaths as tendons pulled tight in his neck.

"Use me," I said, "Let me use you. I can take whatever you have because I know you love me."

"Once I start..."

I moved my hand faster as the cock in my grasp turned to steel. "I'll beg if that's what you want."

Reid didn't speak, turning me quickly toward the wall. My fingers splayed on the tile and my diamond ring sparkled as he pulled my ass toward him and kicked my feet apart. My breathing hitched as his finger found my folds and plunged inside.

My gasp echoed against the tile as a second finger with the perfect curl was added. My knees bounced at the unbelievable friction.

"I love your cunt." Reid turned his hand as his thumb pressed against my tight ring of muscles. He pushed his thumb deeper, penetrating my anus.

"Oh," I panted as I pushed toward his touch.

"Your ass is so tight." His lips came to my ear as his large body enveloped mine. "Sweetheart, if I wanted to punish you, that's what I'd do."

My fingers grasped at the tile as a strange chill flowed through me. I wasn't sure where it came from. We'd done anal before and it hadn't been punishment. I knew and trusted my husband. However, before I could respond or analyze my reaction, Reid plunged his cock between my folds and deep into my core.

There was no inch by inch, no slow burn. In record time, he was balls deep. One of his large hands wrapped around my waist while the other came to my back, bending me so he could get impossibly deeper.

Willingly, I complied, my core stretching with each thrust and my breasts swaying with his rhythm. "Yes," I panted as heavy breaths added to the shower's steam. In and out, over and over, he plunged.

I could lose myself in not only the mindboggling sensation, but in the emotion. The closeness was what I'd been ready to beg for. The intimacy we shared. Throughout the years, Reid's love had given me what I never realized I needed or what as a child I could not have even imagined existed. In return, my love for him had grown each day.

Together, we were unstoppable.

Holding my hips, he moved faster and faster. Each plunge caused my fingers to blanch as he dove in and out. This wasn't making love. This wasn't a tender reunion. This was fucking. This was spearing me to my core, splitting me open only to put me back together.

Harder and harder.

My pussy clenched as an orgasm exploded without warning.

"Reid...oh my God..."

He didn't slow as I struggled to keep my footing, and my hands slipped over the wetness.

Again, wrapping one arm around my waist to hold me steady, he also reached for my chin and pulled my face backward until his lips were again at my ear. His breathing sent warm puffs of breath through the shower's mist over my sensitive skin. "No one touches you, no one but me."

"Yes." It was all I ever wanted.

Still holding my chin, he continued to pound, our wet skin slapping against one another. "This cunt is mine."

"Yes."

"Say it, Lorna. Say it out loud."

"It's yours. I'm yours. All of me."

"Your cunt. Say it."

I was lost to his deep tenor, his demanding thrusts.

His hand slipped to my neck. "Say it."

"My cunt."

"Who touches it?"

"You." My pulse raced as I complied, feeling not only

adoration for his possessiveness, but as if I were on a precipice where a deep dark hole could take it all away.

His hand slipped to my breasts, pinching and tweaking my hard nipples. Pain shot through me and straight to my core. My mind was totally back on him.

"And these, who touches these?"

"You, Reid. Only you."

His hands slid lower over my skin until he again gripped my hips. His thrusts slowed as his breathing grew deeper. Sliding one hand around to my stomach and lower, he found my clit.

I called out his name, my voice reverberating through the shower stall as a new orgasm overtook me.

Reid's roar joined the echo as my body detonated. Fireworks exploded behind my closed eyes. Shock waves caused my core to clench around his pulsating cock. I had no control as my body spasmed and I panted for breath.

Easing himself from me, Reid wrapped his strong arm around my waist. Without it, I wasn't sure I could stand. The next thing I knew, the water no longer flowed, and I was lifted from the floor, cradled in Reid's arms.

As water dripped from my long hair, I laid my cheek against his wide chest. He opened the shower door. Once we were in the bathroom, he gently sat me on the vanity. Spreading my legs, he stood between them. With a sly grin, his stare moved painfully slowly from my freshly fucked core, up over my breasts, and finally to my face. As if his dark eyes had lasers, his gaze left my flesh warmed in its wake. My nipples grew taut and my core throbbed as I scanned all of his perfect nakedness. If we were done, his cock was unaware.

Palming his cheek, I smiled. "That was...exactly what I needed."

"Now that I fucked you, I want more."

Placing my arms behind me, I leaned back, purposely pushing my breasts toward him. "I'm glad. I want more of you too."

His smile faded as he ran a large finger over my left cheek. Even without seeing, I knew that he was looking at my worst bruise, the one with the deepest discoloration. Before I'd awakened, a plastic surgeon had reconstructed my cheekbone.

I reached for his hand. "Please don't."

"It makes me so damn angry."

"Reid, please see me, not the bruises. I know it's not easy, but I need you to stop looking at me with disgust."

"Disgust?"

"I see it in your eyes."

"Bullshit." He took a step back and scanned me again. "There is nothing about you that disgusts me. You're fucking perfect. It's at me, Lorna. You are..."

"A mess," I offered.

"*My* fucking mess." He reached for a plush towel and helped me from the vanity. "I'm wrapping you in this because if that pink pussy stares at me for another second, I'm going to fuck you again." He tucked the edge of the towel under itself.

In my mind, that dark hole was still too close. I didn't know what memories I had buried, but I knew with my man I was safe and secure. He'd keep me from falling. He'd hold me tight. He'd love me as he always had. For that and so much more, I wanted to show him that I was still me, his wife.

My lips curled upward as I reached for what he'd just secured and loosened it. As the towel fluttered to the floor, I grasped for his hand and tugged him toward the bedroom. "Last night, you said I could be on top."

REID

*A*s the steel door opened onto 2, the room and its occupants came into view. This was my sanctuary. It was where I had done some of my best work. Whether it was cracking security, breaching firewalls, increasing the Sparrow assets, or utilizing government satellites and metropolitan traffic cameras to discover someone's identity or location, I had done it. I'd developed programs that were far more advanced than some of the highest-touted systems in the world. And yet as I stepped into our oasis and took in the familiar scents, technological sights, and overall atmosphere, my usual sense of ease was replaced with my burning need for revenge.

While it was still early, Mason was dressed in his casual daily attire, not much unlike mine. Blue jeans, cowboy boots, and today it was a thermal shirt. It was autumn in Chicago, but no matter the season, when it came to dealing with capos and business around the city, Mason preferred to keep his tattoos covered. His long hair was damp from his shower and loose, framing his face. My difference was a short-sleeved shirt, canvas loafers, and dry hair.

Lorna and I had made our bed a detour following our shower.

Patrick on the other hand was wearing his customary gray suit with leather shoes. Today's suit was a lighter shade of gray and his tie was a solid darker gray. I imagined his closet looked more like a store rack with the same clothing repeated over and over. The only significant color change came in his tie collection.

"Nice of you to join us," Mason said as he lifted a mug of coffee to his lips.

Palming my hot mug, I sneered. "Fuck off."

"I see you woke on the wrong side of the bed...again," Patrick said as he typed away on a keyboard.

I hadn't awakened on the wrong side of the bed. And if I had, it was quickly reversed. Fucking Lorna was the best medicine in the whole damn world. Watching her come apart in the shower and again in our bed as her vibrant emerald eyes rolled back, her neck arched, and her breasts hung precariously close over my face, was something I could do every damn minute.

She'd asked me to see her, not her injuries.

I did.

My wife was an amazingly strong, stunningly beautiful, intelligent, independent woman. I saw that. I wanted to lavish her with adoration for her survival of what many couldn't endure. I also saw my failure in her wounds.

Mine not hers.

Instead of responding to Patrick's comment, I walked behind him and peered at the screens before him. "What do you have?"

The screens were filled with graphs and tables. There was a search engine running with numbers flowing at untold speed, looking for a match on something.

"Mason's working on some shit that went down in Garfield Park last night. Two rival gangs decided to fuck each other up. Afterward, a clerk and customer were shot at a liquor store."

I walked to my chair and sighed. Placing my coffee mug on the desk, I said, "Tell me that someone gives a shit about who took the ladies. Tell me that is someone's fucking priority besides mine."

Halfway through my speech, the steel door opened again, and Sparrow entered. Dressed to the nines in attire and accessories that cost as much as a small country, he was ready for Michigan Avenue. It was the first time he'd been dressed for Sparrow Enterprises since I'd returned to Chicago with Lorna.

"You're leaving the tower?" I asked.

His head nodded. "Yes. My assistant has been on my ass about meetings I've missed." That would be Sparrow's personal assistant at Sparrow Enterprises, the legitimate side of Sparrow. She'd been with him since nearly his acquisition of and ascension in the real estate empire, and she understood the balancing act Sparrow performed while not being fully informed as to what he did outside the office—that he literally ran a city and fought constant battles for that supremacy.

"Araneae told me to go and put out fires," Sparrow said, going to the coffee machine, placing a pod inside, and hitting the button. When he turned, he had a lopsided grin. "If you assholes must know, I think her words were something about my hovering becoming overbearing."

Mason scoffed. "Sterling Sparrow—overbearing. I'm glad that overdue news bulletin finally came through." He shook his head. "I wasn't sure how much longer we could keep it under wraps."

Sparrow darted a dark-eyed glare toward Mason, but instead of responding, he turned to me. His expression was again serious. "It's my priority. Finding the identity of the kidnappers is all of our priority. I get that Lorna has needed you. We do too. Last night while the shit was happening at Garfield Park, the preliminary lab results came in from the forensics team we sent to the underground bunker."

Our capos had discovered two underground bunkers in the wilderness of Montana. The trackers in our wives' shoes had lured them there. Mason recognized the setup and thankfully, we didn't lose Christian or Romero to the trap. One bunker was blown to rubble. The other was able to be searched.

Patrick hit a few keys and the large overhead screens that had been rotating images from around Chicago, now filled with a photograph of what appeared to be a cell. "Mason, do you want to tell them what Laurel said?"

Mason leaned back in his chair. "Doc said she believes Araneae and Lorna."

My eyes narrowed. "Why the fuck wouldn't she?"

Mason raised one hand as he stood, his chair rolling the opposite direction. "Let me finish. She said that she believes the women don't remember anything. She's been running tests on their blood draws. I don't get all of it, but she's been able to identify some similar compounds to her formula. She says the amounts..." He took a breath and shrugged. "Fuck, she can tell you herself." He looked at me. "I'm sure you'd get it better than I do."

We all had our specialties. Intelligence wasn't lacking in any of us. Our differences strengthened our team, not weakened it.

"What did she say?" I probed. "Tell us what you can."

"It appears that they were both given similar dosages."

"What does that mean?"

He shook his head. "We don't know. It could mean that whoever had them has perfected the formula."

Rightfully so, Laurel would be more concerned with the formula. My focus was on my wife and Araneae. "Will they get the memories back?"

"Doc said they could. She said one of the most...fuck, she had a word. Basically, the best stimulus for memory is from our senses. Smell is the most powerful. The next is sound and then sight. Taste and feel fall near the end. So a smell could be the trigger to retrieving their memories, or a sound, like a train whistle or even a phrase. Last of the prominent senses is sight."

"That's where these pictures come in," Patrick said.

We all looked up at what appeared to be a cell.

"Laurel," Mason went on, "believes that the ladies should be shown the pictures to see if they elicit something."

"No." The answer came resoundingly from both Sparrow and me.

Mason was still standing. "Hear me out. Laurel said she could introduce them in one of their sessions."

"They're not fucking sessions," Sparrow said. "My wife doesn't need therapy."

His denial made me bristle. The little bit of talking Lorna had done with Laurel seemed therapeutic. I didn't give a damn what they called it. I was for it. However, at the moment, a battle over semantics wasn't worth fighting

"Fine, when they *chat*," Mason replied.

I looked up again at the picture. It wasn't the first time I'd seen it. "You said that lab results came in from the forensics team?"

"Lorna's blood was found in this cell room along with someone else's." Patrick hit a few keys. "We're doing a search of the data banks to see if we can get a DNA match."

"It wasn't Araneae's?" Sparrow asked.

"They found Araneae's in a hallway near the entry. Since most of her wounds were on the soles of her feet, we're thinking that's why her blood was there." Patrick let out a long breath. "Lorna's was found in a greater quantity along with the unidentified individual's."

"Could it be Nancy Pierce's?" Sparrow asked.

Laurel had worked with Dr. Dixon to determine that the

woman found did have significant genetic markers in common with both Mason and Lorna. There was no question: she was their mother.

"No," Patrick replied definitively. "The other larger splatter was most definitely from a different individual. Currently, individual X."

I recalled Lorna's dream. "I need to talk to Laurel. Is she staying here today or going to the institute?"

"Here," Sparrow said. "Laurel is the target. She made a list of some essentials she needs from her lab at the Sparrow Institute. Mason and I have Sparrows collecting whatever she wants."

"Her and Mason's apartment isn't big enough," I began, thinking of the logistics. The space she had at the Sparrow Institute was so large, most wasn't even utilized.

"There's room on this floor," Sparrow interrupted.

"This floor?" Patrick and I questioned together. This floor had always been only us. Always. The four of us, no one else.

Sparrow turned his stare to us. "Don't we have other things to discuss?"

From the look on Mason's face, I had the feeling that Patrick and I were the only uninformed participants in this conversation. The decision had been made.

"What do you want to ask Laurel?" Mason inquired.

"I want to better understand what you're saying." It wasn't one hundred percent accurate. I wanted to be more specific with Laurel about Lorna's dream. Casually bringing up the subject of Missy, Mason and Lorna's sister, wasn't what was needed to keep us focused.

Sparrow looked at his watch. "My day is fucking packed." He looked at me. "Are you up for a trip?"

"A trip?" I wasn't ready to leave Lorna.

"DC."

"A visit with Edison Walters?"

Edison Walters, a senior legislative aide, has been a staple in Washington DC for over thirty years. During that time, he has worked closely with various legislators from all parties. He's stayed securely in the background, helping to research and draft various bills.

The seemingly benign aide had an alternate identity that was known to very few. He was, in reality, Top, the top commander of the Sovereign Order. The man had more power than five-star generals or even the president, and yet in his everyday life, he answered to junior congressmen and - women. Little did they or most know that Walters could say the word and World War III would begin, top dignitaries would disappear, or crowned princes would meet their demise.

"I don't like this," Mason said. "Top doesn't welcome visitors. I should go alone."

"It's time for breakfast," Sparrow said, tilting his chin toward the steel door. "Lorna was up there when I left as was Araneae. If they can both be out and about, we're giving them a full kitchen. This discussion can wait." He turned to Patrick. "I hope Ruby will be there. It's nice to have her home."

The worries of the world momentarily disappeared from

Patrick's blue eyes and a smile spread across his lips. "I'm learning that teenagers and mornings don't always mix."

We began to collect our coffee mugs and head for the door when Patrick added, "I don't think Ruby is as upset about being summoned home as Maddie expected. Ruby was happy to be back at the academy, but she's also excited to welcome her new brother. This way she has an excuse to stay near Maddie."

As Sparrow placed his palm over the scanner, Patrick's computer made a noise.

"What?" I asked.

Patrick quickly returned to his screen. "There's a match on the DNA found in the blood that was in the cell with Lorna's."

LORNA

A feeling of warmth came over me as everyone from throughout our tower gathered for breakfast. The aroma of food filtered through the air, sautéed onions and peppers as well as bacon. Greetings came as each person entered. As coffee and juice were sought and the constant chatter came from around the large kitchen, I took a moment to take in what at one time had been routine—the beginning to another day.

I turned as a gentle hand came to my shoulder. Araneae's soft brown eyes glistened with unshed moisture, yet her expression was filled with happiness.

"It feels good, doesn't it?" she asked softly.

"Being here?" I confirmed her meaning.

She shrugged. "All of it." She looked over the room. "I can't help but think that we could have lost this."

Swallowing a lump growing in my throat, I nodded. The

men had all entered, their discussion on the surprise ending to a football game as they all took turns refilling their coffee mugs.

"Reid rarely watches football," I whispered.

"Neither does Sterling."

"I've never seen Patrick watch either," Madeline added as she reached for a large platter of scrambled eggs cooked with chopped vegetables.

Araneae shook her head. "They're keeping things from us."

I had taken a quick look at the news on my phone before coming up to the penthouse. I spoke louder. "Oh my. Did you see the play where the Bears' quarterback was injured?"

All four sets of male eyes turned my way before murmurs arose as they exchanged glances amongst themselves. "I-I..."

"You didn't watch the game," Araneae chastised the men as she carried a bowl of fruit and placed it on the large granite table.

"The quarterback was injured?" Laurel asked. "I didn't know that."

"He wasn't," I answered. "It was a ploy to call these poor actors out on their attempt to keep all of us shielded from the truth of what they were discussing ten seconds before they entered the kitchen."

"Hockey," Mason volunteered. "The Black Hawks—"

"Liar," I replied, interrupting my brother. "You can't lie to me. I know your tells."

Madeline smiled. "He tilts his head slightly to the left and his lips thin."

"I do not," Mason replied, lifting his coffee mug to cover his lips.

We all laughed.

"You're right," I told Madeline.

Her brows arched as her gaze widened. "That's my thing."

"Mine too," Patrick said. "Of course, I never used it to win poker tournaments."

"Except the one where you beat me," Madeline said, feigning a frown.

Patrick reached for her hand. "It was the best win of my life."

Her frown turned upside down as pink filled her cheeks. "I'm not complaining—now."

"Where's your daughter?" Araneae asked as we all took our seats.

Madeline sighed. "I'd assume Ruby is still asleep."

"She's on a forced vacation," Sparrow said. "Let her sleep."

"Are you going to be as accommodating to our child?" Araneae asked.

Sparrow flashed a grin at his wife. "You know me. I'm always accommodating."

"Well, we're not," Madeline said.

"The academy sent her schoolwork so she wouldn't fall behind," Patrick added. "Not really a vacation, forced or not."

The conversation stayed on the mundane, and as it did and I listened and participated, I realized that I was perfectly all right with the theme. I imagined scenes and players as Madeline told stories about the poker circuit and tournaments around the world. We shared our enthusiasm as

Araneae shared news about a new line of merchandise her fashion company Sinful Threads was about to showcase for the holiday buying season.

As we ate the food Madeline and I had prepared together, I sipped my coffee and relished the simplicity of this time together while simultaneously wondering how very close we had been to losing it.

While we—the Sparrow women—lived in our bubble, we weren't without knowledge. Despite the sparsity of information shared by our men, we were aware of the fires beyond our walls. We ladies knew that we were sequestered within for the foreseeable future, yet complaining or arguing was not on any of our agendas.

After whatever Araneae and I had been through, we were home and safe. Despite my outward appearance, I was loved thoroughly by my husband and also by the family surrounding me—the sense of camaraderie felt special in a way I couldn't describe. The recurring thought returned.

I am somebody.

A sudden chill replaced the warmth.

"Are you all right?" Laurel asked.

Pushing the odd thought away, I nodded. "I really am."

As plates and mugs emptied, the men began bidding their goodbyes. Sparrow was off to Michigan Avenue after first whisking Araneae off to the other room. I could imagine their discussion. The queen was reassuring the king she would survive for a few hours out of his sight. It wasn't one he would appreciate having overheard, as in his facade, all decisions were his alone.

When she returned alone and winked my direction, I knew without a doubt, she'd sent him away to do what he needed to do. Mason kissed Laurel as he mentioned doing some work around the city. That was a broad statement that never came with any further explanation. As Patrick and Reid stood to leave and the four of us began clearing the table, Ruby entered.

"Good morning, sleepyhead," Patrick said.

At eighteen, Ruby was beautiful beyond her years. With her father's vibrant blue eyes and her mother's delicate features and long dark hair, even in soft pants, an oversized shirt, and bare feet, she was truly stunning.

"I was awake. I was checking email."

We all turned her direction.

She lifted her hands. "Steady. I didn't reply. I know I can't."

"We'll get that set up," Reid volunteered. He was working on resetting the VPN and upgrading all of our security.

"Thanks, Reid," Ruby said with a grin as I handed her a mug of hot chocolate. Her gaze met mine. "Thanks, Lorna. You don't need to wait on me. I can get it."

"I like making it. The chocolate smells heavenly."

She lowered her lips to the rim and sipped. "Tastes that way too."

"There's still food on the table," Madeline said as she gave her daughter a plate. "Then you can help us with dishes."

"Or I can do my schoolwork." Her cheeks rose with a grin. "But if you don't want me to do my schoolwork…"

Patrick laughed. "Have you decided on a major yet for next year? I'm thinking law. You make convincing arguments."

Ruby smiled as she dished herself some fruit.

"I'll be in and out of the tower." Patrick reached for Madeline. "Call me if you feel anything or you need anything."

"Five more weeks," she said, laying her hand over her enlarged midsection.

"Promise you'll call."

"She will," Ruby added as she settled with her hot chocolate, fruit, and toast and lost herself to whatever was on her iPad.

Similar to her emails, Ruby was in full voyeur mode online until Reid had the security on all her devices updated. No chances were being taken online or in person.

As I reached for empty plates, Reid reached for my hand and gave it a squeeze. "You don't need to do anything you're not up to doing. Everyone wants to help. You can head back to our apartment."

Shrugging, I looked around the kitchen. "I think I want the company."

"We won't let her overdo," Madeline said with a grin.

"You're the one who should rest," Laurel scolded.

"Come with me," Reid said, tugging me from the kitchen.

REID

*L*orna followed, her hand in mine.

The opulence of Sparrow's penthouse or even the changes that Araneae had made over the last few years were lost on me. My mind was vying between the woman with me and the computers down on 2. While Lorna had been my top priority since before I asked her to marry me, the importance of what was waiting on 2 was magnified due to its connection to her.

The DNA results would give us a name—the name of a dead man walking—because he wasn't long for this world. Same as the other men had given their wives a nonspecific description of their daily whereabouts, I couldn't say with certainty that I would remain in the tower. First, once it was scheduled, I would attend the meeting with Edison Walters in DC. Second, once I had a name to go with the blood found near Lorna's, I would search heaven and hell; I wouldn't spend my day sitting behind a screen in the tower.

Dark crimson colored my thoughts as I contemplated the future. I'd killed before, in the war for our country and in the war for this city. Though Sparrow may claim that I was deadliest when behind a screen, with what had happened, I would no longer maintain that distance. This time, as Lorna and I came to a stop and I peered down at her healing face, I was determined to be the one who watched the asshole who hurt my wife take his last breath.

I was assuming it was a man.

Truly, it wouldn't matter.

When it came to enemies, women were hardly the weaker sex. No one, male or female, would get away with harming anyone in our world simply because they had two X chromosomes. Actions had consequences—for everyone.

Images of destruction momentarily danced in my mind's eye.

A pull of a trigger and the echo of the blast could combine to give me the satisfaction of witnessing the shower of brain matter splattering over the walls. Or maybe a twelve-inch blade would be my weapon of choice. Once in Iraq, my platoon came across a man in an abandoned building, one who had been sliced through his gut. In the heat, his remains baked as insects feasted. The horrendous odor has stayed with me, petrified into my memory. I also recalled how his intestines and bodily fluids had spilled from his body. Terror still showed on his face as he died with his hands unsuccessfully holding back his protruding insides.

A bullet would end his life with only seconds to contemplate his final moments.

Slicing his gut would not be fast. That means of execution was deliberate and slow, allowing the victim to remain conscious. It definitely held a certain kind of appeal.

I imagined looming over the faceless man who'd harmed my wife and watching as he died, his mind full of things he should or shouldn't have done.

Then again, maybe there wouldn't be a weapon. I could use my hands, doing to him what he'd done to Lorna, beating him repeatedly with my fists as his bones cracked and splintered.

Yes, I'd given these possibilities much thought.

"I'll be fine," Lorna said, tugging on my hand and bringing me back to present. "As long as I know I have you."

Running my finger gently over Lorna's cheek, the lightness that dwelled within her shone like sunshine streaming from her emerald stare. Though the consuming darkness that fueled my innate need to avenge her was near, reverberating through my circulation, in her presence I could keep it at bay.

"I fucking hate leaving you."

"You're not. You're going to be on 2, doing what you do."

The potential inaccuracy of her response made me want to bristle. Instead of confessing my possible alternative whereabouts, I replied, "That's where I'm going now."

Her gaze narrowed as if she heard my unvoiced dissent. "Now? Are you leaving? No, Reid" —her words came faster— "if you leave this tower" —her tone changed— "please tell me."

I placed my palm over her cheek as the warmth of her soft flesh radiated to my hand. If I closed my eyes, I could imagine the woman I married, her undamaged skin, her contusion-free appearance. But my eyes weren't closed. They were wide open. "I don't want you to worry about me or where I am. I can't stand to cause you any more pain or worry."

She reached for my hand. "Reid, I have worried about you and what you do from the day we met. What happened to me hasn't changed that. Now I'm afraid you'll do something because of me that will put you or any of the others in danger. Don't do that."

"Don't create possibilities that don't exist. This isn't our first fight. Lorna, we're fucking good at what we do. The four of us didn't get to where we are today by taking stupid chances. Besides, we have Sparrows all over who will follow through on our orders. None of that is your concern. You concentrate on healing." I feigned a smile. "I wish I could stay with you and make sure you followed my orders."

There was a second of question before her lips curled, her fist went to her hip, and her eyebrows arched. "Your *orders?*"

I nodded.

"And what would we do all day, Reid? Watch movies on television or binge a new series?"

"Actually, I was thinking that we could spend the day as we had earlier this morning."

Her arms relaxed as pink filled her cheeks. Its hue clashed with her bright red hair, making her blush more noticeable as the soft crimson radiated upward from her neck.

I lowered my volume. "I figured we could spend the day

assessing all the possible positions I can take you in repeatedly, positions that have your tight cunt at my disposal and positions that make you scream in ecstasy, not pain."

As her stare held mine, she shifted her feet. The movement made me grin. Lorna and Madeline had mentioned Mason's tells—his unconscious outward signs that gave away his inner thoughts. Lorna had them too. When I said or did something that turned her on, she would fidget.

It was cute in a sexy way that went right to my cock.

"Reid..." She turned toward the kitchen.

Leaning down, I brought my lips to her ear, exaggerating each word as my warm breath tantalized her sensitive skin. "Like you did this morning."

Her breathing deepened and her nipples tented her blouse.

My voice went even lower. "Mrs. Murray, are you wet for me?"

Lorna brought her finger to my lips and took a step back. "Stop. Ruby is a room away."

"You didn't answer."

"Yes, I am, and I will be tonight when you and I are home —alone. Now you need to go do what you do. You have a job. All of you have jobs that need to be done. Like I said before, I don't need a bloody head on a platter at my feet." Her nose scrunched. "I don't want that. I want to know that whoever did this" —she passed her hand from her head downward— "won't be doing it to anyone else."

My teeth came together as my jaw clenched.

Lorna may not want a bloody head, but I fucking did. I

wanted it—needed it—as much as I needed to fuck my wife. The latter would have to wait until I knew more about the first. Standing taller, I reached again for her hands. "Promise me you'll rest if you get tired."

She nodded. "Yes, I promise."

"I don't care if you're sore, I'll spank that cute ass if you don't listen."

Lorna scoffed. "I think year nine of a marriage is a little late to add kink to our sex life."

The bloody head on a platter at Lorna's feet was momentarily replaced by thoughts of my wife bound to our bed, her legs spread, her body exposed, and all her sensitive areas vulnerable to my every whim. "I can do kink."

"Well, *Sir*" —she emphasized the title in a way that erotically combined her response with the images of her straining against satin restraints, sending my circulation straight to my dick— "I will behave. After all, I can't leave the tower, so if I need rest, there's no reason I can't get it."

"When this turmoil is settled, we need to investigate these roles more fully." As the unknowns of the turmoil came to mind, my tone changed, reflecting the seriousness of our reality. "It doesn't fucking matter where I am, if you need anything, call or text. You're not alone and you're safe."

My wife nodded.

"Follow my orders."

Lorna stood taller on her tiptoes, placing her hand on my chest and peering into my eyes. The intensity in her emerald stare made me want to shy away. The way my wife was looking at me was as if she could see my thoughts. Maybe after all these years she could. Currently, I didn't want that. I didn't want her to see the dark thoughts swirling through my mind. Reaching for the back of her neck, I brought my lips to hers.

When we pulled apart, she said, "Reid, don't do anything that you'll regret."

I'd gladly kill for you without regret. My wife didn't need to hear that; instead, I said, "My regret is not keeping you safe."

"You saved me. I may look like it, but I'm not broken."

My palms went back to her cheeks. "Fuck that, Lorna, you don't look broken. You look like a fighter. And I'm so damn proud of you for fighting. You're here, and as your husband, it's my fucking right to worry about you. Just promise me you'll never stop fighting."

Her eyelids fluttered and her lips turned upward into a sexy grin. "Even when you want me to role-play?"

Yes, this fiery, beautiful, and sexual petite woman was definitely the light I needed.

I returned her grin. "Especially then. Fight me so I have reason to punish you."

Lorna shook her head. Placing her hands on my shoulders, she whispered, "Go, because even though I'm uncertain how I feel about that idea, in another minute I'm going to need to change my panties."

Our lips brushed one another's in a chaste kiss before she shooed me toward the elevators on the other end of the penthouse.

"Do what you do with no regrets. I love you, too."

I didn't have time to revisit the words she'd said about role play. I also didn't have time for my dick to be thinking about them. With each step, the hardness faded as my circulation resumed its normal flow.

It was difficult to maintain an erection while simultaneously contemplating a killing.

Scanning my palm near the elevator, I waited for the doors to open and then stepped inside.

In no time, I was down two floors and entering our command center—2.

Three sets of eyes met mine.

"What the fuck? Don't you have places to be?" I asked.

"Garrett's waiting in the parking garage," Sparrow said, glancing at his watch.

Mason's eyes met mine. "Andrew Jettison, sergeant major."

My gut twisted. "Tell me he's alive so I can fucking kill him."

"He died in battle," Sparrow said.

"Six years ago," Patrick added.

LORNA

*A*s Reid turned away, his broad shoulders straightened in a nonverbal show of determination. That wasn't all that left me uneasy. There was something in his tone and expression. Yes, he'd joked and left me with unmet sexual tension and desire, yet he'd also given me a glimpse of his vendetta, his need to punish. I knew my husband well enough to recognize his projection. If and when we ventured into any type of role play, it would be pleasure he delivered, not pain. Reid's current desire to punish wasn't directed toward me but to whoever hurt me.

I didn't doubt his or any of the other men's capability. It was that I didn't want to lose my husband or anyone in our family because they sought to avenge me. The worry twisted my stomach as I wrapped my arms around myself and watched him disappear beyond the stairs toward the elevator.

"Please keep him safe and let him concentrate," I whispered. "And bring him home to me."

"Lorna?"

I turned to the sight of the only teenager in our tower, the one whose presence I'd warned Reid about. "Ruby, did you overhear?"

"What?" She shook her head. "No, I was hoping I could talk to you, and I waited until Reid left."

Ruby's kind heart was the crowning jewel to her outward beauty. It would have been easy for her life to have turned out differently, or her outlook to have been soured by the circumstances around her, yet it hadn't. I was certain her mother, Madeline, was responsible for the well-rounded young lady before me.

I lifted my hand to her. "Of course we can talk. It's great to have you home."

Ruby reached toward me, our hands meeting, not in a shake but a squeeze of familiarity. "The more I'm here, the more it feels like home."

"Good."

"I-I'm sorry about what happened to you," she said.

"I know I look like I lost the heavyweight championship."

Ruby laughed. "Try lightweight."

"The truth is that I don't remember a thing."

We both sat, each in one of a pair of plush chairs near a wall of windows. The morning sun streamed through the tempered panes as far below leaves turned from green to orange, yellow, and red. Autumn was upon us.

Time continued to move despite my memories or lack thereof.

"When you do—remember," she began, "please talk to Reid."

I sat straighter. "Are you giving me life advice?"

"If you want to hear it."

Leaning back in the chair, I grinned. "When did you become so worldly?"

"I think since I was born," Ruby said, her back straight and legs crossed at her ankles, reminding me of her mother. "I know you all see me as a kid," she went on, "but when we first got here—when Mom got here, too—it was like a faucet opened inside of her or a dam broke. She had so many memories, things she'd packed away." Moisture glistened in her eyes. "I love her, and yet I didn't know what to say to her or what to do."

"I'm sure just having you here," I offered, "and knowing you and she were safe—"

Ruby shook her head. "No, it was all Patrick. He got to her. I mean they hadn't been together in seventeen years and he..." She grinned, taking a deep breath. "To be perfectly honest, I don't want details of what he did. I just know my mom. I know that never before in my life had she been anything other than...perfect. It probably was what Andros expected. No matter why, I never saw her cry or get upset. I saw her try to hide her fear when she was scared, but no matter what, she was always in control of her own emotions. She used to say that only you have power over yourself. Of course, I didn't know what had happened through her life."

Madeline's past was a complicated story unto itself.

"Ruby, it wasn't your burden to carry."

"I know that. I also know that when my mom finally allowed herself to remember and feel, the memories threatened to drown her. There were so many that they were overwhelming, taking her down an emotional spiral she may not have come back from."

"No," I said, "your mom is strong. She's a survivor."

Ruby reached over to my knee. "So are you, Lorna. Aunt Araneae told me about Mason, that for years he was gone. She even mentioned a sister who you lost when you were young. And through it all, you survived. I know Mom's story is different, and she chose not to face her memories. Your loss of memory isn't a choice. Which is..." —she shrugged— "maybe worse because you can't decide when they will come back."

I hadn't thought of that.

"But please," Ruby implored, "if and when your memories do come back, grab a life raft. Hold on to Reid, or" —she motioned toward the kitchen— "anyone in there. This place is super weird."

I scoffed. "Weird?"

"Yeah, it's like we're all family. Every one of you rallied around my mom even before she was ready to tell you her story. But everyone has a story. I mean, Uncle Sterling thinks he rules the world. Patrick enables him. Aunt Araneae has, like, dozens of names. Laurel is some kind of genius. Reid can do anything on a computer. I bet he's a whiz at hacking. And your brother was an assassin for hire."

I shook my head at her voicing what was never meant to be uttered. "Ruby, we don't—"

"I'm not dumb," she interrupted with a grin. "I think it's all cool, and I know not to say anything. I mean, I may be young, but after growing up in the Ivanov bratva and moving here, I pick up on more than the average eighteen-year-old.

"No one in this tower has lived an unscathed life, even me. I still sometimes think of watching Oleg die." She forced a smile. "That's what makes it" —she paused and looked around the luxurious room— "perfect. Because people here accept things that others might not. No matter what you remember or when you remember, everyone here will still love you."

Her words prickled my skin and brought unshed tears to my eyes. Listening to her wisdom, it was easy to forget I was speaking to a teenager. Her life truly had made her wise beyond her years. "I'll remember that. Right now, I really don't remember."

"When you do, don't do it alone."

Madeline came around the corner with a sigh, a kitchen towel in hand. And with the light from the archway, her baby bump appeared more like a round beach ball beneath her sweater. "Is everything all right?"

I smiled. "I'm getting great life advice from Ruby."

Madeline's head tilted to the side.

I reached for Ruby's hand. "Thank you." As we stood, we reached for one another and embraced. I stifled a small wince as she applied pressure to my sore muscles.

"Oh shit. I'm sorry," Ruby said as she hurriedly stepped back.

"Ruby Cynthia," Madeline corrected.

"Mom, update, I'm an adult. Adults say *shit*."

Araneae and Laurel came from the kitchen.

"What do adults do?" Araneae asked.

"Cuss," Madeline and I said together as Ruby repeated, "say shit."

Araneae's hand went in the air. "I do." Her expression changed. "Wait, am I the aunt who's a bad influence?"

Ruby went to Araneae and wrapped her arm around her waist. "You're my only aunt, so I think that makes you the best influence." She turned her blue eyes to her mother. "And don't get mad at Aunt Araneae. I learned all the cuss words from Andros, others at school, and...well, life."

Madeline laid her hand on her midsection and smiled at Araneae. "Maybe we can work on not saying them as much for these next little ones."

"I know, we can have a cussing jar," Ruby volunteered.

Araneae smiled. "Great idea. Now, is it possible that I could arrange an automatic thousand-dollar deposit the first of each month and call it even?"

"It's only a dollar a word," Ruby explained.

"Well, fuck" —Araneae's hand flew to her lips— "I better make it two thousand."

Laughter, unforced and natural, filtered through the penthouse, a comforting melody to remind me of our shared connections.

"Did I miss dishes?" I asked.

"All taken care of," Madeline said. "And we started a big

pot of chili for lunch. I guess we can all rest." She looked around. "Or do schoolwork, or work-work."

Araneae's and Laurel's technology was already upgraded for safety as they both had work outside the tower that they needed to access.

Rest.

A sigh escaped my lips as I turned toward the glistening waves of Lake Michigan, suddenly dreading spending time alone.

"What is it, Lorna?" Laurel asked.

"A lot of things. I wasn't going to say anything" —I winked at Ruby— "but a friend just gave me some great advice. Would you mind if we talked for a little bit? Or do you need to do work?"

"Let's go downstairs. My place or yours?"

"Yours would be good." I peered around the penthouse. "I need a change of scenery."

*M*y steps staggered. "He died six years ago?"

Mason's complexion paled as he dropped into his chair and laid his head back against the leather. "This is all on me. I brought the Order into this world. How in the fuck did I think they'd let me go?"

Sparrow took a deep breath. "We need to deal with this. But right now, I have to get to the office. Hell, I'm already behind on meetings. Shit doesn't stop just because more is coming our way. It just piles deeper." He looked at Mason. "Get this pity-party shit out of your system because we need you. We need your understanding of the Order and what we're dealing with. We have the DNA of a dead soldier who obviously missed the memo of his death."

Mason's jaw clenched. "Been there."

"Yes, and we took you back. *I* took you back." Sparrow emphasized the personal pronoun, "You didn't lie to me or us.

You didn't downplay the Order. We knew what it meant to have you here and we chose you." He stood taller. "So if you want to blame someone for bringing the Order to Chicago, blame me. The fucking buck stops here."

"I'm also to blame. I had a say," Patrick said.

"Me, too," I added. And then a thought occurred to me. "Maybe you should stop being so damn narcissistic."

All eyes were on me.

I walked closer to the group and my desk area. Before sitting, I turned to Mason. "Hear me out. Even if this is the Order, they don't want you."

Mason's green eyes, so much like his sister's, opened wider. "They want Laurel."

"That's why she's not leaving the tower and you can," Sparrow said.

"Did you introduce Laurel to the Order?" I asked, already knowing the answer.

He hadn't.

"Fuck," Mason said as he stood again and began to pace before the rows of active computer screens. "I've been so focused on the fact this could be the Order and that they could have taken Lorna and Araneae, I wasn't seeing the entire picture." He spun toward us, running his fingers through his untethered hair. "I didn't—introduce them to her. The Order had a tracker on her for years."

"Because?" I asked, also knowing this answer.

"Her compound. She—the tracker—was fucking there when Laurel was recreating..." His sentences weren't keeping up with his thoughts. It was all right. We could fill in the blanks.

"Why is Laurel alive today?" Patrick asked.

When Mason hesitated, Sparrow answered, "Dr. Laurel Carlson wouldn't have lived if she'd been with any other person, male or female, in the entire world. I wouldn't have understood who was after her. Reid or Patrick wouldn't, and you know we're about as badass as they come. You were able to save her because you understand the Order. You're not the weak link here. You're the fucking asset." Sparrow looked again at his watch. "I need to be downtown." He took a step and stopped, staring us all down. "I want intel today. Nothing but intel. No one takes off for DC or anywhere outside our city. No rogue shit. Am I clear?"

We nodded.

"Learn for sure where Walters is. Is he in DC? If not, where?" Sparrow turned to Mason and Patrick. "We need to put out these little fires everywhere around my city. Get on the street. Talk to capos. Check with the informants with contacts in the gangs. I want to know why we're on the edge of a constant battle. This is our city. I make the rules.

"If any of this annoying shit is coming from within our ranks, we have a round of housekeeping to do. I don't want to lose Sparrows, but I won't stand for insubordination in the lines." He straightened the cuffs of his starched shirt visible below the cuffs of his suit coat and righted the gold and diamond cuff links. "Tomorrow, we're going to Walters."

"All of us?" I asked.

His dark gaze met mine. "I sure as fuck plan to look in the

eye of the man who was ultimately responsible for my wife being taken. Was I wrong to suppose you felt the same?"

"Not at all."

"I need to be there," Mason said.

We turned to Patrick as Sparrow spoke. "Patrick, we need your skills, but we can have them from here. After you meet with the capos and street gangs, get back here with Reid so we can rely on you to shoot us whatever is necessary from this command center. Also, line up a handful of Sparrows to join us on our trip and give them orders. I want them to arrive before we do and secure every loose end. We'll need a private location to meet and the assurance of staying under the radar. Walters won't want to be seen with me any more than I want to be seen with him."

Patrick nodded.

It was no secret; Patrick didn't want to be distanced from Madeline. Leaving her in Montana happened because we convinced him that it was for her good. We were wrong. Now she was safe in this tower. It wasn't only her location. As he'd mentioned privately to each of us, Madeline gave birth to Ruby over six weeks early. He refused to not be present and at his wife's side when his son entered this world.

None of us could blame him.

The world's fires would rage as would those in Chicago. That didn't mean our priorities weren't constantly changing. It wasn't that we cared less about the Sparrow Empire; it meant we also had other concerns.

Settling in my chair, I lifted my chin to my brother-in-law. "I could use you to stay here for a bit."

He nodded as Sparrow and Patrick disappeared behind the closing steel door, leaving the two of us alone.

"I want to know everything I can about Andrew Jettison, sergeant major."

Mason wheeled his chair closer to my workstation. "Since his blood was found in that bunker five days ago, I think we can safely say that he didn't die six years ago in combat."

"You found his DNA match..."

"It was matched through government records." Mason leaned back in the chair, bringing one of his ankles to the opposite knee. "Even the Order hasn't figured out how to completely erase someone's identity. They've been content to end it, to declare the man or woman dead."

I hit a few keys, making my way into the program Patrick had run. A summary of Andrew Jettison's education and service record appeared, and I began to read. "Jettison was a member of TACP, tactical air control party specialist."

Mason grunted. "Sounds like a man who could handle flying a chopper."

I continued reading. "His family received what was left of his remains in a ceremony in DC after his plane was shot down during airstrikes over Iraq and Syria. Jettison was honored for his service. The airstrikes took out a huge weapons depot." My mind went to Lorna, how she'd bravely gone to the coroner's office and identified the charred remains we'd been led to believe belonged to the man now sitting beside me. "Jettison had an impressive history of service with a list of commendations."

"The Order only spends its resources on the best."

My lips twitched. "A little full of yourself."

Mason shook his head. "I don't envy Jettison."

"No," I replied, "because I'm going to make him suffer."

"I'm certain he already has."

When I turned to my side, Mason's gaze was distant. From my vantage, I imagined that his mind was immersed in a cloud of memories. "Man, are you all right?"

Abruptly, he stood, his chair scooting across the cement floor. "Talk to me and then I need to get out to the docks."

"Talk, be more specific. I was talking."

Mason took a few steps, his boots clipping across the floor. "I don't want this to sound wrong."

I waited because his change in tone and demeanor already sounded...not right.

"Doc wants to help Lorna and Araneae any way she can," Mason began. "She's also practically elated over the drug that they were given. She's been up late researching the toxicology reports and writing in notebooks—plural— all full of notes." He stopped walking. "You have to understand, we've devoted our lives to Sparrow and the outfit. We have done a shit ton of good, an equal amount of bad, and made some great money along the way." He gestured around. "This life we live is nothing like what Lorna and I had when that bitch-on-ice gave us life."

Bitch-on-ice—Nancy Pierce. My mind went back to Lorna's dream—Missy.

"Laurel's whole life," Mason continued, "has been about helping people. Even as a kid, she'd accompany her dad—"

"Lorna told me," I interrupted, trying to move his story forward.

"Okay, so when she was an undergrad, Laurel was selected for a project. It was very secretive."

"That's where she first heard the theory that led to her compound."

"Right," Mason confirmed. "The project was cut short. She eventually made it her life's work to do what that project didn't accomplish, or what she thought it didn't."

"But it had succeeded."

"Right again, but it was so top secret, no one outside the Order knew about it." He tapped his chin as he tried to put it all into words. "I can't fully remember, but whatever I was given wasn't a onetime dose. And it didn't eliminate only recent memories. It took them all—every fucking one. I was a man with absolutely no past other than what I was told."

I had never had this specific conversation with Mason. My knowledge came through Lorna and comments Mason had made on and off. Though he hadn't told me all of this history, he'd been completely open with Sparrow. Patrick and I made a pact not to push. Maybe now was the time to start. "Yet you knew how to soldier. You knew languages. You knew technical maneuvering. You knew how to kill."

"I was retaught." Mason shook his head. "The Order determined that reteaching what someone previously knew has been more effective than teaching someone who never knew. It's the premise upon which they select the soldiers they do. Each one has the knowledge and abilities the Order wants; the soldiers just need to be reminded."

"Lorna remembers everything from before we all went to the ranch," I said. "Everything."

Mason nodded. "That's what fascinates Laurel. At the Sparrow Institute she's made progress toward reaching the place she had been at the university, but this drug—whatever the ladies were given—is more refined or fine-tuned."

"So if they're ahead of Laurel on their compound, why do they want her?"

"We don't know," Mason admitted. He pulled a hair tie from the pocket of his jeans and secured his hair at the nape of his neck. "I'm headed to the docks. Learn everything you can about Jettison. Laurel brought my memory back by bringing back my past. If you really want to fuck Jettison, do the same. Remind him of who he was before you kill him for good. If you kill him as he is today, it won't make a damn bit of difference."

"What do you mean?"

"He has nothing to lose. He's already dead."

As Mason began to walk away, the cold reality of his words settled over me. I watched as he scanned his retina to open the steel door. "Mason, Lorna needs to know about Nancy."

"It can fucking wait."

"I don't think it can. I'd be happy to bury it and her, but that's not fair to Lorna."

"Let me face Top first. Then I'll face my sister."

It was easy to think first and foremost of Lorna, but the man walking away had lived two lifetimes. He, too, deserved to face the reality of Nancy in his own time. "Fair enough."

LORNA

*L*aurel opened the door to her apartment and gestured for me to follow. Whenever I entered one of the other two apartments, the difference in decor and personality always struck me. Essentially, we all had the same floor plan except ours was the mirror image—flipped. Still, we all had a living room and dining room that flowed into our kitchen. We also all had a master bedroom suite, two additional bedrooms, an office, and an exercise room. Laurel and Mason had made one of the spare bedrooms into an office for Laurel. She'd shown it to me a while ago.

I stopped and took in the view, the other amenity we all enjoyed from our walls of windows. Laurel and Mason's living room and master bedroom looked out onto the Great Lake. After Mason *died*, Reid and I discussed switching apartments as ours lacked the lake view. It truly wasn't much of a discussion. This apartment was Mason's. I wanted and needed to begin my life with my new husband in what would always be our home.

"May I get you anything?" Laurel asked.

"Is it too early for alcohol?" Since we had just finished breakfast, my question was meant as rhetorical.

Laurel smiled. "There are no wrong answers or questions in therapy."

The word made me shudder. "Is this...that—therapy?"

"We can call it whatever you want, but I don't want to mislead you. I want to help you, as a friend and as a person educated in psychology and psychotherapy. And whether it's me or someone else—Araneae has some fantastic therapists, psychologists, and psychiatrists on staff at the Sparrow Institute—I think talking to someone is best. With the knowledge that stays in this tower, I volunteer to be that person. But I'm sure Patrick could vet the right therapist if you'd prefer."

"I talk to Reid."

Laurel smiled as she pointed toward the L-shaped sofas. Their walls were covered in a light shade of gray with white trim. Upon their walls were large photographs of Chicago and the ranch, in black and white. They fit perfectly with the clean minimalist decor.

"Well," Laurel said, "we can sit here and watch a movie."

"I want to talk. I think..." I began as I sat on the soft sofa. "I have questions about memories."

"I'm going to get some more coffee. Are you sure you don't want a cup?" she asked as she walked into the kitchen.

"Memory is an all-encompassing subject. I'll share what I can. What do you want to know?"

What did I want to know?

The list was long and the more questions I voiced, the more came to mind.

I appreciated Laurel's candor. When she knew an answer, she gave it. When she didn't, she didn't try to sugarcoat or pretend that she had the answer wrapped in fluff. Her analytical mind knew more than I could comprehend. Maybe it was her years as faculty in higher education, but she had a wonderful way of explaining.

"How long can memories stay suppressed?" I asked.

"There's no way to answer that."

The clock moved and we continued to talk. Eventually, our conversation led to amnesia, how it occurred and why.

"You do realize," Laurel said, "you and Araneae don't fit into any of the categories I just mentioned."

"You don't think our minds are suppressing a traumatic experience or experiences?"

Laurel thought for a moment. "Lorna, I would never be dishonest with a patient or a participant. I won't be with you.

"You and Araneae were taken from our ranch. You know that. We have seen the security video. You were both unconscious before the two men entered the kitchen."

"Do you think we were drugged?"

"Yes." She nodded. "I didn't realize you hadn't been told."

I lowered my feet to the floor and sat taller.

"A canister was found placed in the main house's

ventilation system. It had a remote start to release its contents of what is known as knockout gas. After we'd all eaten lunch, Madeline went upstairs to rest. I went to the office."

"And Araneae and I stayed in the kitchen."

"Are you asking or do you remember?"

"I don't remember. But as you said, I've seen the video."

Laurel nodded. "So to answer your earlier question, yes, your and Araneae's minds have every reason to block out those memories. You were kidnapped. That is traumatic."

"Then why don't we fit?" I asked.

"We've told you both—the toxicology report shows the presence of unique chemicals, numerous ones identified that I've used in my formula and compound."

We'd received information in small snippets. I was having trouble retaining it all. "I remember that now. So you believe we were given your formula?"

"Not mine. Whatever you were given is further advanced. With whatever you were given, they were able to disguise a very specific segment of your memory. Think of blacking out at a party."

A smile came to my lips. "That's funny. Araneae said something similar."

"This is similar. Can you think back to when that happened?"

I shook my head. "It never has."

Laurel's blue eyes opened wide as she set her coffee mug on the nearby table. "Well, good for you. I can't say the same thing."

"Really? I can't imagine you..." *Goody-goody Little Mary*

Sunshine. I sat taller, wondering why that would pop into my mind.

Laurel was shaking her head. "I know people assume I was all about studies, but I was a young adult too. Experimentation is a normal and educational part of growing up."

"I'm sure if you tell Patrick that, he'll be open to Ruby experimenting."

"No, he won't," she replied matter-of-factly. "No parent is and in reality, while experimenting is normal, it is also dangerous." Laurel took a deep breath. "In alcohol or drug-induced blackouts, such as with the date-rape drug known as GHB, the chemical enters the bloodstream, usually through ingestion. That begins the process of covering memories. In many cases, the person to black out will remember up until a particular moment and then nothing. That nothing point is when the drug or alcohol took over."

I tried to understand. "You think whatever was in the ventilation system began the process of our hidden memories?"

"I don't. Madeline and I both inhaled the knockout gas and neither of us is missing weeks of our lives." When I didn't respond, Laurel went on, "And both you and Araneae are missing time before the kidnapping."

"That's true."

"I believe you were given a formula that has the ability to specifically block a defined time period. Unlike the alcohol example, whatever they have created in this formula is capable of going back in time." She exhaled. "I'm fascinated.

I'd love to know what you last remember and if you've had any flashes of memory."

"I last remember life here, in our tower." I furrowed my brow. "What do you mean, flashes?"

"Part of what I do at the institute and what I want to do with my formula someday is to help people live in conjunction with their traumatic memories. I don't want to wipe the slate clean as was done to Mason. I also don't want to suggest or plant memories that don't exist. In order to do that, the participants in my studies must feel comfortable enough to speak freely with me and identify specifically what they want to forget. As they recount that, I record their brain activity. Later, I watch the brain scans for electrical activity as they recount the memory. Unfortunately, recounting is a traumatic process, almost self-defeating to my work."

"What if they don't remember...like it's blank?"

"Like you feel now?"

I nodded. "What do you see on the scans?" I asked.

"I can identify the areas of the brain that, in the simplest terms, light up while recalling the events. Then I know where I need my formula to work."

I stood and began to walk around Laurel's living room. "But...I don't think any of that happened."

Laurel stood and came toward me. "That's what's so fascinating. The specificity of your memory loss is well directed without making you endure the memories."

For a moment, I stood at Laurel's window and looked out into the sky. Large white clouds floated overhead. From our height, I could look down and see the shadows they cast. As if watching the clouds move, the shadows also moved.

While I appeared calm from the outside, inside, I felt as if I were in a tug of war.

I turned back to my friend. "What if I'm afraid to remember? Could that mean my memory loss is me and not the chemical?"

"There's no way to know whether you're experiencing natural amnesia due to your traumatic experience or chemically induced memory loss. Or a combination."

"Will the chemical go away?"

"In my study, my goal is that it won't. I would like to provide one dose and help those living in fear for the rest of their lives."

"Don't people do that every day?"

"Yes, a vast majority of the population develops their own coping mechanisms. The human brain is truly capable of so much. We see it all the time, especially in children." She shrugged. "It's the other people who need our help, the ones who are unable to deal daily with debilitating memories."

I gave that some thought.

Don't most people have experiences they don't want to remember?

Is that what was living in the black hole I fear? Is it filled with memories?

"What if..." The realization I was about to voice surprised me as much as Laurel. "...I'm afraid now?"

"Are you able to tell me what scares you?"

Tears came to my eyes. "Everything and nothing. Noises and quiet. Being alone and having others around—though today's breakfast was nice. Some things that shouldn't affect me make my heart beat faster or bring on a cold sweat, but I don't understand why. It's like there is this space or maybe the opposite, a void, hiding in my subconscious that I'm afraid to face. It's right there and as much as I think I should acknowledge it, I want to run far away. My sleep has been shit. I think it's because I'm not on guard in sleep and weird shit comes to my mind."

"What kind of *weird shit?*"

I inhaled as I shook my head at last night's dream. "Don't tell Mason."

Laurel smiled. "I'm very honest with my husband, but if it's important to you, I can keep whatever it is you tell me confidential until you're ready to share it with him."

"There's no reason to ever share it with him." Sometimes omission was best. I sighed. "I told Reid, and I'm going to tell you so you can see what I mean about totally wacky thoughts." I turned to her, our gazes meeting. "I dreamt I spoke with my mother."

Laurel's expression blanked. It was as if all emotion and thought were gone or masked.

"What's wrong?" I asked, my pulse increasing at her odd reaction.

Her smile returned. "Tell me about the conversation you had with her."

"It wasn't her," I corrected. "It was a dream, and in it, she was old and thin…" I walked back to the sofa and sat with one leg beneath me. I wrapped my arms around the other knee as I drew it close to my chest. "I'm sure there are volumes of psychology textbooks written on all the ways parents screw up their children." I put my chin on my knee. "They should all end with 'use birth control and don't have children.'"

Laurel followed me to the sofas and sat on the one she'd been on before. "There are many theories on psychosis that stem from childhood experiences. But" —she grinned— "not all human beings exhibit psychosis, so I don't think reproduction is the issue."

I scoffed. "I don't need to tell you about our mother." Thoughts that I hadn't had in years seemed to rear their ugly heads. I pushed them away with generalities. "You knew us back then at the Boys and Girls Club, one of the places where we could find meals and support. I'm sure Mace has filled in the blanks."

"I'm more interested in your dream," Laurel said.

The memory came back. Nancy Pierce's gaunt features, paper-thin skin, and fragile appearance. "My mother spoke to me in an odd old voice. She apologized for being a shitty mother." I forced a grin. "I'm paraphrasing and probably projecting."

Laurel nodded. "You're allowed. Anything else?"

"I think she died."

"In your dream?"

I swallowed emotions I didn't understand as I hugged my knee closer. My voice began to quiver. "I shouldn't care if she's dead or alive."

"She's your mother—hypothetically, in your dream," Laurel added.

"She never cared about us. It was all about her. I shouldn't care what happened to her." I rubbed my hands together as if they were suddenly cold. My empty mug caught my attention. "Would you mind if I got another cup of coffee?"

"Of course not." Laurel began to stand.

"No, let me." I needed to move. Taking my cup, I went toward their dining room and around their breakfast bar into the kitchen. Having similar floor plans and familiarity made navigating easy. It was like being home in the upside down, without all the colors.

Once the coffee maker stopped and my cup was filled, I reached into the refrigerator for the creamer. As I added the liquid, my hands trembled. Wrapping my fingers around the mug, I relished the warmth coming from within. Yet as I walked toward the living room, my trembling turned to shaking, the caramel-colored liquid sloshing near the rim.

"Lorna, are you all right?"

"Probably too much caffeine."

Laurel stood, took the mug from me, and reached for my hand. "Let me help you."

My mind filled with memories, good and bad, of the woman who gave birth to me.

"Our grandma had to claim me from the hospital when I was born," I said as Laurel led me back to the sofa. My head shook. "I'm sorry. I have no idea why I said that." As Laurel put the mug on the table, I resumed the embrace of my knee.

"It's true?"

I nodded.

"Then that's why you said it."

"This is what I mean. I'm afraid to remember. Not

remembering the last few weeks has brought a slew of other memories up from where they were buried." I sighed. "Are dreams memories, or are they just crazy thoughts brought on by the drugs I was given?"

"I can't answer that."

"You won't or you can't?" I pushed.

"I can't. It's not easy to discern."

My temples began to pound as I closed my eyes. "I'm sorry."

"Lorna, stop apologizing. You should never be sorry for what you can't control. Was there something else about the dream or simply the presence of who you believe is your mom?"

"Other than I think she died?" I asked a bit sarcastically.

"There's no wrong answer. You don't need to say anything you don't want to say."

"Maybe if you could hook up one of those scans," I suggested, "you could erase everything about my childhood, about my mother, about our sister, and about..." I didn't want to finish that sentence, fearful it could lead to a place or places I didn't want to recall.

"It's not erased..." She swallowed. "Lorna, maybe you should rest. I can take you to your apartment or you can rest here."

"No," I said as I sniffled my emotions and runny nose. "I don't want to sleep. I don't want to see her again or hear her lame apologies or confessions."

"Confessions?"

From where I was seated on the sofa, the door to the

apartment was behind me. I couldn't see and didn't hear the
door to the common area begin to open until the next
sentence was off my tongue. "Yes, confessions. Nancy Pierce
claimed Missy wasn't kidnapped. She was sold, probably for
money for drugs and alcohol."

"What the fuck?"

Laurel and I both turned to over six feet of rage. Mason's
green eyes were focused on me. With his long hair tethered at
the nape of his neck, the muscles in the side of his face
pulsated. Colorful tattoos leaked from the collar of his shirt,
and tendons pulled tight in his neck.

"Mason," Laurel said as she quickly stood. "Why are you
home?"

"I came to get—" He held out his arm, stopping his wife
from getting closer as he turned to face me. "Lorna, what the
fuck did you just say about Missy?"

LORNA

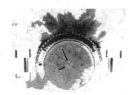

I jumped to my feet, meeting my brother's unnecessary rage. "What the hell? Why are you angry about a dream?"

Mason's jaw clenched. As he took a step back, his eyes moved from Laurel to me and back to his wife. "Fuck," he muttered.

"Mason."

I turned to Laurel, wondering what I heard in the way in which she said her husband's name.

"Is there something you aren't telling me?" I asked, uncertain who I was addressing.

Mason tried to reach out, but I stepped away.

"Lorna" —he took a deep breath— "What about Missy?"

My head shook as I shut my eyes. There was so much that didn't make sense. My temples resumed throbbing as the breakfast I'd eaten sloshed and twisted with the cups of coffee in my stomach.

I heard Mason and Laurel call to me as I pushed past them to their hall bathroom, certain I couldn't make it to my apartment in time. As soon as I closed the door, I fell to my knees and gripped the sides of the toilet seat.

"Lorna." Mason's voice came over the pounding of his overzealous knocks.

My chest ached along with my head as the contents of my stomach emptied into the toilet bowl.

As I opened my eyes, for only a millisecond, the nice bathroom around me was gone, the pretty tile work, the plush towels, and even the word art upon the wall. My entire body shivered as concrete blocks replaced reality. And then the illusion was gone.

The bathroom was back.

"Lorna." This time it was Laurel's voice.

"Just a minute," I called as I forced myself to stand and walk to the sink.

Cupping the water in my hands, I rinsed and spit. When I raised my gaze to the framed large mirror, the coldness returned to my skin. I splashed more water on my face, turning up the heat until my hands and cheeks registered the warmth.

Opening the door, I anticipated seeing two sets of expectant eyes. Instead, the hallway was empty. Taking a deep breath, I pushed forward, making my way back to their living room. "I-I…"

"Come sit down," Laurel encouraged, patting the sofa near her.

I came to a stop at the end of the hallway. "I think I better go home. Maybe it's the medicine. I'm having difficulty keeping food down and" —I turned to Mason, fighting the tears— "I'm not ready for anger. It was a dream. I know you hate the subject of Missy. I wouldn't have said anything if I knew you were here."

"So you'd lie to me? We don't lie."

My lips came together. "Like that's fair? It was a dream." I felt like I'd repeated that phrase more times than necessary.

"You didn't tell me."

"Do you tell me every dream you have, Mace?"

My brother looked at Laurel and me. "I guess..." He seemed to not only be searching for words but also doing his best to moderate his voice, toning down the anger and soothing a volatile situation as he had over the course of our lives. "You mentioned Missy. Tell me, what did she say she did?"

"Who? I didn't see Missy in my dream, and you know as well as I do that Nancy Pierce has probably been dead for years—she deserves to be. Missy is gone. People don't turn up twenty-five years after they disappear."

My hands went to my stomach. The soreness of my ribs along with the nausea made for a sickening combination. "Laurel, I know I said I don't want to sleep, but I haven't." I shook my head. "Not really. I think it would be best if I could take a break from the memories and uncertainty. Is there anything you can prescribe?"

Laurel stood. "I can't do that. I can call Dr. Dixon if you'd like. She can coordinate with the other medical professionals on your team to determine what would be best."

"Best," I scoffed. "I don't know. How about you give me some of your formula to make it all go away?"

"That's not my goal and we're still in trials."

"Then let me be in a trial."

"Fuck, Lorna," Mason said, "what the hell happened? You seem...on the edge. What did she say?"

The emotions were there, bubbling out of the black hole. I didn't want them or the memories that lurked in its depths. "It's all catching up and I don't think I'm ready." I tried to give Laurel a smile. "Maybe talking wasn't a good idea."

She knowingly nodded. "We can do it again when we're alone."

"What?" Mason asked. "Now, I'm an intruder with my wife and sister?"

"Mason." It was again her one-word warning. "I would agree that the two of you should talk."

He looked at his watch. "I'm late."

"Then leave," I said.

"Tonight," he replied. "I'll talk to Reid."

"Reid?" It was my turn to question. "What does he have to do with it?"

Mason's jaw clenched. "We're fucking drowning in shit." He disappeared down the hallway and came back with a black box. "This is why I came back. Fuck, carry on. Don't let me intrude in my own damn home." His gaze came at me. "You and me are going to talk. I want answers."

A million thoughts were loose in my mind. Untamed and wild, they stampeded toward an unknown destination, chased by a hidden predator. "I don't have answers, Mace. That's the problem. Hell, I don't even have questions." I remembered something Ruby said. "I'm swimming and there's no shore." When neither of them replied, I went on, "It's like I don't remember if I can swim or if I'm afraid of sharks and why. Maybe I'm a talented swimmer. I just don't know." Tears prickled the backs of my eyes. "I am the one who needs answers. I don't care if they're from one of you or Reid. I need something."

Mason ran his hand over his tethered-back hair. "Tonight, after I'm back from some meetings I can't ignore, we'll talk."

Laurel exhaled.

"I'm not a child, Mason," I said. "I'm an adult and you keep forgetting that."

"You can be one hundred and ten fucking years old, and I'll still be me and you'll still be you."

"You can stop protecting me."

He took a step closer. "That's not in me."

"Your meetings," Laurel reminded Mason as she stood and offered him a kiss. "Stay safe. I love you."

Their eyes met. "I love you, Doc. Don't..."

She shook her head.

"Just don't," he said.

Once he was gone, I turned to her. "Don't what?"

She feigned a smile. "Leave the building. Go to the institute...try to learn baking, set the apartment building on fire. I could probably go on forever."

I crossed my arms over my chest. "He's lying and so are you."

"We haven't lied."

"So it's almost the truth? Isn't that the same as a lie?"

"Lorna, when you're ready, you can tell Mason more about your dream, and he can fill you in on a few things they decided could wait."

"They?" I said too loud.

Laurel didn't respond.

"The men. That's who you're referring to as they: Reid and Mason. Are they alone or are Sparrow and Patrick in on it too?"

Her lips flattened.

"Of course they are. The four of them share a damn brain. They all know something, and for the last four days they've kept it from me" —my head tilted— "and from Araneae?"

"It doesn't apply equally to her."

"They know who hurt me?"

She shook her head. "They haven't said."

The black hole returned. No longer satisfied with a low bubble, the emotions within grew in intensity, the bottomless pit of dark beginning to boil. As I blinked my eyes, there were images.

Was this what she meant when she asked about flashes?

There was the old woman. There were stars. I saw a man with black hair. His complexion was light yet his expression was...I was afraid.

My fingertips went to my cheek. Placing gentle pressure, I

felt the soreness. I fell back to the sofa. I blinked again. The walls were covered in paneling and the stench of cigarette smoke hung thick in the air.

The flashes seemed unrelated, and yet I didn't want any of them. "You mentioned blacking out with alcohol. I never did, but there are blanks from before—long ago—things I can't remember."

"No one remembers everything," Laurel said. "That's normal."

Again, I stood. The small hairs on my arms stood to attention and my skin bristled.

"Lorna, are you all right?"

I brushed invisible predators from my arms.

"There's nothing on you."

The offensive smoke scent faded. I looked down at my arms and pulled the sleeves of my sweater up. The bites were healing, yet they weren't gone. However, there was nothing else on me.

I turned to my friend. "Laurel, what happened to me?"

Suddenly, a thought that had not occurred to me before this second seemed obvious—as obvious as the insect bites on my skin.

Why hadn't I thought of it before?

"Do you want to rest?" Laurel asked.

Instead of answering, I asked, "Was I...raped?"

Oh God.

Was that why Reid didn't want to have sex?

Were there diseases?

Taking a few steps toward their dining room, I had to keep moving. My words came quicker, in time with my steps along the shiny wood floor. "I need to know. I need to know if I was assaulted...sexually."

"We should contact Reid."

"Why? No." My volume rose. "It isn't his decision." I reached for my phone in my back pocket. "I'll call Renita. It might be too late to test." Reid and I had just... My hand with the phone fell to my side. "Shit. It probably is too late."

"If she's at the hospital, you can leave a message."

"No," I corrected. "I mean too late as in...too much time since I was found."

"It isn't."

"This morning...Reid and I..."

Laurel smiled. "I'm so glad."

Her response made me grin. "What? Why do you care?"

"Because, psychologically, the fact that you're ready to be intimate is a good sign. It's a very good sign."

"But because we had sex, they can't test." I let out a breath and sat again. "Why didn't I think of this before?"

Laurel sat beside me, placed her hand over mine, and squeezed. "We don't need Reid present. That is your choice. You have every right, legal and otherwise, to learn this information on your own. I simply believe that it's good to have support when faced with difficult situations."

"Difficult..." My pulse kicked up, adding to my throbbing temples. "Do you believe I was?"

"Assumptions aren't necessary."

"What do you mean?" I asked. "How long does it take to get results?"

"You've already been tested."

I sat taller. "When? How?"

"You were unconscious. As your husband, Reid had the right to authorize medical procedures. Some couldn't wait, like the plastic surgery."

"And a rape kit?"

Laurel nodded.

I fell back against the soft sofa. Reid thought I'd been raped. "Wait, has he seen the results?"

"No. He specifically said no one could see them until the time came, if it ever did, when you asked. He said it didn't matter to him."

"Didn't matter?" My lip slid between my upper and lower teeth as I gave that some more thought.

"Lorna, it matters. He made it clear that he wouldn't love you any less or think differently. The only thing he was told about the kit was that you tested negative for STDs."

I let out a long breath. That was good. "I'll call him and let him know that I want to know."

"Okay," she agreed.

As I reached for my phone, I confessed, "Laurel, I feel like there are so many things I should know and remember, and they're right there. I can't let something this large be within my reach without getting an answer. I'm sinking and now I have one thing I can control. Whether Reid can be here or not, I need to know."

"I understand."

I activated the screen of my phone and entered the pass code. "I'll call Renita first and find out when she can be here and then let Reid know. Either way, I'll have at least one answer today."

REID

*A*fter Mason left and I was alone on 2, I forced myself to stay focused. It was too easy to slide into my thoughts of how I would avenge Lorna. Yes, Araneae was part of the equation. I wasn't minimizing her kidnapping or anything that happened to her.

When it came to our women, the four of us weren't teenage boys in a locker room. There was no boasting of conquests or discussions of what occurred in the privacy of our marriage vows. That wasn't necessarily because we were upstanding individuals. The truth was we all had done things in our lives we would rather not bring up at the dinner table. It was that within this strange family we'd begun in this tower, our wives weren't simply present for fucking. They were not and never were considered less because of their gender. They were a part of the greater us.

Lorna shared with me how Sparrow had said something to

her not long after our wedding. It was when he talked to her about her role in our lives. I supposed that talk should have come from me, but when it came to the group as a whole, it was Sparrow's show. I had made it clear that Lorna wasn't leaving. I did all I could to show her she was loved and wanted. He took it a step further, imploring her to be a part of not only my life but everyone's.

For six years, we were married before any of the other women joined this castle in the sky. It would have been shitty of me to bask in an active sex life while the others were most hopelessly devoted to their hands and cold showers.

No, they didn't say that.

While Mason was a mystery until he returned with Laurel, I knew of times Sparrow and Patrick had gone off the grid without explanation. It wasn't often—but it happened. I'm a man and knew that they were calmer upon their return. It was usually after a big event in our world.

Our wives weren't stress relievers, though Lorna's and my morning hit that mark.

My point was that Sparrow hasn't shared personal knowledge of how Araneae was dealing with what happened. I knew facts. Her pregnancy was progressing. She had the same compound in her system as Lorna and had no memories since before the women were taken to the ranch.

Did she wake crying?

Did she startle at normal noises?

I didn't have those answers. I knew my wife and saw the unjust fear in her eyes when a tea kettle began to whistle. I found her crying in our shower and saw the effects of her captivity on her skin.

It wasn't that I didn't want retaliation for what had been done to Araneae. It was that I needed it for my wife.

As the morning turned to afternoon, I fulfilled my checklist.

Utilizing travel records in and out of Dulles International and Ronald Reagan Washington National, I successfully tracked the comings and goings of senators who worked with or near Edison Walters. Over the years, he'd worked as a senior legislative aide for many senators in all parties. It was his knowledge and dedication that they wanted, not an affiliation to party. Whatever the newest hot-button issue was, Edison Walters and his staff were the go-to aides. Their experience with compiling bills and wording and presenting them in committee made them highly sought after.

While the bipartisanship of yesteryears was in a wane cycle, with people like Edison Walters, he'd been around long enough to believe the wax cycle would return. He'd personally walked the halls of various buildings within the Capitol complex during the administration of the last seven presidents.

It would be wrong to assume that Edison Walters had simultaneously held the position of Top during all of over forty years. If that were true he'd reached pinnacle status in his twenties. Of course, there was no way to research the history of the top administrator of a governmental agency that didn't formally exist.

If I wanted to take the time, I could verify the money

trails and determine that additional funding was allocated before Edison Walters entered the congressional chambers. The congressional summer recess was about to conclude.

There'd been no official documentation of Walters leaving Washington DC during the break; however, utilizing different cameras around the city, establishments he frequented, and a stoplight near his home, I learned he'd been off the grid for the first three weeks of August.

A week and a half ago he returned.

I can only assume his travel wasn't commercial but facilitated by the Order.

The bunker where Christian and Romero found the ladies' shoes was near Anaconda. I cross-referenced facial recognition software with the stored data I had from tracking down the old Ford truck.

Simultaneously, I compiled as much as possible on Sergeant Major Andrew Jettison. Patrick and Mason had compiled most of his service record. I went back further, remembering Mason's advice: if you really want to fuck Jettison, remind him who he was before you kill him for good. If you kill him as he is today, it won't make a damn bit of difference—he's already dead.

Unlike all of us who had been born in and around Chicago, Andrew Jettison was born in Sacramento, California, to David and Melissa Jettison. He was the third of four children. They all survived him.

"Oh fuck," I said as more information came up.

My phone vibrated with a text message. My wife's name came upon the screen. I hit the green icon.

. . .

"I CONTACTED RENITA. SHE HAS MY TEST RESULTS AND WILL BE HERE AT FOUR. I'D LIKE YOU TO BE WITH ME, BUT I'M GETTING THE RESULTS."

I continued to stare at her words.

Test results?

There was only one test we hadn't mentioned.

Rape kit.

How did Lorna know Dr. Dixon had the results?

Crimson flowed over my vision. Lorna wasn't ready for this information. Only this morning she was crying in the shower.

How in the hell did she learn there were results to be had?

Not only wasn't she ready for this information, fuck, I wasn't ready.

And then I had a thought—we had Jettison's DNA. The kit would provide DNA if she was...I couldn't even make myself think the word. My teeth ached as I applied pressure.

If the DNA matched...

Andrew Jettison was already taking his last breaths. If this could be added to his list of sins, there would be no salvation. And now I had more information. I'd fucking work overtime to bring back his memories, reminding him of who he was before killing him for good.

Taking a deep breath, I laid my phone on the desk and pushing back my chair, I stood.

The tension and tightness could be felt in my muscles. I hadn't moved from that chair in hours. Walking away from the monitors, I stretched my shoulders. One arm over my head, I pulled my elbow upward. Closing my eyes, I pulled harder, relishing the burn. Next, I did the same with the opposite arm. Rolling my head from side to side, I knew it would take more than a few stretches to work out this tension.

I wasn't willing to devote the time to the weight bench or treadmill. My muscles could coil into a massive ball of yarn before I devoted more time to anything that didn't work toward my ultimate goal.

Finding Jettison.

Meeting with Walters.

And ultimately learning why the Order was after Laurel. That still seemed like a missing piece of our puzzle. At first, we assumed it was her formula, but why would they want her when it appeared as though they had a superior compound?

The clock in the large screen above told me I had half an hour before Dr. Dixon would arrive to the apartments.

Shaking my head, I hit call.

"Lorna." I spoke as soon as the phone connected.

"Did you get my text message?"

"Yeah, I was wondering—"

"Reid," she interrupted, "I can't stand not knowing. I'm having what Laurel calls flashes—small snippets of memories. But they don't make sense. I can't place them or connect them. There is so much that I don't know. I need to know something, to have an answer."

Her fucking voice tore at my heart. She was fighting thoughts and feelings because of me.

If she'd been kept safe...

My grip of the phone grew dangerously tight.

"Reid?"

I wanted to ask her how she even learned of the kit. I wanted to reassure her that I loved her, yet as guilt morphed into self-loathing, I turned to the six-year-old picture of Andrew Jettison.

"Reid, are you still there?"

"Tell me what you want, Lorna?"

She cleared her throat. "I want to wake up and have it be three weeks ago. I want no blanks in my memory and not to hurt with every step. I want to go back to believing that despite the danger in the world, I'm safe. I want to not feel vulnerable. I'm not, Reid. I'm not. I am strong, and I want to feel that way."

Fuck.

I walked over to the computers and hit a few keys, putting my screens to sleep while keeping programs running. "I'm coming up."

LORNA

Twenty-six years ago

After our grandmother died, Mason, Missy, and I moved in with our mother, Nancy Pierce. It was the first time we'd lived with our mother, other than when she would stay at Grandma's. When she finally claimed us, she wasn't living alone; she lived with a man named Gordon Maples and his two daughters, Anna and Zella.

Mom told us and the lady from Children's Services that we would all be a family and made it sound like a story from a book.

While Missy was excited, Mason and I were weren't sure how it would work. Why after having three children, the oldest one eleven, would she suddenly want us?

When the car pulled up to the large white house, Mason and I looked at one another with a seed of hope. Maybe this would work. Maybe our mom could keep us and we wouldn't end up in foster care or separated.

It was clear even to me that Mr. Maples wasn't pleased about the extra mouths to feed. It wasn't unusual for one or all of us to be sent to bed without dinner. Even though he had a large house with four bedrooms, the three of us were given the attic as our room. If we behaved to his approval, we would have light. If not, there was one window and a streetlight below.

There were ever-changing rules and long lists of chores.

Not meeting his expectations led to punishments. Mason took the brunt of the beatings, but no one was immune from Mr. Maple's belt, not even our mother. There were times I'd preferred the belt to the humiliation of standing in the corner of the living room while Anna and Zella watched television and laughed at me.

Mr. Maples came up with what he called punishments to match the crime.

One time after I'd completed washing the dishes, he found a glass I'd missed. That night, I was made to stay up all night and wash every dish. I'd put them away and he'd empty another cupboard. By morning, everything had been washed and dried five or six times. Another time it was floors that needed scrubbing.

Days turned into weeks, weeks into months.

My tenth birthday came.

Then one night as I was about to sleep, the door to the attic opened. His outline appeared in the light from the stairwell. I reached for Missy, who was asleep next to me.

"Lorna." Mr. Maple's voice was thick, the way it became at night after he'd drunk beer.

Mason's head lifted, but I shook mine at him, telling him to stay quiet.

I'd probably need to clean some mess or apologize for something Anna or Zella did. That degradation would be less humiliating than involving Mason. He'd surely end up with a bloody lip or black eye.

Leaving Missy asleep on the mattress we shared, wearing my nightgown, I quietly walked toward the doorway.

"Follow me."

It was his only directive as we climbed down the narrow attic staircase into the hallway on the second level. We passed Zella's bedroom and then Anna's. My heart beat faster as I followed him down the bigger staircase that led to the living room on the main level.

I scanned the room, wondering what was out of place, what I would need to do.

He didn't speak as we walked through the kitchen. Again, my eyes searched the counters, unsure what my task would be. The only things out of place were empty beer cans scattered about.

The question of what I'd done or what I needed to do was on the tip of my tongue. It stayed there, unspoken. I worried that saying it would make him mad. Judging by the number of beer cans, he'd had a lot to drink. We then entered the rear living room, the one with the television. A cloud of cigarette smoke hung near the ceiling. My gaze went to the corner.

Would I need to stand there?

I told myself that it wouldn't be as bad with Zella and Anna upstairs.

Whatever was playing on the television echoed off the paneled walls. Every few seconds the fake sound of laughter came from the speakers. My steps stopped when I saw my mother. She didn't see me. Her eyes were closed and her mouth open as she slept on the long plaid sofa. On the carpet, near where her hand dangled was an empty wine bottle. Mr. Maples lifted one finger to his lips before gesturing toward his and Mom's bedroom.

My stomach twisted and my hands trembled with each step. He was leading me into the unknown. We'd physically passed by all his normal punishments. This was different. I didn't know what I'd done, but whatever it was, I believed in my soul that punishment was coming—I just didn't know how he would deliver it.

As I walked past my sleeping mother, I wanted to shake her, to wake her, and to ask her to help me.

Would she?

She'd probably do as she usually did, tell me to be nice, listen to Mr. Maples, and do as he says.

I came to a stop at the threshold of their bedroom. It was the one room we weren't allowed to enter. My eyes quickly scanned the room. The bed was unmade. The carpeted floor was stained and littered with piles of clothes, overflowing hampers of dirty laundry, cigarette butts, and other trash.

There were more beer cans.

"Go-on," he urged, his two words slurred into one.

My heart beat faster. Once he closed the door with both

of us inside, I turned and apologized for whatever sin I'd committed.

"No, Lorna. Stay quiet."

Though I had a strange feeling, my lips came together, obeying as I nodded.

"I like you." His voice held an odd tone. "You like me, don't you?"

I wanted to scream no. I don't like you. But instead, I again nodded.

"Good." He smiled, his teeth stained yellow from cigarettes. "You and me, we're going to share a secrct." The stale scent of beer and cigarette smoke surrounded him as he came closer. "You like secrets? Don't you?"

My trembling increased as I tried to back away.

He shook his head. "You can't tell anyone about us. That's the rule with secrets."

"Mr. Maples...I need to go to bed. I have school."

His glassy gray eyes scanned as I stood in my nightgown. The way he stared felt wrong in a bad way I didn't understand. I wasn't sure why I didn't like the way he was looking at me, but I didn't. It sent a cold chill over my body as small hairs stood up on my arms and legs.

"You look real pretty, Lorna. You look like your momma." He came closer and lifted a strand of my hair between his fingers. "You have her pretty red hair."

I stood frozen. It wasn't that the room was cold—it was much warmer than up in the attic. It was as if I couldn't move. Mr. Maples was talking to me, telling me about secrets and special friends, telling me how nice he can be and how I should appreciate his compliments.

"Don't you like to hear how pretty you are?"

I didn't, not from him.

"Don't be scared, Lorna. We're going to be good friends." He continued to touch my hair and talk about the color. It was when he asked me if I had pretty red hair between my legs that my eyes filled with tears.

"No, I'm not old enough," I answered.

"I'd like to see."

I shook my head. "Grandma taught us that anyplace that a bathing suit covers was our private areas. Those are only ours and no one else's."

As he wiped away a tear from my cheek, I noticed his dirty fingernails and grimy skin. "It's okay, Lorna. You and me, we're friends, and friends can share special things and special places—even private places." He reached for his belt buckle.

Before he said anything else, I jumped backward and tripped, falling backward. "Please." I knew the sting of his belt, not as much as Mason, but I did.

"Shh," he said with a laugh. "No, Lorna. I'm going to show you what friends do. I'm going to show you my private place, and then you can show me yours."

Still sitting on the floor, I lowered my chin, not sure what to do. I closed my eyes, wishing for anything—lightning to strike him, lightning to strike me, or maybe my mom to wake.

"Stand up."

My heart beat so fast, the room swayed as I stood.

The stench of stale beer grew stronger as he whispered

close to my ear. "Be a good friend, Lorna, and this will be our secret. If you tell anyone, we won't be able to be friends. I'll have to make Missy my friend."

I sucked in a breath of the sour air.

"Open your eyes."

I had a brother only a year older than me. I knew that boys and girls were different. But I'd never seen a grown man's penis. Instead of it lying between his legs, his was ugly, big, and sticking out like an angry stick with a mushroom-shaped top.

Mr. Maples had asked me about hair between my legs. I didn't have any, but he did. My nose scrunched. It was black and curly. It wasn't only between his legs. A line went up his fat belly, and his legs were also covered, just not as thick.

"Do you want to be my friend, or do you think it should be Missy?"

Although I didn't know exactly what the future held, I knew that my job was to protect my sister. "Me," I answered, my voice barely audible over my pounding heart.

He smiled in a scary way like the villains in comic books. "So you want to be my special friend?"

I nodded.

"Tell me, Lorna. Let me hear you ask me."

"Can I-I...?" my voice stuttered.

He reached for my chin and spoke slowly. "Please, Mr. Maples. Let me be your special friend. I promise I won't tell anyone. I promise I won't break your trust."

LORNA

Twenty-six years ago

The dinner I'd eaten long ago churned in my gut. I wasn't sure how I did it, how I repeated what Mr. Maples said, but somehow, I made the words come out. "Please, Mr. Maples. Let me be your special friend. I promise I won't tell anyone. I promise I won't break your trust."

"Now that we're special friends, you can touch my private part. Only good girls get to touch it."

I knew in my ten-year-old heart that it was wrong. I was wrong. This was wrong.

However, I'd asked for it, and I was too scared to stop, terrified of making him mad. I'd seen him mad. Whatever this was that he wanted me to do wouldn't be as bad as his belt or some of the other punishments he could invent. I could do this and go back to bed.

That was what I told myself.

My hand shook as if the temperature of the room had dropped to below freezing as I reached toward him. The tips of my fingers made contact.

"That's it. Really touch it."

I did. It felt...weird.

He covered my hand with his and curled my fingers around his private part. "Let me teach you how to make a friend feel good."

I didn't speak as he moved my hand up and down. As he did, he made strange noises as his eyes closed, his legs shifted, and his breathing became weird. It sounded as if he'd been running and was out of breath. Beneath my hand, his penis moved and twitched.

"Please let me stop," I pleaded as my stomach rolled.

"Not yet."

Again, I closed my eyes. He squeezed my fingers tighter and moved my hand faster. The skin on his penis stretched under my touch. His feet staggered and more cuss words came in a mumbled whisper, yet he didn't slow. I was afraid to look at what was going on under my grip, and then *it* happened.

My first thought was that he'd peed.

I jumped back as warm liquid hit my feet. "I'm sorry." I knew how embarrassed Missy was when she had an accident. Mr. Maples was a grown man. Surely, he'd be angry that I saw him do this. "Please don't be mad."

He breathed in and out. "I'm not mad, Lorna. What

happened is a good thing. You did such a good job, you made me come."

His words didn't make sense.

Come?

Where was he that he came?

Why wasn't he mad?

Mr. Maples tilted his head toward the attached bathroom. "Go fetch a washcloth and clean this up."

As if I was in a daze, I obeyed. My entire body trembled as I stepped around the wet spot and the debris littering the carpet of their room. In the bathroom, I found a twisted washcloth in the bottom of the tub. I quickly saturated it with water and carried it back out.

Mr. Maples's penis was still in his hand as he pointed to the carpet. "Clean that up so we can keep our secret."

Tears flowed down my cheeks, dripping from my chin, as I scrubbed the carpet. I wasn't sure how one stain was different than the other, but I didn't stop scrubbing until he told me I could.

"Look up here."

Still on my knees, I turned. His penis was now in front of me.

"Are you going to keep our secret?"

"Yes."

"Who will you tell?"

My head shook. "No one. I promise."

The hand that had been holding his penis was wet and smelled. I shivered as he used it to cup my cheek, concentrating on not pulling away.

"I sure do like having this private secret with such a pretty little girl. Do you want to stay my special friend?"

"Yes." It wasn't what I wanted. I wanted to go back upstairs to our attic. I wanted to be back with our grandmother. I wanted to pack all our things and run far away.

I wanted anything, anything at all, except to be his special friend.

"Next time," he said.

Next time?

I didn't want there to be a next time.

His hand was back to moving up and down his penis. "Next time, you can show me that you don't need my help. You can be a good girl on your own." He took a step closer. "Now, let me tell you another secret." I didn't speak or move. "Secret friends kiss good night."

That was the last thing I wanted. I didn't want to kiss him or for my lips to touch his. I'd seen the gross way he and my mom kissed.

I'd been wrong in thinking that was what he meant.

"See right on the tip." He directed my eyes to his penis. "See how it's still wet. Give it a kiss and lick away the wet. Good friends finish the job."

I couldn't do it. It was right before me, but I couldn't make myself do it.

Until...

"Oh, Lorna, maybe I was wrong about you. I'm sure Missy would do better. She's a good girl."

No, I was strong. Grandma said I was. I could do this for Missy.

Closing my eyes, I puckered my lips and leaned toward him. As I did, the odors made me want to gag. Instead, I held my breath. The instant my lips touched his private place, I felt the moisture and pulled away.

"Yeah, that's it. See, you can be good too." He petted my head as if I was a dog or cat. "I like your kiss, Lorna. Now, I want you to lick it—like you would an ice cream cone. Once you do, then you can go to bed."

Dinner or something else bubbled in the back of my throat. My body trembled as I stuck out my tongue.

The urge to spit and cough was right there, yet I didn't.

His hand came again to the top of my head. "Yeah, that's so good. One more lick."

More tears spilled from my closed eyes as I obeyed.

"What flavor of ice cream do you like?"

What?

"Tell me."

I leaned back. I hadn't had ice cream since Grandma died. The lady from Children's Services who took us away from her house gave all of us ice cream. It was vanilla inside a hard chocolate shell. "Strawberry," I said.

"That's it," he said, his yellow teeth smiling down at me. "It will be our secret-friend game. We'll pretend you're eating a strawberry ice cream cone. Go ahead and show me how good you lick."

I didn't have it in me to protest. I'd gone this far. All I

wanted was to be back in bed with my sister. My tongue went forward.

His legs quivered.

"Good girl. I'm very happy you want to be my secret friend." Mr. Maples took a step back and offered me his hand.

Not taking it, I stood. "Can I go now?"

"This is our secret. Remember, if you tell, you'll break our special friendship, and then I'll need to find a new secret friend."

"I won't tell. I promise." The truth was I'd say anything at this moment to get away from him.

"You know, your momma would be mad at you if she knew."

"Mad?"

"Yep. She wants to be my only special friend. She doesn't like to share, especially not with someone so much younger and prettier than her." His lips came together as he shook his head. "Yep, she'd be hollering mad. I'd bet she might just want to make sure it don't happen no more. She'd probably make sure."

"How?"

"Send you off to foster care."

The chill returned to my skin.

Mr. Maples reached for my shoulder. "Now, Lorna, I don't want that. Do you?"

"Away, without Mason and Missy?"

"Yep. All by yourself."

The three of us had never been apart except for a very brief time after Grandma died. "No, please."

Mr. Maples pushed his penis back into his pants, zipped the zipper, and fastened his belt. He shrugged. "It's your choice, Lorna. Once your momma sends you away, I'll just have to teach Missy what I'm teaching you."

My head shook.

Mr. Maples lifted his dirty fingers again to my hair and tugged on a curl. "I can teach you so much." He tugged again on the curl. "Tell me you want to learn."

The words burned my throat and tongue. "I want to learn."

Walking past me, he opened the door to the living room. "Be quiet now, you don't want to wake your momma. She'd be mighty upset about what you did."

My escape was in sight.

Quietly, I hurried as fast as I could, barely glancing at my sleeping mother or the empty wine bottle. When I got to the second floor, I ran to the bathroom and shut the door. My cheeks were still wet from my tears, and my eyes were red around the green. Turning on the water, I cupped some in my hand and rinsed my mouth. Then I brushed my teeth and rinsed again. I loaded the toothbrush with more toothpaste and brushed again.

Afraid of Mr. Maples hearing the shower, I took off my nightgown and using a washcloth and soap, cleaned myself. Even though he hadn't touched me or seen below the nightgown, every inch of me felt dirty. I washed away the smell and even his stare. Over and over, I scrubbed my foot where the white liquid had fallen until the skin was red and raw. By the time I was satisfied, my crying and trembling had stilled.

Slowly, I crept up the steps to the attic.

"Where were you? What did he want?" Mason asked as I opened the door.

"I was in the bathroom."

"What did Mr. Maples want?"

"He made me clean up a mess." It wasn't a complete lie. At the same time, it was the least truthful I'd ever been with my brother.

I told myself not to think about it.

I wrapped my arms around my sister and with my lips near her hair, I cried myself to sleep as I told myself a blatant lie. "That didn't happen. You are strong and a good sister, just like Grandma said. Don't think about it. There won't be a next time."

My new promise repeated until slumber finally came.

LORNA

Present day

The door opened and Reid's eyes met mine. They scanned me from head to toe. Each inch seemed as though he were trying to determine if I would survive the next hour, his gaze debating what could happen.

I took a deep breath as he came closer. The emotion I'd seen up in the penthouse when he walked away was back, swirling in the depths of his eyes. No longer a soft shade of suede brown, darkness and uncertainty brought turbulence to his orbs. He reached for my damp hair.

"You took another shower without me."

It was an odd statement, completely irrelevant, and yet it made me grin. "It was a bath and quicker than our shower."

"I didn't know you wanted quick."

Shaking my head, I lowered my forehead to his chest as he gently kissed my hair.

"Did you talk to Laurel?" His question reverberated through his wide chest as his strong arms gently came around me.

I looked up. In the seconds we'd been close, the storm in his gaze had settled. I doubted it was over. If it were a hurricane, perhaps this was the center—the eye. But I knew better. The four men in our lives were out for blood, and a few days or even a week wouldn't resolve this fight.

"I did," I answered.

"Is that why..." He hesitated. "Who told you about the kit?"

My feet moved me away from his embrace. "If your biggest concern right now is how I learned that a rape kit had been done on me without my consent, then I'm afraid you're missing the forest for the trees."

"I consented," he admitted, standing taller. "Laurel and the doctor said that it might not be possible after you woke. I consented, Lorna. I'm sorry I didn't tell you. I'm sorry this is even a fucking conversation. I'm not sorry I consented to something that could give you an answer if you ever decided you needed it."

Reaching up, I palmed his cheek. "I'm not mad at you. I'm glad you did it because that's exactly what I need—answers." I brushed my lips over his, warm and full. "Laurel told me that you said no one besides me could ask for the results."

"So that's why you contacted Renita?"

With a deep breath, I took another step back. "Yes and

no. We were talking and I realized that I hadn't thought of rape. It hadn't occurred to me." I wrapped my arms around myself. The clothes I'd worn to breakfast were gone. I was now wearing denim leggings and a soft shirt, all covered by a long sweater with fringe. With the position of my arms, the fringe tickled my hands.

Reid's eyes closed as he shook his head. "What you said on the phone, wishing you could go back in time..." He walked toward the windows in our dining room and stared for a minute. "I'd fucking give up everything to make that come true."

"Everything?"

"This" —he lifted his hands high— "money, power, all of it...to grant you that wish."

"And me too? You'd give me up?"

His entire being turned my way, energy surging from his pores. "Fucking never, Lorna."

"I don't want to give any of it up."

Reid's head moved back and forth. "I can't turn back time. Ask me for anything else, anything."

I walked closer, my sock-clad feet sliding on our tile floor as I reached for his hand. "Don't leave me."

"Never. I told you that isn't a possibility."

"Laurel told me what you said, about the results of this test not mattering."

Reid nodded.

A lump came to my throat. No matter how many times I told myself I could handle whatever the future brought, I was failing. I wanted to know something, to have control over some single aspect of my missing past. And now I wasn't sure I'd made the right decision.

What was it they say?

Be careful what you wish for.

"Reid, it will matter to me."

"Oh, sweetheart, I didn't mean the results don't matter. I meant, to me. I love you. I will always love you. The results will matter because if..." —he swallowed, his Adam's apple moving up and down— "it happened, it's my fault."

"If it happened," I said, "I'll need you beside me. I will need you to tell me and show me that I'm still loved, that you don't see me as damaged, as less, as no one."

"Never. I told you, you're a fighter. You're not damaged."

"I'll still need something else."

Before he could respond, there was a knock on the door.

Reid looked down at me, his hands now at my waist. "Tell me what that is."

"I already did."

The knock came again.

He didn't move, not an inch. His grip of my waist solidified, unrelentingly holding me in place as his tumultuous stare continued.

"I said it before. Don't leave me. I don't mean only physically in proximity. I mean here." I lifted one finger to his temple. "I need you with me, not avenging me."

His lips came to mine, lingering longer than the time before.

The door to our living room opened.

Startled, we both turned.

"Sorry," Laurel said with a shy grin. "I knocked. I thought...well, Dr. Dixon called, and she's in the garage. Reid, can you please give her access?"

Letting go of my waist, he nodded as he walked to his office down the hallway. I had only seen the room I refer to as their command center or lair once and it wasn't for long. My husband's office in our apartment was nothing like that. This one was warm, even more than Sparrow's in the penthouse. Reid's love of books was evident as soon as you entered. Two walls were nothing but built-in bookcases filled to the brim. New books were piled here and there. He'd allowed me to add rugs with color and some artwork, but the rest was all him. His desk was often covered in papers and notes. In the corner was an old chair that was in need of replacement, yet he wouldn't part with it. That was my husband and his space. He wouldn't part with what he loved and what mattered.

As I watched him walk away, I hoped that included me.

Laurel reached for my arm. "Did you get any rest?"

Taking a deep breath, I turned. "I don't think much. I soaked for a while in a warm bath."

"That's good." Her smile turned more serious. "Just because Dr. Dixon has this information, it doesn't mean you have to see or hear it."

"I do."

"No, Lorna. There is no timetable you're required to maintain."

I peered toward the hallway to be sure Reid was still out of earshot. "I can't explain what it's like not to know things. I can't even tell myself what did or didn't happen. I just don't know, and not knowing is making me question other things I either don't know or have forgotten. It's a spiral and I'm spinning out of control."

She shook her head. "You feel that you are."

I blinked away tears. "Yes."

"That alone is a sign you're still in control." When I didn't respond, she went on, "A repeated question in psychology is very simple. Who needs the most help—the person who asks for it or the one who doesn't? You see, the person who asks receives counseling or therapy. The one who doesn't ask, who doesn't recognize that there is something amiss, is the one who could need it the most."

"I know that I need control over something. I have no answers." I rubbed my cool hands together. "The answer I get may not be what I want to hear, but I'll have it. I might not remember an assault or how I responded or reacted, but I'll know it happened. That may sound odd..."

Reid's footsteps came from the hallway.

Laurel squeezed my arm. "I want you to know that you don't sound odd. You sound strong. I don't know how I would be if I were in your shoes. I can only hope I would be as formidable as you." She grinned as Reid came closer. "And I would say by the empirical evidence before me, if there was a *him*, you gave him hell."

Reid placed his arm protectively around my waist. "She's a world champion in my eyes."

A new knock came to our door.

"That would be Renita," Reid said.

Laurel smiled. "I don't know the results. I wanted you to

know that." She looked at Reid. "We took your instructions seriously." Her gaze came back to me. "I'm going upstairs to help Madeline and Araneae with dinner. If you don't feel like coming up to eat, text me. We'll bring dinner down to you two."

I nodded as across the room, Reid opened the door.

Renita Dixon had been a friend of the Sparrows since before I met Reid. As a matter of fact, she was at the ball where Reid and I met. I can't remember if she was a fake date for Sparrow or Patrick. Either way, it was clear from that first meeting, she was a trusted soul. Not long after that ball, she finished her degree, earning the title of doctor. Next came her residency in cardiology.

"Lorna," she said with a bright smile.

I returned her grin. Today she wasn't dressed in her scrubs giving away her medical profession. She was simply a beautiful and knowledgeable woman wearing makeup that I didn't usually see upon her dark complexion and a lovely light-pink pantsuit.

Renita offered me her hand.

As we greeted one another, I said, "You know, I was just thinking that you have an overqualified résumé for delivering lab results."

Her smile widened as her cheeks rose. "How are you?"

"I'm in therapy or whatever it is Laurel does."

"That's good. Is it helping?"

"No, not really."

Reid wandered about in close proximity, doing as I asked and not leaving me as Renita and I chatted, creating, despite the circumstances, a sense of both familiarity and calm.

In a way I couldn't describe, just having my husband near as well as Dr. Dixon, the bearer of the answer I sought, beside me brought me a bit of comfort. I wasn't going to learn what had happened from a stranger but from a friend. Truly, in the Sparrow world, the woman now seated in my home was one of my first female confidants.

Dr. Dixon lifted a large magenta purse from the coffee table where she'd placed it upon sitting.

"It's in there?" I asked.

Renita nodded. "I'm so glad you contacted me when you did. Robert and I have reservations for the symphony and with your location, this timing worked well."

Robert was her husband. While I didn't know him well, he'd been at Reid's and my wedding. And through the years, we'd crossed paths.

"I'm so sorry to have upset your schedule."

She shook her head. "No, I'm happy to see you again. The last time you were a bit under the weather."

"Unconscious," I offered.

Renita nodded. "Reid." She craned her neck from side to side.

"I'm here," he said, calling from the kitchen.

"Lorna, I'm assuming you want Reid here with you?"

I nodded.

"Go sit by your wife."

The bossiness in her tone brought a grin to my lips.

Our eyes met as my husband came around the breakfast

bar and dining room before taking a seat at my side. As he sat, the sofa dipped to his weight. Yet instead of emanating comfort, I sensed his unease—the tenseness of his muscles and the way he was perched upon the edge of the cushions, barely sitting.

"She doesn't bite." Renita smiled as she turned to me. "Or do you?"

I looked over at Reid and shook my head. "Not on purpose."

Scooting closer to me and onto the cushion, he reached for my hand. As we connected, our fingers intertwined and his muscles eased.

"That's more like it," the doctor praised.

There were few people in the world who would order around any of the Sparrow men. While she probably wouldn't take the same tone with Sparrow, in the here and now, her taking charge was what was needed.

Settling against my husband, I took consolation in the warmth radiating from his side as we both waited expectantly for the information the doctor had in her possession.

My grip of my husband's hand tightened as she pulled an envelope from her purse.

"Have you read it?" I asked.

She extended her hand and the envelope toward us. "I have."

Reid's grasp tensed.

As if she could hear his unspoken response, she added, "I've found it better to enter a patient's room prepared." She looked around our living room. "That includes a patient's home."

With a trembling hand, I reached for the envelope and looked over to my husband.

"Do you want me to open it?" he asked. The storm that had settled in his eyes was back, the typhoon-force winds swirling violently despite his calmer cadence.

"Maybe we can do it together?"

REID

It took every ounce of self-control to not rip the envelope from Lorna's grasp and stow it away where the contents were incapable of threatening her well-being. As I forced myself to do what Lorna asked—to be present, an unusual memory came to mind.

I was probably eight or nine years old. A relatively quiet child, I was rarely in trouble. Yet that day there'd been something that happened in my classroom. This many years later, I can't recall the exact incident, although I remember the topic: another boy told me I didn't have a dad. I did. He was no longer with us, but I had one.

While the incident remained in my memory, it didn't imprint upon my psyche as much as what happened later at home.

Sitting in the living room of the home I shared with my mother and grandmother, my knees trembled as I held an envelope with my mother's name written in scrolling letters over the surface. My teacher told me to deliver it. Of all the assignments I'd had in my short life, it was the hardest.

In my child-aged mind, whatever was in the letter was going to end so much worse than what happened at school. It wasn't that I feared my mother's or grandmother's punishment as much as it broke my little boy heart to cause either of them distress. They were both still reeling from the aftershocks of my father's death. Even at a young age, I knew they were working to make our lives continue albeit in a way my mother had never imagined, and here I was, giving them grief they didn't deserve.

Mother and Grandmother sat with their eyes fixed on me, not the letter.

"What happened, Reid?" my mother asked.

I handed her the envelope.

"No, son," my grandmother admonished, "your mother asked you a question. We'll look at that letter in time. Now you need to explain what we'll read."

"I don't know what she wrote." I didn't. The letter was sealed. If I'd have opened it, they would've known.

"You don't know what she wrote?" Grandmother asked.

My head shook in time with my hands and knees.

"Bring the letter here," Mom said. Her demand wasn't stern but instead laced with compassion.

I knew from experience that she didn't mean to simply hand it to her but to stand and walk toward her. With my chin near my chest and eyes down, I took small steps, finally reaching the spot before her skirt-draped knees. I lifted the envelope.

My mother took it and placed it on her lap before reaching for my chin and lifting my eyes to hers. "Reid Murray, keep your eyes up. Don't you ever let someone else determine your worth. You're a good boy. You will be a good man. I don't know what this letter says, but I know what's here" —she laid her hand on my shirt over my heart— "and here." She touched my forehead. "Nothing in that letter will change that."

"I'm sorry, Mom."

"Good, son. There isn't anything wrong with an apology, especially if it comes from your heart. Real men can be sorry," Grandmother said. "But it takes more than saying it. It takes an honest heart. Apologies are useless if you don't learn from your mistake and decide to do better in the future."

Mom lifted the envelope. "Did you learn anything today from whatever your teacher is going to tell us?"

"Yes."

"And you'll try to do better the next time?"

"Yes, ma'am."

"Then it's a good day," Grandmother said with a smile.

As Lorna's arm beside me tensed, I had no idea why that memory had returned at this moment. It had been a long time since I'd remembered our home and the wisdom of my mother and grandmother. And yet in barely a second, that entire scene had sped through my thoughts.

Lorna placed the envelope in my hand and folded back the flap.

It wasn't sealed.

I reached for her hand as our eyes met. "Sweetheart, I want to tell you something I just learned, just now." I didn't care that Dr. Dixon was listening. My confession couldn't wait.

"Reid, the results..."

My finger came to her soft pink lips. "I learned something I have known but now is reinforced. I know something I already knew, but now it's overwhelming."

Lorna swallowed as a rogue tear slid down her battered cheek.

"You are the strongest woman I've ever known. I'm so fucking lucky to call you my wife, and I will love you every day I take a breath. I'll be here while you read this. I'll hold you and love you. I'll spend every fucking day making up for my lack of protection, but not one second will be spent disparaging the greatest woman I've ever loved."

The envelope fell to my lap. As Lorna lifted her arms around my neck and buried her face in my shirt, my embrace surrounded her. If only I'd been with her. If only I would have protected her. For a moment, I held her as her breathing steadied. When she pulled away, her eyes were dry.

"I love you. I need to know this."

We both turned to Dr. Dixon who nodded.

Lorna lifted the envelope from where it had fallen and again lifted the flap. The report within was four pages and stapled in the corner. There were numbers and percentages. There were listings for the different tests ran.

Surface DNA as well as internal.

Collection data.

Presence of spermicide.

Discussion of clinical observation and results.

Lorna scanned the first page and then the second. Her eyes met Dr. Dixon's. "It says you took pictures."

"It's standard. I didn't include them in the report, but I can get them."

Lorna's arm began to tremble as she turned the final page. "It says 97.9 percent?"

Dr. Dixon nodded. "It is unusual to have one hundred percent in these types of reports."

"Why is there any doubt?" I asked.

Dr. Dixon sat taller. "Lorna, it is my medical opinion that you were not raped in the common understanding of the word." Before we could question, she continued, "There was no trace of spermicide or evidence of prophylactic usage."

My wife exhaled as her hand returned to mine.

"While you suffered an attack or multiple attacks," the doctor continued, "your perineum region was relatively unharmed."

"Relatively?" I asked.

"Lorna was injured over her entire body. The injuries she sustained were not consistent with forced penetration."

"Then why doesn't the report say one hundred percent?" Lorna asked.

Dr. Dixon reached over to Lorna's knee. "I *do not* believe you were raped."

Lorna nodded, yet her voice was unsure. "Okay, you've said that. What aren't you saying?"

My arm went around Lorna's shoulder, pulling her closer. "You have your answer."

Lorna lifted the paperwork. "Then it should say one hundred percent."

Dr. Dixon took a breath and sat back, her neck straight. "Lorna, three pubic hairs were found, one on your skin and two in the fibers of your underwear. Those three pubic hairs were not yours or Reid's."

The resolution we'd sought, the one that had been so close, was stained by the presence of three hairs. Red filled my vision as I worked to stay seated.

Lorna's head came to my shoulder. "I'm sorry."

My hands went to her cheeks as I turned her face to mine. "We will find out who did this." Still holding Lorna's face, I turned to Dr. Dixon. "I'm assuming you have DNA or some identifying data?"

"It should be turned into the authorities."

Releasing my wife, I stood. "Doctor, I think you know." I put out my hand. "We are the authorities. No one else needs to be involved."

Dr. Renita Dixon had been involved with the Sparrows for too long not to fill in the blanks. Nodding, she reached into her purse, removed a second sheet of paper, and placed it in my hand.

"Thank you, Doctor." I looked down at my wife. "I told you that you're a fighter." I reached for her hand, encouraging her to stand. Once she did, I stared down into her emerald gaze, wishing I could make all the sadness and indecision disappear. "Sweetheart, you are here with me and that's what matters."

Dr. Dixon also stood. "Lorna, I can imagine these results don't answer all your questions."

"I don't think all my questions will ever be answered." She took a ragged breath. "But this helps. I wasn't raped." She looked up at me. "Thank you for having the kit done."

The last thing I deserved in this situation was praise.

"Sexual assault," Dr. Dixon began, "isn't limited to penetration."

Before she could continue speaking, I stood taller and interjected, "Dr. Dixon, thank you for making a special trip and delivering this information in person. I'm sure Robert is waiting. May I walk you to the elevator?"

She nodded before turning to Lorna. "You have a great support system. That includes me. Anytime you want to talk, Lorna, I will make the time."

"Enjoy the symphony."

"Get some rest."

As Renita and I left the apartment and walked through the common area, she paused. "Reid, I don't expect that I'm saying anything you don't realize, but as I was about to tell Lorna, sexual assault isn't limited to penetration. Your wife was not penetrated. That doesn't mean she wasn't assaulted. Without her memory, we can only speculate at how those hairs made their way onto her body and clothes."

My teeth clenched as she spoke.

"It's a misconception that only the act of forced or coerced penetration is psychologically harmful."

The paper she'd given me with the DNA information on

the hairs was in my front pocket. I patted it. "Doctor, we will take care of this."

Though she wasn't much older than us, her gaze shone with the wisdom that comes from both experience and knowledge. "One day, Lorna may remember. On that day, that minute, that second, she will need to know that even if it wasn't what is commonly referred to as rape, her trauma is real and she should be free to express it any way that will help her deal with it."

My Adam's apple bobbed. "You're saying not to downplay it. You don't need to worry about that. Whoever this DNA belongs to isn't long for this world. Downplaying is not my plan."

Renita pressed her lips together. "You have dealt with trauma too. It's important to realize this isn't only affecting her. I hope that you two can come to the point where you can help one another. What is best for you may not be best for your wife."

I reached out and hit the button for the elevator. Once the doors opened and Dr. Dixon was within, I hit the G. "Thank you. Enjoy the symphony."

As the doors closed, the phone in the pocket of my jeans vibrated.

It was a text message from Sparrow. He was on his way back to the tower and wanted a briefing with all of us.

When I opened the door to our apartment, Lorna wasn't there.

A brisk walk to our bedroom and I found her in the bathroom, pulling her long red hair back into a ponytail. I went behind her and wrapped my arms around her. The top of her head came below my chin as we both stared into the mirror.

"Sparrow wants me on 2."

"That's fine. I'm headed up to the penthouse."

"Are you sure," I asked, searching her reflection for a reaction from the test results. "Laurel said they'd bring food down. I can come back as soon as the briefing is over."

My wife spun in my arms, a new smile on her lips as her petite hands came to my chest. "Reid, I have an answer. I wasn't raped. Now I can search for more with that reassurance."

Her voice was strong and clear, and her eyes were no longer moist. The signs were there that everything would be better, but what if it was a facade? What if, like Dr. Dixon said, even this slice of peace would be annihilated when her memories returned?

"Come up to the penthouse for dinner when you're done on 2," she said, walking into our bedroom before she stopped. "Oh, and tell Mace we can talk about my dream another day."

"Your dream?"

"Yeah, he heard me telling Laurel and freaked. I know he's hiding something, but tonight, I don't want more confrontation."

"Hiding something?"

I knew what he was hiding. It was what earlier today I'd told him needed to be shared.

There was a woman on ice in a makeshift morgue on 1. It was amazing what resources we could find when we needed them. It wasn't like we could take her to the Cook County morgue. There would be questions whose answers we didn't know or weren't willing to provide.

"You know what?" she asked. "Tonight, I don't want to know what he's hiding. No more information. I'm on overload, and this was one bit of good news." She tilted her head to the side. "Can you talk to him and make sure he understands?"

"Sweetheart, if that's what you want."

Lorna came back in the bathroom and after resting her hand on my chest, lifted to her tiptoes and kissed my cheek. "I do. Thank you."

As she walked away, I contemplated a thought I hadn't had since Mason's accident, since Lorna found the tickets to England. It hadn't occurred to me since, but now it was here.

Maybe it was time to take my wife away to someplace safe and leave the dangers of the Sparrow world, the Order, and the underground behind.

While that thought swirled through my mind, the paper in my pocket brought me back to reality. First, I needed to know the owner of the hair.

LORNA

*a*t nearly midnight, with sleep just out of my reach, I stepped from the shower. While steam rippled through the bathroom, water dribbled down my body in small streams to the bath mat below. My nipples hardened from the cooler air as, forgoing a towel, I walked nude to the vanity and turned on a heat lamp above.

Water droplets glistened in the warm light as I stared at myself. I wasn't sure what had prompted me to take yet another shower, but I had. I lifted my face to the glow, taking in the radiating warmth with the knowledge that I was clean.

Returning my line of vision to the large mirror, I took in my reflection. My bruises were still present. Yet I concentrated on other aspects of my image, such as my long red hair piled messily upon my head. I brushed away small wisps of curls clinging to my face and neck as my skin dried, the moisture continuing to evaporate under the warm lamp from above.

As if I were in a daze, each act required thought. It was like I'd forgotten routines I'd done for years. Seeing my toothbrush in its holder reminded me to brush and floss. There was no set time, no number of strokes. Battling thoughts and flashes of memories—ones that seemed disjointed by time and space—I found myself floating in a continuum, unable to make sense of the world in any dimension.

Next, finding my hairbrush, I loosened the hair tie and began smoothing my unruly long locks. The humidity in the shower returned life to the curls, making my mane difficult to tame. I tugged on one strand, brushing and running the tangle-free curl through my fingers.

There was a flash of something. Dropping my hairbrush, I jumped back. My arms reached to cover my nakedness as my skin peppered with goose bumps, and my heart pounded in an erratic rhythm.

Whatever had just happened wasn't a complete thought.

I lifted a strand of my hair and stared down.

That was it, but in the flash, the hand wasn't mine.

It was big and dirty.

As I concentrated on the hand, my body became rigid. The air was no longer filled with the sweet aromas of shampoo, conditioner, or lotions. My nose scrunched at a horrible stench. I closed my eyes as my stomach twisted, and I saw the hand with dirty fingernails tugging on a long red curl.

It was as real as if someone had been right here with me.

And then it was gone—all of it.

My head shook as I reassuringly reached for the vanity and took in our master bath. The scent of lavender from my shower gel returned, suspended in the moist air. The glass stall where I'd been dripped within from the condensation. The tile work throughout was colorful and ornate. Plush towels hung from the racks, and my long robe dangled from a hook. Though my heart still beat too fast, the reflection in the mirror confirmed that I was alone.

I turned a complete circle, taking comfort that my surroundings were not those in the flash.

Was this what Laurel meant?

A flash that made no sense?

No matter how I tried, I couldn't place the scene, the hand, or the feeling.

Taking a deep breath, I willed my heartbeat to normalize as I bent down and retrieved my hairbrush from the floor. Forcing a smile at my reflection, I spoke, "It's the drugs they gave you." Saying it aloud gave my proclamation authority. And though I didn't speak aloud again, my mind continued the conversation, creating plausible answers.

The loss of memory and thoughts of my dream were conjuring up scenes from fiction. Perhaps it had been a book or a movie I'd seen and long forgotten. My mind was simply too tired and confused to differentiate a distinction.

As my skin continued to air dry, I took my time applying lotion gently over the bruises while adding antibiotic cream to the cuts and bites. The scent of eucalyptus replaced the lavender. Clean and fresh, the aroma infiltrated my senses, relaxing me as I reached for the bottle of sleep aids I'd received after asking Laurel.

After filling a cup with water and opening the lid, I shook two into the palm of my hand.

Indecision slowed my movements.

The tablets were white and round, yet I worried how they'd affect me.

I recalled the scene of terror at the flash I'd just experienced.

If perhaps I could sleep without dreams...

With a shake of my head, I placed one back in the bottle and hurriedly tossed the remaining tablet into my mouth, taking a drink of water, and swallowed. As the ajar door to the bedroom opened wide, I spun, facing the intruder and bringing the bottle and my arms to cover my breasts.

"I expected you to be asleep," Reid said. His tone was a mix of emotions. Fatigue combined with a whirlwind of others swirled in his gaze.

A wave of relief flowed through me at the sight of my husband.

"I'm about to go to bed," I replied. Holding up the bottle, I added, "I decided to give these a try and see if I can sleep for longer than a few hours."

With each step toward me, lust overruled Reid's exhaustion. "Seeing you here all sexy and naked...I have another suggestion to help you sleep."

Reid's voice deepened with each step. Once his massive frame was before my nude one, he reached for a tendril of my hair and twisted it around his finger. For a moment, my breath caught, and as quickly, the uncertainty the flash had caused moments ago was lost.

This hand twisting my hair was not the same one as in the flash. Reid's was large but clean. His skin wasn't covered in grime, and the color was different than the one with dirty nails.

I reached for the hand of the man I loved and looked up into his eyes. The heat from his gaze scanned over me from my head to my toes; the longer it lingered, the more it twisted my core.

My breathing deepened as hardness returned to my nipples. "Please, Reid, take me." It was one thing to hold his hand in mine, but I needed more. I needed to focus on reality and push away the uneasiness that lurked in the shadows.

"I...Dr. Dixon—"

Lifting myself to my tiptoes, I covered his lips with mine, stealing his words. Like a statue of granite, his hard body remained still as I surrounded his neck with my arms and pressed my naked breasts against him. Reid's hands went to my hair as moans came from our throats and our kiss deepened.

No longer did my scalp send waves of pain at his touch. Instead, our closeness sent sparks igniting my nervous system and tingling each synapse. Small detonations, one after another, exploded until moisture flooded my core. I pulled him closer, pushed me closer, made us closer, until my entire body melded against his.

The need within me surpassed physical desire. It was

primal. Such as a wild animal in heat, I needed Reid inside me to survive. More than that, I wanted him to eclipse the revelations of the day and of what was to come. No longer did I think about Dr. Dixon's report or a flash I didn't understand.

As my empty core clenched with unmet need, my only thought was Reid.

"Fuck, Lorna," my husband growled as he seized my shoulders, pushing me to arm's length.

His handsome face was all I could see. The bathroom was gone. The flashes were gone. It was only the man I knew and loved. Though my request was that of a desperate woman, my voice was strong. "Show me I'm not damaged. Show me I'm someone."

In one swoop, Reid released my shoulders and pulled the hem of his shirt over his head. The aroma of deodorant and cologne mixed with the eucalyptus. His toned massive chest filled my vision. Before I could speak, he lifted me to the vanity and spread my legs. Tugging me forward, he brought my ass to the edge and sank to his knees. "Hold on, sweetheart."

"Oh God." It was a prayer or a decree of worship, I wasn't sure which, as my fingers gripped the edge of the granite, and his warm breath skirted over my wanton core.

Reid's secure grip held me in place, keeping me from falling. Without hesitation, his tongue delved between my folds. The day's beard growth abraded my sensitive skin. I gasped as a shiver ran through me, prickling my flesh and curling my toes.

"I love the way you taste."

I did my best to stay upon the edge of the counter, yet as he continued to ravish my core and the lamp from above shone over us, my skin covered with perspiration, making us slick as I panted for breath. Kisses and nips came to my thighs as he spread my legs incredibly wider until I was fully bared to him. My eyes went to his short dark hair and the bobbing of his head. Noises I created and some he produced echoed off the colorful tile as he lapped and licked. It was as his tongue swirled my clit and he teased with his teeth that I knew my orgasm was near.

Instead of allowing me to fall into bliss, Reid stood, lifted me from the vanity, placed my feet on the floor, and spun me around. I was beyond comprehending his movements as he brushed my toiletries away from the counter, some falling to the floor while others found their way into a sink. Like putty in the artist's hands, Reid molded me to his desired position, pressing my lower back over the counter, flattening my breasts, tugging my backside to him, and moving my legs apart.

"Don't move."

From my vantage, if I lifted my head slightly, I could see the man I loved and the man who loved me, in the reflection. There wasn't time to be uncertain or uneasy. I was his, and despite my obvious submission to his desires, he was mine. Anticipation and trust as well as his command kept me in place, awaiting his next move.

Reid's eyes no longer swirled with turmoil as they had for the last few days, but in the reflection, they shone with love, lust, and desire. His broad chest glistened as his mahogany skin covered in dew from my shower and perspiration from the heat coming from above. It was the sound of his zipper cutting through the din of our breathing that electrified my flesh and flooded my core with new desire.

"You asked me to take you."

My breathing accelerated seeing in the reflection that his hard cock was now in his hand. I bit my lip, watching the way his arm moved as he pleased himself.

"You made me hard, your sexy body, your pleas..." He trailed the tip of a large finger down my spine. "So hard I fucking ache." His finger trailed lower. "Is that what you want, for me to ache?"

My head shook. I didn't want that.

"You want me to fuck you?"

"Please."

His finger moved lower until it was close to my need. "Is that still what you want, my dick buried inside you?"

My stepping fidgeted, hoping for his touch to go lower still to meet my goal.

His large hand came to the small of my back. "No moving. No one satisfies that tight cunt but me."

I exhaled an exasperated breath. "Reid."

Without his realizing it, he'd done as I asked, focusing my attention and my need on only him. In the reflection his arm moved. My lip went between my teeth, as desire and jealousy raced through me. He was pleasuring himself in a way I wanted to only come from me.

"Sweetheart, I can last all night. Answer my question. Do you want me to take you?"

"Yes. I need you inside me."

LORNA

*T*here was strength in voicing my requests and power in making my wishes known. I was a woman with desires; claiming my sexuality and needs was empowering. It wasn't one-sided. Reid also had needs and wants. We'd never shied away from being honest with one another.

Reid's finger roamed lower, each movement sending shivers over my flesh and electric shocks to my core. I struggled with staying still as his touch moved between the cheeks of my backside, inciting trembles of anticipation.

It seemed like forever as he taunted and teased.

"Oh God."

I cried out as his fingers finally plunged deep inside my core. My walls pulsated, no longer empty, as he tantalized and tormented. It was perfect and yet I wanted more.

"Here?" he asked, his fingers curling.

"Yes."

"You want my dick here?" He continued his taunting.

My answer came in between gasps. "Yes."

With one large hand upon my lower back holding me against the counter, another finger pressed beyond the tight ring of muscles. "Here?"

I gasped as the intrusion caused me to rise up on my toes.

He dipped another finger again in my essence before adding it to his claim.

My eyes closed as I took in the fullness of his fingers, knowing his cock would be so much more. A third finger entered as he worked to loosen the muscles' fight. "Here? Answer me."

Words were out of reach as I savored his invasion.

Reid's chest came over my back, his breath at my ear. "I want all of your thoughts on me, Lorna. Only me."

"Yes."

"My cock wants inside this tight ass."

I nodded as much as possible.

"Answer me."

"Yes." I wasn't an anal virgin curious of my first experience. I was a wife, a partner, a soul mate who trusted her man, her husband, and her lover completely with every part of her. This wasn't uncharted territory, and I knew without a doubt, Reid was skilled at making it pleasurable for both of us.

He eased his fingers out.

Reid's rock-hard cock pushed against my lower back as his hard body stayed folded over mine. One hand came to my neck, stretching and pulling my face upward. Our eyes met in the reflection. "You're not damaged, Lorna. You're perfect in every way. You're also mine and always will be."

"Yes." It seemed to be the only word in my current vocabulary as I reveled in the protective cocoon he'd made. Wrapped in his body, I was safe and secure, with pleasure on the horizon.

"Perfect," he said again as he took a step back. In the mirror I watched as he scanned my backside. "Your pussy is pink and wet."

I didn't know how I should feel about the things he said. Was it supposed to embarrass me? It didn't. I heard his observations as praise.

"It's like it's begging for my dick."

My feet slid on the tile as I contemplated what he was about to do. "Yes," I moaned as his cock found my center. My back arched as my lips formed an "o."

"Best cunt in the world."

I sucked in a breath. With my essence easing his plunge, he thrust without hesitation to the depth of my core. My muscles stretched to accommodate his perfect size. Width and length, he moved in and out, penetrating me over and over. My bruised hips banged against the granite as our bodies slapped one against the other.

Though we were covered in perspiration, my thoughts were consumed with the amazing friction within.

"You're someone. The most important *someone*." Reid's words and phrases recounting my worth came and went, floating through the air and in and out of my consciousness.

The world was a cloud and we were the only two inhabitants.

One of his hands found its way to my breasts, tweaking and pinching my hardened nipples until my breasts engorged, making each ministration both erotic and painful. I longed for him to stop while praying he never would.

"You're so wet, sweetheart."

I knew what he was going to do next; this was his prelude.

Leaving my nipples unattended, his hand dipped between us. Without missing a thrust his rhythm continued as he smeared our essences over my ass and pushed his thumb in and out of my tight hole.

"Tell me and I'll get lube."

"Don't stop. Take me, Reid. I'm all yours."

As he pulled out and the large tip of his cock pressed against my back hole, I knew this was what I wanted and needed. I wanted my husband to re-stake his claims, to take away any thoughts that there had been anyone else.

I held my breath as Reid took what was his and his alone. My body instinctively fought, but there was no resistance that would hold him back. I bit my lip as the pressure built.

"You're so fucking tight."

Still biting my lip, I held onto the edge of the counter and pushed back until he stilled. With only a small bit of his destination accomplished, our eyes met in the mirror. His were glazed with the sexiest sheen of desire. Though mine were moist, I knew what I wanted. "Don't ask me, Reid. Take me."

A shrill scream escaped my lips as he did exactly as I

wanted. Pain and pleasure. My grip tightened to a vise on the edge of the counter. He stilled again. "Sweetheart, it feels too good to stop. Relax. I'll make it good."

I breathed in and out. "I don't want you to stop."

His fingers found my clit, rubbing small gentle circles. It wasn't enough to bring me to climax. However, it was perfect to gather my attention. My knees began to keep time to the rhythm he created. The more and more he pleasured, the more endorphins flowed through my circulation. With my concentration elsewhere, his cock continued its invasion.

Each time I hesitated, he stilled. It was a dance, and while he was leading, he was also listening, not only to my words, but to my sounds and the way my body moved. Reid knew me better than anyone in the world. It was why I trusted him to take this part of me and make it good for both of us. "God, Reid, I'm so full."

"Just a little more."

My wish had been granted. There was no one in my thoughts but him, here and now. I concentrated on his touch, the way he orchestrated my clit and dipped his fingers inside me. As my body was at battle with his incursion, pleasure won the war.

Starting at my toes, a new and more powerful climax built within me.

"Fuck, it feels good." His deep baritone filled with satisfaction was the last ingredient to my complete indulgence.

"Yes. So good." And it did.

Reid craned my neck toward him as his lips seized mine. His tongue tasted like me.

As he continued to work me, stoking the fire inside me, he filled every one of my senses until I was consumed with the overwhelming sensation of him.

Reid's hands went to my hips as he steadied his footing. In and out he thrust, slow and steady. Fire burned while pleasure contained the flames. No longer were there unwanted thoughts or questions swirling in my mind. There was no one or no place other than here. I was incapable of living outside this moment.

"Touch yourself."

My nipples turned to diamonds at his command.

I didn't question his meaning as my fingers went to my clit, resuming what he had started. The smoldering coals that had been burning ignited. The extra fuel from my own touch was the accelerant to an out-of-control blaze.

Volcanoes erupt with less pressure.

I screamed out my husband's name as Reid's rhythm increased. I was above the clouds, dancing with the stars as supernovas continued to explode within me. Their blasts ricocheted throughout my circulation.

How I remained standing was a mystery.

It had to be Reid. He wouldn't allow me to fall, not from outer space.

Faster and faster he pumped until a deep guttural roar reverberated throughout the bathroom. It might have gone farther. Beyond our apartment, our floor, or out of the building.

Did pedestrians on the street, ninety-plus stories below, hear the rumbling roar and assume a storm was brewing?

My body lay prone, my chest to the counter, as Reid again folded his massive body over mine. With his cock still buried deep inside me, his arms wrapped around my waist. "I'm keeping you right here, forever."

Though my energy was gone, I smiled and made a sorry attempt to wiggle my ass. "Did you say no moving?"

"If you keep that shit up, there will be a lot more moving." Slowly, he eased back, separating our connection, and making what had been one, two. I was left with an emptiness where only seconds before I had been overflowing.

"Don't move." He playfully slapped my backside. "This time I mean it."

I wasn't sure I could physically disobey.

I didn't know if it was the orgasm still sparking through my body's nervous system or the sleeping pill I'd taken. Either way, I obeyed his command without hesitation, closing my eyes as in the distance I heard the sound of running water.

A warm cloth came to my sensitive flesh as Reid tended to my well-loved and tender core. "I love you, Mrs. Murray." His deep voice settled around me like a warm blanket. "Never forget you're mine."

My eyes opened to see his handsome face before mine. "I'm pretty sure I'll remember every time I move tomorrow."

"Come here."

I forced myself to stand, pushing away from the vanity. The reflection in the mirror still displayed bruises in a variety of colors, yet there was more. My flesh was dotted with red where his beard growth had abraded it, and my eyes were glassy with complete satisfaction. I turned around to face my husband.

I wasn't sure when he rid himself of his jeans and shoes, but as I scanned my man up and down, taking in his naked perfection, I saw what God intended when he created man. Reid's toned muscles displayed his recent workout. His arms were defined and his abs rippled. His thighs bulged and his cock stood ready for a second round.

I longed to run the tips of my fingers over every crest and crevice.

Yet before my mind and hands could coordinate, I was lifted into the air and cradled in his arms. My cheek fell to his wide chest as he carried me to our bed.

As he walked, the world passed by in familiar scenes—our bedroom, windows, furniture, and bed. There was nothing that didn't belong.

Keeping me cradled, he scattered the throw pillows, mumbling under his breath at their quantity, and pulled back the covers.

With the gentleness of caring for a newborn baby, he laid me upon the soft sheets. It was an about-face from the way he'd just ravaged me minutes earlier, and at the same time, it wasn't. I blinked up at my husband. "I've never loved anyone like I love you."

His brown eyes glistened as his cheeks rose in the bedroom's dim light. "That's good because I love you, and don't get any ideas because, sweetheart, you're stuck with me."

When he stepped out of my vision, a cold chill returned. I felt their presence. The thoughts, images, and memories were back, hiding in the shadows, ready to strike and obliterate my bliss.

Pulling the blankets to my bare chest, I blinked away a man with black hair.

Another blink, and a sickening scent of staleness filtered in and out of reality.

My hands came to my ears as the old woman's crackle rang within.

"No." I didn't know if I spoke aloud. "Stop."

"Lorna."

I opened my eyes as Reid's large hands framed my cheeks.

"Me. Think of me," he commanded, his tone steady in the sea of my dark thoughts.

My chest ached. "I'm trying."

"I'm here, sweetheart. I'm not going anywhere."

"Hold me? Please. I need to feel you with me."

Reid nodded as the turbulence returned the storm to his dark orbs. "All night, Lorna. I won't let you go. Let me turn off the rest of the lights and I'll be back."

As the room went dark and Reid's side of our large bed dipped, I scooted closer, meeting him near the middle. It wasn't until his strong arms surrounded me that I closed my eyes again. Though I knew without a doubt that the darkness lurked beyond our dimension, I concentrated on the man holding me.

With his front to my back, and his massive body curved around mine, he reassured, "I'm here."

"Please don't leave." It wasn't a request I often made. I knew he had work. I knew the Sparrow world needed him. However, at this moment, I needed him too.

"I'm not leaving you, Lorna. When you wake, I'll be here."

I felt the release. Call it residual bliss or the effect of the sleeping pill. Either way, it moved through me until my limbs and eyelids grew too heavy to move, and I was lulled into a dreamless sleep.

REID

*H*ours after my wife woke from one of her longest and most uninterrupted nights of sleep in recent days, I left her. It wasn't without warning. I left her awake and in the penthouse, surrounded by those who loved her.

Currently, I was soaring above the clouds on the way to our destination, Washington DC. With Sparrow and Mason discussing logistics, I was communicating via the computer with Garrett, our top Sparrow on the ground. Much as we'd done nearly two years ago when we'd gone to DC to claim Mason's freedom, we had Sparrows already in the city, setting up our hotel suite and securing the safety of the location.

In an attempt to keep this visit under the radar, we weren't currently riding in the bird plane. This one was smaller with two sets of seats facing one another. For a less-than-two-hour flight each direction, the luxurious accommodations of the larger plane weren't exactly needed. That wasn't to say we were flying in a tin can, far from it.

Marianne was piloting—as was usually the case when Sparrow was aboard. Keaton was also present and in the aft cabin ready to see to our needs, not that we had many. It was simply standard to have at least one flight attendant when the king was present.

Patrick and I decided that a hotel would work best for the rendezvous point. A large elite establishment held many options. Comings and goings were less noticeable. The reservations were made under the guise of a difficult-to-trace LLC. The rooms were booked from yesterday to two days from today. Securing a booking for longer than required was also common. If word got out that Sterling Sparrow was coming to the city—any city—this extended booking made it more difficult to pinpoint his arrival and departure.

It was becoming increasingly annoying that the Sparrow entourage would be met with a gaggle of reporters. The legitimate side of Sparrow, the work of the Sparrow Institute, and the availability of social media spotlighting the name Sparrow, all garnered the increased attention. While the reporters' questions were most commonly of no significance, their presence was unappreciated, especially when meeting with someone like Edison Walters.

One difference with today's meeting versus the one nearly two years ago was that this time Mr. Walters knew it had been called by Sterling Sparrow. And while we had a cover for the press should we be questioned, Walters was equally aware that we weren't arriving to discuss funding for lobbying on a hot-button issue.

Nevertheless, for appearances, the subject made a good cover. After all, the most obvious reason for Sterling Sparrow to meet with a legislative aide would be to discuss something relative to Chicago commerce.

Recent modifications in regulations increased the amount of emissions that were now considered acceptable. Sterling Sparrow, the real estate tycoon, was among a list of prominent donors, as well as local and state political officials—the mayor and Illinois governor—who opposed the recent relaxed standards based on the environmental impact. Yes, the change gave perks when it came to big business. However, with their nationwide passing, that wasn't a boon to Chicago alone and despite promises, those perks hadn't trickled down to the workers who kept Chicago's economy going.

Edison Walters was involved with a congressional oversight committee designated to monitor the impact of the recent changes. Simultaneously, he was securing donors to fight for new stricter regulations. Some would see that as a conflict of interest.

In a nutshell, our meeting would appear to be nothing more than a legislative aide meeting with a prominent donor of one of the growing lobbyist PACs aimed at pressuring Congress to revisit the recent modification.

There was more to it—as was often the case with these kinds of issues.

The corporations that benefited from the adjustment didn't add to the state and city tax base. Many had unexpired exemptions that they were no longer honoring in deed. Sparrow's mother was among the aldermen willing to accept the regulation change as long as the tax revenue was increased accordingly. To say this was a simple two-sided issue would be erroneous.

In reality, we weren't here to discuss any of that. It made an acceptable cover for our meeting.

I turned from the monitor to the two men with me. "Garrett has the presidential suite at Mandarin Oriental secure."

"Do we have the space we need?" Sparrow asked. "I thought it was booked."

"Garrett was convincing in his request."

"Does he have it wired?" Mason added. "I want a transmission going to Patrick in real time, and we don't have time before Top's arrival to do much of anything."

"Yes," I answered Sparrow, "regarding the space. It's their largest suite with over thirty-five hundred square feet. Two bedrooms." I turned to Mason. "One is already wired for the on-site command center. Garrett has it manned, and there are Sparrows scattered around the hotel and on the street. If you'd rather sit at a table, there is a dining room that will work."

"We're not entertaining," Sparrow replied, his tone clipped and gruff.

He wasn't the only one on edge. We were all mentally preparing for what could go down. This wasn't going to be a simple meeting. A man who maintained an alternate clandestine personality as possibly the most influential person in the world doesn't negotiate easily, even when that negotiation is with a man whose own clandestine role was that of the kingpin of the underground of the third-largest city in the US.

Of course, Sparrow came to this meeting prepared with more than his own influence. He'd worked diligently since returning to Chicago to secure support from other leaders throughout the country's underground forces. Without giving much detail or ever calling out the Sovereign Order, Sparrow implored the other leaders to consider the benefits of forming an alliance to fight a possible common enemy. He was forthright about the threat that had been made to his queen and the wife of one of his top men.

The world of the underground went by many names: Mafia, Cosa Nostra, bratva, brotherhood, or cartel, to name a few. It was dark and dangerous. People died. Property was destroyed. Fortunes were stolen. And yet a key connection was family.

Sterling Sparrow's wife had been threatened.

There was no greater call to unity.

Mason stood. "He knows this isn't about the emissions."

For this occasion, Mason was more formally dressed than usual. His blue jeans were replaced with dress trousers, and his thermal shirt by a button-down under a sports jacket. It wasn't exactly a suit, there wasn't a tie, and his cowboy boots were still present; nevertheless, for Mason Pierce this was as close to formal as he usually came.

Of course, Sparrow was dressed like the Chicago royalty he was: dark blue suit, striped shirt, and silver tie. The cuffs of his pressed shirt glittered with expensive gold and diamond cuff links. His family's crest shone from the gold ring on his right hand. And his loafers and belt were made of the finest Italian leather. At one glance, there was no question that he was a man of importance.

I'd also dressed for the meeting. While I hadn't been in the room with Edison Walters the last time we all met, I had been present. This time would be different. This time I too would demand answers.

Mason paused as he peered out a small rectangular window. With blue skies above, the clouds below moved ominously, churning in peaks and valleys. "The forecast is for rain."

No one responded.

"Fuck," Mason said, turning back to us. "The tension is thick in here."

He was right. Like a stagnant cloud, the stress combined with the importance of this meeting hung in a thick blanket around us.

Sparrow stood, pacing between the window and seats. "Here's what we know." He crossed his arms over his chest. "Our only evidence of a connection to the Order is Andrew Jettison. We can imply and make assumptions, but if Walters is the man you say" —he was looking at Mason— "the only case we can make is with the DNA match."

"I want to know," I said for not the first time, "why? What is the endgame?"

"That's our angle—*mine*," Mason corrected. "Listen, I know you want revenge for your wives. I get it. But the reality is that Walters could be as responsible for the ladies' kidnapping as Sparrow is for a gang shooting on West 87th."

Sparrow bristled at the analogy. "I learn," he said. "I don't always know they're going to happen, but once they do, I see the data. You're the one who's proclaimed the Order's control. Do you think that my wife and the wife of one of my top men—forget that, the sister of one of the Order's previous soldiers—were kidnapped and *Top* doesn't know or wasn't informed?"

Keaton entered the cabin with a knock coming from the door in the aft. "Excuse me. Marianne asks that you all take your seats and fasten your seat belts. We're about to descend and she expects turbulence."

LORNA

Twenty-six years ago

*D*ays and weeks passed.

We'd been with Mom, Mr. Maples, and his daughters for over five months. The warmer days and nights of autumn slipped into winter. Holidays came and went. Mr. Maples didn't believe in wasting money on decorations or a tree. There were no stockings like we'd had at Grandma's. Thanksgiving came and went like any other day. He'd managed to recognize the gift-giving tradition of Christmas. While Missy, Mace, and I received a few gifts, we were expected to sit and watch as Anna and Zella opened the bulk of the presents.

I couldn't explain how I felt with each passing day. If I did, I would tell things I wasn't allowed to tell. I'd divulge secrets that could mean the end to my life with my brother and sister.

The best description for my feelings was that I had none. None was easier to deal with than some.

While at school, I rarely participated. Lifting my hand to share an answer, even those I knew, terrified me. If I did that, the teacher would call my name, and the other students' eyes would turn to me. I avoided the spotlight at all costs.

If people looked at me, would they know what I did?

The only time I felt like me was in the attic with Mason and Missy. Quietly, the three of us would make up games. We'd tell stories and smile. Sometimes we'd eat the food Mason brought from his job at a nearby convenience mart. It was something he'd do when we were sent to bed without dinner. He'd climb out the window and an hour later return the same way with brown bags in hand. They were usually cold sandwiches or apples, but they were food and that's all that mattered.

The time in the attic was the closest we had to what life had been like with Grandma.

The biggest issue with the attic was that it was winter in Chicago, and the three of us slept in a drafty, unheated attic, often without light. Since no one came into our room except us—Mr. Maples only came to the doorway—we dug through the boxes of discarded clothes to create layers of mothball smelling material to protect us from the cold.

Through it all, I kept the secret of Mr. Maples's and my continued friendship. With time I noticed that each time I followed him down to his room, not only was there a wine bottle by my mother as she slept, but also a bottle of sleeping pills.

Each time that we entered his room, Mr. Maples made me ask to be his friend.

Each time the words came out, I knew they were wrong, that what I was saying was a lie. I also knew I was wrong for saying the words and for maintaining this secret. Yet each time the lies came easier.

It wasn't only for me, but for Missy and Mason. Unlike secrets around holidays and gifts that filled others my age with anticipation and hope, my secret dimmed the world around me. Day after day—even without being required to go to his room—the secret dulled everything. A smile would quickly fade as the secret lingered just out of sight.

I was stuck in the darkened world, sinking deeper and deeper, and I didn't know that there was a way out. After all, I had asked. I agreed. Of course, my mom would be mad.

I didn't want to be sent away.

Sometimes at school, I'd look at the other girls and wonder if they had secrets too. I wanted to ask, but then it would ruin the secret. And then I'd see them laugh with their friends and I knew they didn't.

I didn't laugh.

There was no pattern to Mr. Maples's visits to the attic to retrieve me. Sometimes I'd follow him one night a week for two or three weeks in a row. Sometimes two or three weeks would pass before he showed up at the attic door. I'd grown used to what was expected of me—I had to touch him. I had to make him come.

I now understood what that meant.

While he wanted my hands on him, he always made me

use my mouth. Kiss and lick. It was what he told me to do. When I did, it was like I went away. I was no longer in their dirty bedroom. I forced myself to think about other things. I would remember how Grandma would cook and bake. As my body performed the act, my mind would be away and my stomach would growl for the cookies and cakes we no longer were allowed to eat.

As long as Mr. Maples and I stayed in our secret routine, I could pretend it never happened.

I'd walk by my sleeping mother after I'd cleaned up his mess and not think about how upset she'd be if she knew what I'd done. I'd climb the stairs and slip into the second-floor bathroom, clean myself from head to foot without thinking too much about why I needed to be clean. And then I'd enter the attic and climb under the layers of old clothes and blankets, wrap my arms around Missy, and tell myself it hadn't happened.

It was someone else who did those things.

It was Anna.

I had a reason for choosing her.

One night, a night I wasn't summoned to Mr. Maples's room, Missy woke me, needing to make a trip to the second-floor bathroom. As we left the bathroom, we heard something odd coming from Anna's room. We both stilled, scared if Anna saw us, she'd tell Mr. Maples.

"Is she jumping on her bed?" Missy asked in a whisper.

Why would she do that late at night?

"I don't know."

"If her dad wakes up, he'll be mad."

He would. Hearing those words from my little sister, I knew she was right.

Yes, Anna was older than me, three years older, and mean. She and Zella belittled and made fun of me and my siblings any chance they had, but this night, she sounded...I didn't know—upset. Maybe she was having a nightmare. Missy had them. Sometimes, while totally asleep, she'd thrash about. I had learned how to calm Missy.

"Maybe she's having a nightmare," I said to Missy.

"Wake her up. It's always better when you wake me up."

My sister's large brown eyes stared up at me with more faith than I deserved.

I nodded, not because I wanted to help Anna, but because Missy believed I could.

My heart pounded as the squeaks of the bed and Anna's cries grew louder.

"Please," Missy pleaded in her little-girl whisper, "Lorna, help her."

Taking a deep breath, I walked Missy to the stairs. "Go up to bed. I'll help Anna and be up in a minute."

My sister nodded, her smooth long dark hair moving in a wave over her slender shoulders. "She needs you."

I kissed Missy's head as I sent her up to the cold attic. "Cover up."

She smiled down at me as she opened the door at the top of the stairs.

In the dim hallway, I walked as quiet as a mouse to Anna's bedroom door. With each step, my hearing listened to the noises behind her door. I tried to match them with what I knew. I couldn't.

The doorknob creaked as I turned it. Her cries were louder as were the groans of her bedsprings. I was about to speak, to tell her I'd help, but once I had the door open and the dim light from the hallway shone over her bed, I couldn't move.

Much like during my times in Mr. Maples's room, I was unable to move. The sounds I couldn't identify mixed with my rapid heartbeat, echoing in my ears. I held my breath as Mr. Maples spoke. It wasn't to me but to Anna.

The bed continued to bounce as she cried. He used the voice he sometimes did with me. "It's okay. You're my special girl."

I thought I was your special friend?

It was an irrational thought, but at ten, it was there.

Mr. Maples and I may be friends, but he'd never done to me whatever he was doing to Anna. His hairy butt was out of his pants. He was lying on top of her as they bounced.

"Stop, Daddy." Anna's voice was filled with tears. "It hurts."

"No, Anna. This is what grown-up girls do. It's my job to teach you. You want to be a good grown-up girl, right?"

My stomach twisted in knots. I didn't want to know her answer. Quietly, I shut the door. For a moment I hesitated at the bathroom, wondering if I'd be sick. The noises continued. If I stayed I might be caught.

What would happen then?

Swallowing back the yucky taste in my mouth, I made my

way back up to the attic. As I climbed the steps, I decided that I was a better friend. Sometimes I cried, but not as loud as Anna.

After that, whenever Mr. Maples would tell me to kiss or lick, I pretended to be Anna. I was better at it than her, but I was her. It made it easier to wash and go upstairs. Instead of it being me, I'd watched him again with her. He'd told *her* to kiss. He'd made *her* lick him. He'd told *her* to wrap *her* lips around the end.

As much as I hated what *Anna* did, when I was called to his room, I still didn't tell. It was more than that I'd given my word. I also watched the way Mr. Maples looked at Missy. How sometimes he'd run his dirty hand over her long brown hair or ask her to sit on his lap.

I told myself I could do what he asked. I could be a good friend. I could be better than Anna and Mr. Maples would stay away from Missy.

Almost another month passed without him coming to the attic. Maybe he was busy with the real Anna. I could pretend that was all he'd done. I was beginning to believe I never did those things. I never made promises I didn't want to keep. I never touched, kissed, licked, or sucked on a grown man's penis. I never left Missy's side. The lies I told myself convinced me that it never happened. It wasn't me. And then one night, later than usual, the door opened.

LORNA

Twenty-six years ago

Five months and seventeen days we'd spent in Mr. Maples's house. I knew the date because six months ago, exactly, the lady had come to Grandma's house and taken us away. She'd given us ice cream and promised us that everything would be all right. Missy and I had gone to one house and Mason went somewhere else. It was almost two weeks later when the lady returned, not alone but with our mother. That was the day we came here.

My breathing caught as the door to the attic opened wider. Mr. Maples's shadow stood in the doorframe as the dim hallway light from the second floor shone around him. He rubbed his hand over the front of his pants before calling my name.

"Lorna."

Without a word, I climbed out from under our pile of material and left Missy and Mason behind. Neither Mr. Maples nor I uttered a word as I followed him through the house. He seemed different, gripping the banisters tighter, unsteady on his feet, and swaying from one side of the hallway to the other. As we went down the stairs to the living room he missed a step and cursed loudly. Once we got to the light, his clothes looked dirtier than normal. His shirt was stained and he had spots on his pants. Maybe he had an accident or he came with them on.

That wasn't a normal thought for a ten-year-old, but I had it.

"Bitch," he muttered as we walked past my sleeping mother.

Once the door to his bedroom was closed, a stronger odor hit my nose. I didn't recognize the strong smell. It was different than beer. I held my breath as I tried to get used to it. He didn't seem to notice the smell as he began the same questions. His words slid together, but I knew the routine.

Are we still special friends?

Have I kept our secret?

Do I like touching him?

And then the questions stopped.

He unbuckled his belt, unbuttoned the button on his pants, and lowered the zipper. He held on to the dresser as he kicked off his shoes and pants. Though I wasn't used to him taking them completely off, I was no longer shocked by the way he looked. His hand moved up and down his penis, making it stick out. His glassy eyes focused, perhaps really seeing me for the first time in the light. "Why are you in clothes? Where's your nightgown?"

"It's so cold up there."

His head shook as his gray gaze narrowed. "You're a tease. Just like your momma."

I didn't know what that meant.

Did I tell jokes?

I'd never told Mr. Maples a joke.

He took a wobbly step toward me and reached for my chin. "Is that what you are, Lorna, a tease?"

My head shook as much as it could in his grip.

He went back to holding his penis. "You've seen my private parts. More than seen, I've let you touch because that's what friends do." His hand moved faster. "It's time I see yours. You don't want to upset a friend? Do you, Lorna?"

I didn't want to upset him.

He let go of me and took a step back. "Tonight, we're going to play a game—a secret-friend game. Do you like games?"

My mouth went dry and my stomach felt sick, but I made myself nod.

"Here's how we play. First, you take off your shirt and then you come over, get on your knees, and kiss my special place. Then you'll stand and take off your pants and come over and kiss it again. We're going to keep going until all your clothes are off. And then we will have fun."

My heart beat so fast I was afraid it might jump from my chest like it did in cartoons. This game wasn't our routine.

I couldn't pretend this was Anna.

It wasn't. It was me.

"Grandma said—"

Mr. Maples's hand came out, slapping my face before I could finish.

I reached for my cheek as the sting brought new tears to my eyes. "I'm sorry."

"Who makes the rules here?" His voice was louder than normal.

The tears overflowed, running down my cheeks. "You."

"Now, play by the rules, or I'll take those clothes off for you." He forced a smile. "I don't want to punish you again." He made his voice sound nicer, but I knew he didn't mean it. "I want us to have fun, Lorna. Be a good friend, or I'll have to go get Missy."

With shaking hands, I lifted my shirt over my head. Underneath I wore a t-shirt. It was old and too small. The bottom edge came to my belly button, and there were small straps that barely fit over my shoulders. It wasn't much, but it gave me a layer against the cold. I dropped the top shirt to the dirty carpet.

"Come kiss me."

I walked closer and knelt down.

"I'm Anna." The reassuring voice was in my head.

My tongue went out.

Mr. Maples grabbed my hair, making me look up. "Kiss, not lick. Follow directions."

My lips puckered as he released me. I leaned forward until I contacted his skin.

He tugged on my hair. "Get up. Now take off the pants."

I did as he said. Leaving my pants on the floor, wearing only my t-shirt, panties, and socks, I walked back and knelt, puckering my lips.

When I stood, he asked, "You getting breasts under there?"

"No."

"How about hair? Got any yet between your legs?"

"No."

"I think you're lying to me. A pretty girl like you, I bet you're growing some soft peach fuzz."

I shook my head.

His lips curled into a scary grin. "We're going to stop this game. I'm ready for fun. How about you?"

"I-I..." Words were failing me.

He reached for a strand of my hair and pulled the curl between his dirty fingers. "Be a good friend. Get up on the bed and show me your private place, like I've shown you." He reached for his penis, now bigger than it had been. "And then we touch each other."

When I didn't move, he added, "If you're good, I'll let you come."

I had no idea how I could do what he did.

Was it like peeing?

His hand moved faster. "Climb on up there."

"I'm Anna." The voice in my head repeated.

However, as I climbed onto the bed, I didn't want to be Anna. I didn't want to pee or come. I didn't want him to lie on top of me. I didn't want him to bounce on me.

My entire body shook as I settled onto the mattress where he and Mom slept.

Mr. Maples's hand continued moving on his penis. The veins looked angry and the top was leaking like it did before he came.

I laid my head back on the pillows and closed my eyes.

The bed leaned to one side and the smell got stronger, letting me know that he'd sat on the edge of the bed. He ran his finger over my cheeks and over the t-shirt. My entire body stilled as I willed myself not to feel his touch. His words broke through my defense. "You're a pretty girl."

I didn't answer.

"I'm so glad we are special friends." He ran his hand over my cheek again.

It took all my willpower not to flinch.

His hand went under my t-shirt and moved over my stomach.

"Open your eyes and mouth, Lorna."

I did as he said.

"First, I want to see your private places. Then" —he stuck his dirty thumb in between my lips— "we'll make each other feel good. Show me how you can suck on my thumb."

I'd been taught too well. Obeying didn't take thought. My lips closed as the taste of dirt and grime came to my tongue.

"That's it." He stood back up. "Now pull down your panties."

Though my eyes were still open, I imagined I was in the attic. I imagined the scent of Missy's hair after we washed it and how the fine strands could tickle my nose.

"Don't make me repeat myself, Lorna."

This isn't me.

As I reached for the waistband, the door behind him opened. I saw it, but I couldn't respond. It didn't fit with our routine. No one ever came in. I looked up at the ceiling as I began to pull my panties. The whistle of the bat slicing through the air returned my eyes to Mr. Maples.

The next few seconds happened faster than I could comprehend.

Before I could identify who had entered, the baseball bat came down from behind, striking Mr. Maples's head.

I saw it strike, but it was the gross sound, like dropping an egg on the floor, that pulled me away from my thoughts and back to reality. With my hands still gripping the waistband of my panties, I sat up and leaned forward, staring as Mr. Maples crumpled to the floor.

The baseball bat shook in Mom's grasp as she swayed, stepped back, and reached for the doorframe. Her glassy eyes scanned the room—Mr. Maples's pants and shoes in a pile on the floor, my shirt and pants. It was as if she saw clues but couldn't figure out the puzzle. I sat up, scooting toward the top of the bed, grabbed one of the big pillows and pulled it over me.

Finally, her green eyes came my way. Her gaze narrowed as one eye blinked and stayed shut. "What the hell are you doing, Lorna? You can't be in here." Her teeth were a shade of purple, bluer than her pink nail polish.

"Nothing, Mom." I pushed the pillow away and got off the bed. Hurriedly picking up my clothes, I began walking around her. My attention was on Mr. Maples, the blood oozing from his head and the moans coming from his throat.

Mom seized my arm. "What were you doing?" This time her voice was louder.

My head shook faster and faster. "Nothing, Mom. Really."

She pushed me to arm's length, her pink-painted fingernails dug into my arm as her voice seemed out of place. "Baby," she said, all calm. "I need you to make me a promise."

My entire body shook as if I were back upstairs in the freezing attic. "Please don't send me away, Mom. I'm sorry. I don't want to leave Mason and Missy." Each word came quicker than the one before.

Mr. Maples's moans continued as his arms and legs twitched. It was his penis that caught my attention. It wasn't sticking out but wrinkled and small. I thought about how the teacher told us that raisins were dried grapes. His penis was now a raisin.

Mom looked from him to me. Her neck straightened. "You are going away, Lorna."

My knees wobbled. "Mom, I'll be good. I promise."

"We're all going away."

"What?" I didn't understand.

Mom's voice became even calmer. "Go upstairs. Be very quiet so you don't wake Anna or Zella. Get Mason and Missy and all you can carry." She looked down at Mr. Maples as her nose wrinkled. The grip of my arm painfully tightened as her stare came back to me. "Listen, Lorna. You can't tell anyone about this..." She took a deep breath. "...about him. Nothing ever happened. If anyone finds out about any of it, they'll take

you away from me. If we're going to make it, I need the
checks. If you tell them—anyone—and they take you..." She
let me fill in the blanks. "Do you understand? Missy and
Mason." She swallowed. "The people who take kids, they'd
take you all away."

I nodded.

I did understand.

It was what Mr. Maples had told me, but different.

"Promise me, Lorna. Nothing happened. You weren't
alone with him—ever. You were asleep. I woke you and I told
you we were leaving."

"Yes, Mom. I was asleep..." Repeating lies had gotten
easier with time.

Her green eyes blinked as she finally released me. "Get
your clothes on. Tell no one, not even Missy or Mason. Do
you understand?"

"Yes, Mom."

Mr. Maples groaned louder.

"Hurry, Lorna. We need to be gone when he wakes."

REID

Present day

The plane rolled right and pitched up before rolling left and pitching down and dropping, losing altitude. It was a strange and uneasy sensation, such as a silver ball in an old-fashioned pinball machine. The crosswinds were the paddles, thrusting the plane about. Thankfully, we didn't have rubber bumpers to bounce.

Gray veiled the world beyond the windows as large raindrops pelted the reinforced glass. Lightning streaked, momentarily brightening the clouds before thunder rumbled, echoing as the plane shook. My grip of the armrest tightened as two sets of eyes met mine. The three of us and Patrick had been through too much to be taken out by a storm. It would take more than a force of nature to bring down the Sparrows.

If my life passed before my eyes, half of it was spent with these three men. We'd met at eighteen years of age. Here we were eighteen years later. As days turned into months, time became more difficult to track—basic training, our first deployment, and then our second. We came back to Chicago, attended college, and that was when the real work began.

As the plane bobbed and weaved and we neared Washington DC, I came to the realization that I'd spent as much time with these men as I had with my mother and grandmother. Before this moment, I hadn't put it in that perspective.

It wasn't the only thought that came to mind when assessing my life. While my focus for nearly the last two decades revolved around Sparrow, my existence was so much more than what I did or who I was as a top member of an outfit. The light that shone upon me day and night, the reason for everything from waking to going to sleep was Lorna. When I told her that I didn't need to lose her to know her worth or my love, I was as honest as I could be.

Gasps came as the plane dropped. The phenomenon was referred to as an air pocket. No matter what you called it, it was fucking unsettling to suddenly drop hundreds of feet. Marianne steadied us.

My grip tightened, not because of the turbulence, but with the knowledge that the intersection of the two most important sectors of my life was what brought danger and harm to my wife.

The three of us remained silent, possibly lost in our own

thoughts of Sparrow, family, and future as the plane finally broke below the clouds. No longer submerged in the clouds filled with electrical charges, natural light shone through the small windows, illuminating the cabin. Though the rain continued to fall, the increased light brought a sense of confirmation that we would survive. We would make it to another day, another week, another month...

"Marianne deserves a raise," Mason said with a sigh. "That was..." He didn't finish but we all knew what it was.

"Fuck, I'll give her a year's salary," I volunteered.

Sparrow didn't respond to Mason's comments.

While Sparrow employees weren't officially paid through our outfit, they were well compensated. If he had responded, years of experience allowed me to fill in the blanks. Sparrow would say that neither Marianne nor anyone else deserved a raise for doing their jobs. What he wouldn't say was that she was financially secure, not only for her piloting abilities but more important, for the loyalty she'd shown and her willingness to bend to Sparrow's ever-changing schedule.

It was as if the prolonged minutes within the storm were gone and forgotten, never to be mentioned.

Would that happen once we had our revenge?

Would Lorna be able to sleep without medication?

Would I again see the light in the world?

Sparrow spoke as we neared landing, asking about the hotel and the waiting cars.

A feeling of unease itched just below my skin. "I know I'm usually back in the tower, but I'm not comfortable with the two cars." I was talking about the plan to get us from the airport to the hotel.

"We do it all the time," Mason said. "It's less noticeable when we don't arrive together."

"I'll ride alone," I volunteered.

"No," Sparrow responded. "I'm the one who will be recognized." His intense stare scanned Mason and me. "Reid, you're part of the shadows of Sparrow. People aren't used to putting your face with us. And" —he shrugged— "few have gotten Mason figured out."

It was because of his extensive reconstructive surgery that he defied facial recognition programs.

"Being seen with me," Sparrow went on, "will make it more difficult for you to be seen in the future. The two of you will enter the front door of the Mandarin Oriental, and Garrett will take me around back to a secluded entrance. We'll meet in the suite."

I looked at Mason who nodded.

My head shook as the landscape of Washington DC came into view. "I admit it's less stressful in the tower."

"Are you kidding me," Mason said. "Everything rides on the man in the control center. Every bit of data, every question, and every retrieval of intel. This should be a ride in the park for you."

"Patrick can handle the control center," I said.

"He can," Sparrow said, "but not like you. Don't forget that."

There was a reason we had our roles.

The three of us silenced as the wheels touched down,

bouncing before settling on the runway. A rush of air filled our ears as the flaps moved and brakes engaged. Finally, we came to a stop.

The cabin filled with clicks as seatbelts were unfastened and Keaton joined us. His face was unusually pale. "Marianne said to tell you that she will refuel and be ready to leave as soon as you return."

Sparrow nodded. "I don't expect this to take long."

The Sparrow who drove Mason and me from the airport to the hotel filled us in on recent changes in logistics. The Sparrow tail on Walters had him in view. He'd spent the morning in the Hart Senate Office Building. His official calendar stated he had a meeting this afternoon regarding a coalition of Illinois donors.

That would be us.

Mason continued text contact with Sparrow as I did with Patrick. We may not all be in the same car, but we were on the same page.

The car pulled up to the front beneath the flag-adorned awning of the Mandarin Oriental. An attendant in hotel uniform opened the back door and welcomed us as we stepped onto the sidewalk. He held the door as we entered. The floor within glistened and dark and light pillars held domes of ornate design and artificial light. We bypassed the desk and made our way to the VIP elevator, prepared that it took a special key to access the presidential suite.

We'd received our keys in the car.

I offered it to the attendant at the stand. "Presidential suite."

The older man nodded, slowly taking the key from my grasp as he looked from me to Mason and back. "Sirs, your names?"

"We gave you our key," Mason replied.

The attendant went to his stand and brought a tablet to life. "We have been told that security is tight lately."

This imbecile had no fucking idea how tight the security was. "Phillip Kennington." I nodded toward Mason. "And Joseph Swills."

The attendant searched his tablet. When he looked up, his eyes met mine. "I will need to see identification to confirm."

Mason and I both reached for our wallets. To say the Sparrows were always prepared was an understatement. We removed the fake identification cards from our wallets. Phillip, a.k.a. me, was from New York. Joseph, a.k.a. Mason, was from Miami. We could both rattle off our information as if we were underage college students ready to confirm our illegal ability to drink.

The attendant spent what seemed an excessive period of time scrutinizing the IDs before he handed them back. "Hmm. I can't find anything out of order." Though I'd been the one to give the attendant the key, he handed it back to Mason. "Sir." With his eyes straight ahead, he moved beyond the stand and activated the VIP elevator that would take us directly to the presidential suite.

Once we were in the elevator, alone but probably being filmed, Mason handed me the key. I took it with a huff and placed it back in the pocket of my suit coat. I could mention that I'd never witnessed Sparrow, Patrick, or Mason having an extra layer of security before, but honestly, the hotel employee didn't deserve more of my time or thought. His opinion didn't affect my worth.

We had more pressing matters.

When the elevator opened, Mason and I stepped into another glistening tile hallway. Our only option to proceed was an entry, consisting of two grand doors with a plaque near the doorbell. It read *Presidential Suite*. I removed the key from my pocket and waved it before the sensor. The mechanism within clicked. Once inside we were in a small foyer with two options. There was a door to the right or double doors to the left. Before we had a chance to choose, the door to the right opened.

"Welcome, Mr. Murray, Mr. Pierce," Romero said as he led us into what appeared to be a bedroom—or that was what it normally was. The two beds within were pushed against the window, and in their place a large computer center had been created.

Exhaling, I took in the welcome sight. As the man in the tower, the makeshift field command posts were something I didn't often see. "Damn, I'm impressed," I said as I walked around the setup. "You did well."

"Thank you, Mr. Murray. I didn't do it alone."

Christian sat in front of multiple screens, his fingers on

the keys, and earphones over his ears. I stepped behind his chair. "There he is," I said to Mason.

Mason came up behind me. As he stared at the older man on the screen walking along a sidewalk not far from the hotel, Mason's countenance changed. He straightened his stance and the muscles in his arm beside mine tightened. "That's him."

I looked around. "Show me the security for the suite."

Romero spent the next few minutes showing me all that they had installed from the computers. The entire suite was under surveillance. It wouldn't matter if Walters and Sparrow wanted to conduct the meeting in the living room or dining room. There were cameras and recording equipment covering it all, as well as a rotating feed from the hallway and even the lobby on the first floor.

"So you saw us coming before we arrived," I said with a grin.

"Yes, sir. We saw the asshole at the elevator too."

"He's not worth our breath," I replied.

Romero smiled. "And he can spend the next three hours trying to figure out why Phillip Kennington is in the presidential suite."

"He obviously has nothing better to do."

"Mr. Sparrow?" Mason asked.

Christian had removed one of the earphones and was listening to us as well as his feeds. He hit a few keys and we saw Sparrow and Garrett riding within an elevator.

"Did they stop at the asshole's entry?" I asked.

"No, they came from the basement parking garage. We have access to this feed, but it's blacked out on the hotel's surveillance. When you all leave, there will be no record of Sterling Sparrow ever being in Washington DC."

Romero led us out to the entry and into the doors to the left. It was time to see in person what had been on the screens. I stopped at the threshold. The presidential suite was stunning. I imagined spending a week away with Lorna within a place like this.

The three of us stepped into the living room. The windows lining the far wall looked out toward the Washington Monument. If it weren't raining, we could open the French doors and enjoy an autumn day in our country's capital. To the left, the eight-person dining room table was cleared, with the exception of a centerpiece, ready to be a conference table. To the right was a study, more intimate than the open living room for confidential discussions, and able to be closed off by a set of pocket doors.

Of course, nothing was confidential with the way the Sparrows had this place wired.

We turned as the doors behind us opened and Garrett and Sparrow entered.

"Where is he?" Sparrow asked.

Romero stepped around Sparrow and back to the control room before reentering the living room. "Mr. Walters just entered the lobby and he's alone."

"This will be overwhelming," Mason said. "Four of us, one of him. Let me greet him."

"He's not here to meet with you," Sparrow said. "You two" —he was speaking to Mason and me— "go wait in the study. I'll greet Mr. Walters after Garrett answers the bell. Then,

Garrett will go to the master bedroom and serve as backup. Christian and Romero will be in the computer room watching everything."

"There's a monitor in the master bedroom, too," Romero offered. He turned to me. "Here" —he pulled a phone from his pocket— "this is so you can hear and see from the study."

"It's right..." I didn't finish the train of thought as I examined the phone in my hand. "This is a monitor." I'd said a statement, but there was a hint of a question in it.

"Yes, it is already programmed. Turn it on and use these earbuds. You will hear everything as if you're in here. The monitor is small, but it's better than listening through doors and watching through the keyhole."

Sparrow nodded. "Good that's taken care of. And there are also five more Sparrows in the hotel and more nearby. I'll talk first and then bring the two of you in on the conversation."

Stress rippled off Mason in waves.

"Mason," Sparrow commanded. "Go."

The two men stood at a crossroad staring at one another.

"He's on the elevator," Romero said.

"Go to the computer room," Sparrow directed. "Garrett, answer the door and then disappear." He turned his dark stare to me and Mason. Once Romero had gone and Garrett was in the entry behind closed doors, Sparrow came closer. His tone was low but harsh. "No matter how much power I allow you to have, I give the fucking orders." His eyes were on Mason. "Now isn't a good time to put that to a test."

When Mason turned to me, I nodded and lifted the monitor and earbuds.

Sparrow took a seat on a long sofa near the window. Together, Mason and I stepped into the study. I reached for the pocket doors and pulled them shut as the sound of a doorbell rang throughout the suite.

REID

My brother-in-law paced a few steps in the smaller room before going to the windows and peering out toward the National Mall. "We should have done this alone."

I wasn't confident enough in either plan to agree or disagree.

"I want answers," I said. "No matter if we get them or Sparrow does, I want to know why the Order took my wife and if she's still a target."

Mason let out a breath. "And why they're after my wife."

"I fucking want answers. Lorna got one. It's our turn."

Mason's gaze met mine. He'd learned the results of the rape kit from me, after I left Lorna. While it was reassuring that she hadn't been raped, the fact she needed a kit to determine that coated both of our vision in crimson.

I ran a test to compare the DNA from the pubic hair to

Andrew Jettison. It took less than five minutes for the results to come back with a near percent match. The man who died six years ago recently bled and somehow shed pubic hair less than a week ago.

Mason extended his hand, silently asking for the earbuds. Sitting on a two-person sofa, we both put the earbuds into place, and I switched on the small handheld monitor. The room beside us came into view on the screen.

Garrett was leading Edison Walters toward Sparrow. For a man nearly seventy years old, Walters was formidable. There was no pretension in the other room. Walters didn't need to pretend he was a mild-mannered legislative aide. Sparrow didn't need to pretend that his only concern was real estate. They were coming together with complete openness, a translucency evident in the way Walters walked. He was a man of power.

Sparrow stood, also a man of power.

I hoped the conversation would yield similar unpretentious results.

"Mr. Sparrow." Walter's extended his hand.

Sparrow did likewise. "Mr. Walters." Once they shook, he gestured toward the sofas. "Sit."

Walters stood taller. "Mr. Sparrow, there are few individuals who have access or the ability to request my presence, my real presence. Tell me what this is about."

"Who, not what."

"*Who* this is about," Mr. Walters hesitated. "Is it Pierce? Is there a problem?"

"A problem?" Sparrow repeated. "What sort of problem would you suspect?"

Walters placed his hands in the pockets of his slacks and grinned. "You asked for this meeting. I'm sure you had a topic in mind."

Sparrow walked to the sofa and took a seat. "Thank you for joining me."

Silence filled the room until Mr. Walters took a seat opposite Sparrow.

With a nod, Sparrow began talking. "It came to my attention..."

As he spoke, I couldn't help but think about how different this meeting would be if Araneae were still missing. One of Sterling Sparrow's secrets to success both in real estate and elsewhere was his ability to negotiate. He had an innate sense of the other person's thoughts and motives. It was similar to his aptitude at playing chess. He wasn't one move ahead but four moves. In his mind, he had each possibility planned and countered before those strategies even occurred to his opponent.

"...I want to know why the Order has decided to renege upon the agreement we secured regarding Mr. Pierce."

Walters sat taller. "The Order doesn't renege. Mr. Pierce is no longer a part of any governmental organization, not a legal organization."

"Dr. Carlson, or should I say, Mrs. Pierce?"

Walters sat for a moment, staring at Sparrow. "Mrs. Pierce. Yes, I remember learning that he married. What does...?" His question stopped. "Are you insinuating that the Order is in the process of anything regarding Sergeant First Class Pierce's wife?"

"Yes, I have reason to believe that is the case."

"She was..." Walters faltered a minute. "...I recall, a scientist. She was at the center of the debacle that brought us together the first time." His expression became quizzical. "Part of our agreement was that she would discontinue her research on the compound and formula that she'd been studying in Indiana."

"That research was lost when she had to run for her life."

Walters shrugged. "A fair trade, I suppose."

"You tell me, Mr. Walters, is her life safe?"

"As long as she abides by our rules."

"Then why was there an attempted kidnapping with her as the target?"

Walters shook his head. "I can tell you with complete confidence that I have no idea what you're talking about. I'm sure you pay attention to the world news, Mr. Sparrow. You don't have your head buried only in Chicago."

Sparrow sat taller. "I stay informed."

"Six hostages were rescued a week ago from a rogue ISIS camp. Three weeks before that, a Russian informant was saved from an attempt on his life." Mr. Walters went on. "A month ago, there was a failed assassination attempt on a crowned prince."

"You failed?"

"No, Mr. Sparrow. The prince will be needed in future negotiations on some yet-to-be-discussed diplomacy issues. The assassin failed. The Order doesn't fail—we succeed. If

Mrs. Pierce was meant to be kidnapped, she would have been."

"My wife and the wife of a trusted member of my team were taken."

"My condolences."

"They have been returned."

Mr. Walters stood. "While I am flattered that you assume anyone willing to come against you could only be the Order, we did not and have not prioritized the Sparrow organization. I may not agree with the business you do—"

"Nor I yours," Sparrow interrupted as he stood, "or the way in which you recruit."

"Then we can agree to disagree. As I was saying, despite my personal dislike for organizations that work outside the law, you serve a purpose in your city and beyond. The Order has no urgent or imminent concerns with your business dealings; however, it is wise to remember that you made yourself a blip on our radar."

"Apparently, we have the same radar screen. It is ironic that you would draw an invisible line at legal legitimacy."

"My point, Mr. Sparrow, is do not waste my time again. The Order has much more pressing matters. However, if Mrs. Pierce would decide to go public with a pharmaceutical, a decision that would not be in the best interest of the republic, we would notice. I suggest she use her talents in other means, such as working at your wife's institute."

"Fuck," Mason whispered, ripping the ear bud from his ear. "That was a threat."

Before I could stop him, Mason was up and opening the

study doors. With his feet planted shoulder-width apart, he addressed the man across the room, "Top."

Gray eyes came his way. "Sergeant."

Sparrow took a step back, his displeasure at our interruption well-masked. "Of course, please join us."

Walters looked between Sparrow and Mason and me. "Is this it or will more doors open?"

"This is it, sir," I said. "My name is Reid Murray. My wife was the other woman kidnapped. She was physically assaulted. We have evidence that led us to the Order. It wasn't an assumption that we warranted your attention. Our goal is to work in parallel—we could say on the fringe of perceived legality. The Order has its focus as we do our own."

The man walked closer to me, tilting his head to the side. "You look..." He scanned me up and down. "Murray is a common name."

I wasn't certain where he was headed, but I had a goal. "Sir, I need answers about a soldier that fits the profile of the Order's recruits."

"Yes, your diction is similar." He shook his head as a smile came to his thin lips. "May I ask your parents' names?"

"Top, we need to know—"

Mr. Walters waved Mason's direction. "Of course, it won't be difficult for me to learn."

I scanned the room. All eyes were on me. "My father's name was Rendell and my mother was LaDonna Murray."

Top nodded and turned to Sparrow. "Perhaps we could learn from you, Mr. Sparrow. You do surround yourself with the best, or at least the son of one of the best."

My train of thought derailed. "You knew my father?"

"I did. Lieutenant Colonel Murray is a hero, son, a patriot in the true sense of the term. You should be proud of his dedication to the republic."

"He was part of the Order?" I couldn't believe I was asking this.

"Things operated a bit differently back then. Mr. Sparrow's concern with our recruiting was different. The formula didn't exist."

My mind spun.

Did my father not die in the Gulf War?

Did he choose the republic over his family?

Before I could form questions, Mason drew his attention. "Top, we have recent DNA evidence that led us to a man who served in the army. According to military records, he died six years ago. His DNA was found last week. Even you must admit that sounds like a possible soldier in the Order?"

"And what is this to you, Sergeant? I understand Mr. Sparrow and Mr. Murray." He turned back to me. "Did you ever consider serving your country?"

"Yes, sir. I did two tours in Iraq."

"Branch?"

"Army."

"Mr. Murray's wife is my sister," Mason said, returning the conversation to him. "And as Mr. Sparrow mentioned, we have every reason to believe my wife is the target."

Walters shook his head. "This has been fascinating. Utterly fascinating." He offered me his hand. "It was nice to meet you, Reid. Not all of our recruits come to us" —he looked at Mason— "well, as the sergeant here did. As I said, the Sovereign Order far predates the drug. If you are ever wanting more..."

"Sir, right now, I want answers to who harmed my wife."

"Your father was a family man too." After we shook, he turned to Sparrow and Mason. "I cannot help you. Whatever is being done to you or your wives is not from the Order. I'm certain you have a long list of enemies." He spoke to Mason. "I suggest you rerun that DNA. Erroneous results are commonplace. Obviously, a dead man doesn't leave DNA.

"Goodbye, gentlemen. Don't contact—"

"The women were returned after they had received a similar drug to the one you gave me," Mason said, interrupting. "It's improved. Whatever they were given only blocked out a few weeks, yet they are both missing the same amount of time, and my wife has identified key components to her previous research in their toxicology screen."

Mr. Walters stopped. "That is interesting. I would like to get my hands on that report. I'm sure our scientists would be interested."

Sparrow stepped forward. "Is there any possibility you have another rogue soldier?"

"No one goes against the Order."

Someone had. She'd died in Montana in the fire at Mason's ranch.

"Is it a possibility?" Sparrow repeated.

Walter's gaze went to Mason. "No."

Walters started to walk away. As he did, I felt my chance at avenging Lorna slip away. "Mr. Walters."

He turned. "Mr. Murray."

"You said you wanted the toxicology report?"

"Yes."

"Sir, if you could provide me with the means to reach you, I will send you what we have regarding the toxicology. I'd also like to send the DNA and name and rank of the deceased soldier."

"There can be no record of communication," he said.

"That won't be a problem."

He took a deep breath. "No offense intended, but I don't trust anyone outside the Order. The risk is too great."

"I used to contact you," Mason said.

Walters turned his stare to Mason. "Activate the old address. It's the only way I'll agree."

"Yes, sir. I will," he said.

LORNA

I'd basked in my knowledge that I wasn't raped as I tried to get on with my life. Of course, it wasn't exactly business as usual. We were on lockdown. It made it easier that all of the women were in similar straits, including Ruby.

Everyone did their best to go on with life. Ruby continued her senior year online. Laurel had a new space on 2 that allowed her more room to do what she'd done at the institute. It wasn't as if she could see clients of the institute or check on participants in her study, yet she could access the team she'd been able to assemble and work virtually with them.

Much to Sparrow's chagrin, Araneae maintained her presence—albeit virtual—at both the Sparrow Institute and Sinful Threads. Her friend and co-founder of the fashion design company, Louisa, was more than willing to carry more than her weight. After all, she had been where Araneae was twice. Her little girl, Kennedy, was already four years old and her son, Dustin, had recently celebrated his first birthday. It was right before our trip to Montana. Sparrow, Araneae, and about fifty Sparrows went to Boulder for a first birthday party.

While I couldn't imagine Sterling Sparrow enthralled with balloons and a smash cake, Araneae later said he did well. I suppose that could mean anything from he didn't grunt or he actually enjoyed himself.

Madeline continued to immerse herself in the work around the kitchen. In sharing bits and pieces of her life story, she told me that she had always wanted to learn to cook but had never had the opportunity. I'd found her not only to be a fast learner, but she also had a penchant for Russian recipes, dishes and spice combinations I'd never tried and surprisingly liked. Ruby also liked to help her mom create foods that had been a part of their lives for so long.

That left me to do what I did, maintain the households. While many may think cleaning, laundry, and dishes were boring, I found comfort in the commonplace activities. There was satisfaction in a job completed.

The other ongoing activity left mostly to us women was preparing for our expansion. While Madeline and Araneae were the ones with child, they welcomed Laurel's and my input on all things needed for babies. Laurel at least had a niece to reference. I was woefully detached from all the new and modern baby-care items.

I picked up one of their books and read about care. Simple things like placing a baby in a crib had new rules. They never were to be put on their stomach. And babies no longer wore coats in car seats.

"Are you sure?" I asked Araneae as I considered a newborn in Chicago's winter—not that Sparrow would ever allow it outside the tower until maybe twenty years of age.

"Yes, look." She pulled up a page of baby items on her tablet. "It's because they're too bulky in the car seat."

"Oh," I said, looking at the page. "They have car-seat covers." We both grinned. "With a little place to see their face."

Araneae reached for my hand. "I'm having a few of what Laurel calls flashes."

I nodded, knowing what she was talking about.

"It's like one of those pictures where they use a million other pictures to make one big one. Do you know what I mean?"

"Yeah."

Her lips came together and then slid between her teeth as her nostrils flared. "I'm sorry, fucking hormones."

A grin came to my lips. "Ruby would charge you a dollar."

She snickered, bringing her fingers to her lips. "Oh, damn."

"Go on," I encouraged. "I don't remember exactly where we were, and I only have glimpses of what it looked like. But there's one scene. It was dark. I was all by myself and then you were there. I feel bad when I think about it. I mean, it's only a flash of time, but I shouldn't have wanted you there."

Her hormones were beginning to affect me as I swallowed tears.

"I recall feeling alone and then not," Araneae said. "Thank you. I'm sorry I didn't do more to help you."

"How do you know you didn't?"

"Because I wasn't hurt like you were. I'm so relieved by the results of the rape kit."

"Did you have one done?" I asked.

She nodded. "I did. I asked for it. I wanted not only to know if it happened, but to be sure there wasn't anything, diseases..."

"And I assume you were clear?"

"I was."

"What matters is that your little one is good," I said as I looked down at her growing midsection.

"Do you want to feel a kick?"

"Can you feel it?" I asked.

"Give me your hand." She placed my hand over her blouse. "Don't be afraid to push."

It was amazing to me how solid her growing midsection felt. As I pressed, there was a flutter beneath my palm. "Oh my goodness."

Araneae smiled. "It has been getting stronger and stronger each day." She giggled. "Sterling felt it for the first time."

"I bet he was thrilled."

Her giggle became a full-out laugh. "Without too much detail, I would say he was a bit shocked."

"It happened when the two of you...?"

"Yes. He has started calling the baby 'little cock-blocker.'"

My head shook. "You know it is all about him."

"He better enjoy it because I believe things will change."

The only baby experience I had was with Missy and being only a year older, it wasn't that I was experienced. I also didn't know any of the newfangled swings or bassinets or remember any of that from my childhood.

Thinking of Missy took my thoughts back to my dream from almost a week ago. It made no sense that my thoughts would go that way, but they did.

I hadn't been raped. Was it too much to ask for a little bit of hope that my sister was alive?

One night after dinner in the penthouse, nearly two weeks after I was found, there was a knock on our apartment door. With Reid on 2, I answered it to find my brother.

"Is everything all right?"

"Yeah," he said, his lips thinning as he tilted his head. "Can I come in?"

As sure as Madeline had said a while ago at breakfast, those were Mason's tells. While I let him in, I was pretty sure this visit wasn't to borrow sugar. "Sure." I opened the door wider and stepped back. "Can I get you anything?"

He shook his head. "Is Reid here yet?"

"No, he's downstairs, I figured you would be too."

"I was. I told him I'd come up here. He should be here soon," Mason said as he walked around our living room. His green gaze went to a piece of artwork Reid had bought me early in our marriage. It was an artist whose work had been one of our first-ever conversations. Nevertheless, my brother was doing a terrible job of acting casual. If anything, he was doing a good job of acting nervous.

"Mace, you're freaking me out. What's going on?"

"It's not a big deal."

"Okay, we can rule out life or death," I said in a wasted attempt at humor.

When he turned my way, I realized my sarcasm had landed like a lead balloon.

I walked to the sofa and sat. "Okay, spill."

"Lorna, I should have told you this earlier. I meant to, but there are other things happening. And I kept telling Reid it was you who wasn't ready. He said you were. I think it was me. But, fuck, we need to come clean."

My mind scrambled as there was another knock at our door. My gaze went to the door and back to Mason. "Reid wouldn't knock."

"It's probably Laurel." He tilted his head the direction of the door. "Do you mind?"

"Since I seem to be the only one left out in the cold, help yourself."

Mason went to the door and greeted his wife with a kiss before she entered and assessed the room. "Waiting on Reid?" she asked.

"You are really making me uncomfortable." As I spoke, the door opened again and Reid stepped inside. His handsome face showed the same unspoken stress I was feeling.

"It's about time," Mason said.

"I didn't know you meant *now*."

"I said *now*."

Reid came to my side and sat. "I wanted to tell you this before. At first, I agreed to wait because I wasn't sure, but you're doing so well, and then because you were doing well, I was unsure if this would set you back." He barely took a breath through the entire long sentence.

"Lorna," Mason began, "it's not Reid's fault. It's mine. I take full blame, and if I were honest right now with everyone in this room, I could sleep soundly for the rest of my life not telling you what I'm about to say. Sometimes, omission is a gift."

My hands rubbed up and down my sleeves as his words sent a strange chill over my skin. "What have you omitted?"

Laurel took a seat in a chair nearby as Mason began to share what he wasn't certain I could hear. He was wrong. I could hear it. I just wasn't certain that I wasn't dreaming.

I listened in a state hovering close to disbelief.

LORNA

*A*s my brother spoke, Reid reached for my hand and kept it wrapped safely in the cocoon of his larger one.

Once Mason finished his unbelievable tale, I asked, "What the hell? Can you repeat that?"

Though he was finished talking, his feet were still moving, back and forth on the edge of the area rug defining our living room. When he stopped, he turned my way. "Yeah, I didn't know how to handle it either."

"I don't understand how she was with me. Did the people who took Araneae and me take her? Why?" While those questions should be front and center, I should be concerned about our mother and the confirmation of her demise, including her body in a makeshift morgue on 1, but that wasn't where my mind went. Releasing my husband's hand, I stood "Oh my God. Missy could be alive."

The three of them looked around as if I was speaking of unicorns and pots of gold at the end of rainbows.

"I'm not crazy. My dream could have been real." It was as if they'd all lost the ability to speak. My gaze went from my husband to my brother. "You both knew about this." I turned to Laurel. "And you?"

"It's not her fault," Reid said. "Mason and I agreed—"

"Of course you did." I let out an exaggerated breath as my palms slapped my thighs. "You two decided what I could and couldn't know."

"Lorna," Reid said with the *it was all for your own good* tone. "You were dealing with so much."

"I'm not made of glass." My gaze went to Laurel. "And you. You let me talk to you about my dream. You heard Mace get upset. You didn't think I should know why?"

She nodded. "I did. I encouraged Mason to tell you."

"Almost two weeks later?"

Mason's lips came together. "If you're worried about Nancy, she's not going anywhere."

"Oh." I stepped away from my husband's attempted grasp. "I don't care about *her*."

"What?" Reid asked.

Laurel stood. "Lorna, this information is another shock to your mind in a rapid series of blows. It's okay to be unsure. Don't make rash comments or decisions without allowing this information to sink in." She glanced toward Mason and back to me. "I know that there isn't a lot of love lost between the two of you and your mother..."

I waved my hand toward her. "I'm not rehashing all of

that." Turning a three-sixty spin, my eyes met my sister-in-law's. "Look at this." I gestured between Mason and myself. "We're here. We made it despite her poor excuse at parenting. Hell, maybe we made it because of that. I don't know. Maybe forcing us to grow up as children made us stronger as adults, but even if that's true, I'm not willing to give her credit for what *we* did. As far as I'm concerned, Nancy Pierce is the one who failed. We" —my eyes met Mace's— "survived."

"There is nothing wrong with mourning her," Laurel said.

Still looking at my brother, I asked, "Have you?"

His stance straightened. "Mourned? No."

"Do you feel the need to mourn the woman who birthed you—us?"

"Fuck no."

Turning back to Laurel, I asked, "He doesn't, why should I?"

"There's no should or shouldn't. However, just because he doesn't shouldn't stop you."

Scenes I'd buried for years threatened to enter my thoughts. My hands began to tremble and my stomach twist. The apartment around me was gone. No longer in a castle in the sky, in a flash, I was in a room filled with clothes and trash. Nancy was talking to me. Her face was close and much younger than my recent recollection or dream. And then all of it was gone."

"Lorna?"

Reid's voice filtered into my consciousness. I blinked the unwanted image away.

Shaking my head, my mind replaced the flash with

another scene from my childhood. It was the one-room studio apartment we moved to, about six months after we went to live with our mother. While it was dingy with few pieces of furniture—a table with only three chairs and an old discarded television—it wasn't filthy in the way of that first flash. In this one room, there was only one real bed; a twin-sized one that had a frame where Nancy slept and then, for the three of us, there was a large mattress on the floor.

That memory should be depressing, yet it wasn't. It was the first space we truly had after our grandmother passed away. It was also the last place we shared with Missy.

"Lorna, maybe you should sit down."

"No, don't you all understand?" Excitement laced my words, joy replacing whatever had momentarily sent ice through my circulation. I concentrated on the positive. "If she was found with me, it means that my dream wasn't a dream."

"Lorna," Laurel began, "we've already discussed the unlikelihood of this possibility."

"We? You mean you, Mason, and Reid?"

Sheepishly, she nodded. "I have concerns about what you think you remember. It's inconsistent with your loss of memories. You don't recall going to Montana or being kidnapped, yet you recall a conversation you had while you were drugged, dehydrated, injured, and nearly septic from ant bites."

"What if Missy is alive? What if what I recalled really did happen?"

"What if it didn't?" Mason asked, stepping closer. "Then

after all this time, you're letting that bitch down on
disappoint you again."

"Is that your problem, Mason? You're more concerned
about disappointment than our sister?"

"Lorna," Reid said. "We're still working on who took you.
This isn't a priority."

"My sister isn't a priority?" I stared in disbelief. "And I
suppose the two of you were the ones who determined this
hierarchy of concerns?" Taking in both of the men's
expression, I shook my head. "No, it wasn't only you two.
Sparrow and Patrick had a say."

Mason's lips came together as Reid reached out to me and
spoke, "I'm not saying we won't investigate what you think
she may have said to you. I'm just saying it won't be until after
we have other answers."

"What if you never get other answers?"

"We will," Mason said matter-of-factly. "We've been
working with someone. If it pans out…"

"Laurel," I said, directing my words to her. "You have a
sister. What if Allison had gone missing years ago and you
never knew what happened? What if it was Haley?" Laurel
visibly bristled at the mention of her eight-year-old niece.
"Missy was only a year older than Haley when she
disappeared."

"I'd move heaven and hell to find either of them."

I turned to Mason. "We tried that, remember? But at the
time, we were only kids. We did all we could. I remember you
searching shelters and streets."

He nodded.

"When Mom finally came home, we told our story to the police."

The tendons in Mason's neck tightened.

"What do you mean *when she finally came home?*" Reid asked.

"Oh," I said as casually as possible, "Nancy Pierce was gone as much as she was present, or more." Pity showed from his dark eyes. "Stop. We were fine. We were in an apartment with locks on the door. That was all we needed from her. It wasn't like she read us bedtime stories or came home with bags of groceries."

Mason's tone lowered. "Lorna, stop. This is why you didn't need to know about her. None of us need a stroll down memory lane."

"We aren't kids anymore, Mace. What if what I thought was a dream was reality? What if Missy is out there?" I turned to Reid. "You've told me that you can do anything behind a computer."

He shrugged.

"This isn't the time to be modest," I chastised. "Even Sparrow sings your praises, and in my experience, he isn't one who gives compliments that aren't deserved." No one responded. "I know you want a head on a platter for this..." I waved at my face and body. "I'm healing." I was. My bruises were lightening. Walking no longer hurt. Learning that I hadn't been raped renewed an inner strength I hadn't realized had become depleted. "I want you to find out who did this horrible thing so our lives can go back to normal. But, Reid, I also want to find out if she's alive." Tears prickled the backs of my eyes. "She's my sister."

"Use me," Laurel said.

"What?" Reid and I asked simultaneously.

"I told you no," Mason responded.

"I'm not asking you," she said as her neck straightened. "I'm offering. It's been nearly two weeks. I know I'm not supposed to, but I've heard a few things being discussed on 2."

Mason and Reid stood tall.

"I know," Laurel said. "I'm not trying to eavesdrop. And it hasn't been a lot." Before either man could interrupt, she went on, "I know about the" —she paused— "where you were, Mason. And I knew when Araneae offered me space for my lab that they wouldn't be happy. It now seems, if they aren't the ones who are after me, then they should be after whoever took Araneae and Lorna."

"What?" I asked.

"I don't want to say more than I have, but in a nutshell, the organization for which Mason worked has a similar compound to the one I had created and am trying to recreate. Whoever took you has a superior, or at least, more refined pharmaceutical." She turned to Mason. "If they didn't want me to work on it, they won't want this other one."

"She's right," Reid said.

"So if there are three players in this game, and I'm one of them, use me to lure out the unknown. They're not going to find me locked away in a glass tower with impenetrable shields." It was a joke between all of us women. It started when Araneae arrived. She talked about a force field. "If I am out and about, going to the institute, working with women and children as well as my team of researchers, I will be a target."

"No," Mason repeated.

Laurel looked at me and then Reid.

"Look at what happened to me," I said.

She stepped forward and reached for my hand. "I'm sorry. It was supposed to be me that was taken. I'm also sorry I haven't said that before now. I should have. I guess, I'm trying to help you because you're my sister-in-law and one of my closest friends, and I love and care about you. I think it's also because I can't help but feel incredibly guilty that it was you and not me."

Releasing her hand, I pulled her into an embrace. "Please don't do anything to put yourself in danger. I don't want to be the one home with another one of us gone."

Laurel smiled and looked at the men. "I won't be. This time it will be planned, and I have the best team in the world behind me."

Mason ran his hand over his long hair. His boots clipped the tile floor beyond the area rug. "No. I won't allow it."

My sister-in-law looked my way with a wink. "I think tomorrow I'll be headed to the institute. I can call for a ride. If it doesn't work, I know someone upstairs who will help me."

"Sparrow won't allow her to get involved in this," Mason said.

Laurel looked my direction. In her blue eyes, I saw her unspoken response. Sparrow may be the king, but Araneae was the queen, and as in the game of chess, the queen was capable of more moves. Our money would always be on her.

"Not tomorrow," Mason said with an inflection of resignation. "Fuck, if you're determined to go through with this, we need time to plan. I will fucking have a hundred Sparrows around you."

"That won't be obvious."

He shook his head. "And I need to talk to...the organization. We need all players on deck. I'm not taking chances."

Laurel walked across the room and laid her hand on Mason's chest. "I'll feel safer knowing you're watching over me."

"Fuck, okay. Just give us some time."

Personally, I didn't want Laurel to risk what had happened to Araneae and to me. But that didn't dim my admiration for her desire to help or her ability to manipulate my brother. And maybe if they identified the kidnappers, we would then be able to concentrate on Missy.

My gaze went around the room. "So what's happening with our mother? Please don't tell me that you're going to keep her on 1 indefinitely."

"Not indefinitely," Reid said. "We've run tests on trace evidence to help us find out who took you. There are just so many variables. Basically, we haven't learned more than we did from the forensic search of the bunker where you were kept. It makes sense that everything that would identify the kidnappers was in the other bunker."

"That's why they had the explosives on that one," Mason said.

Reid again reached for my hand. "Do you want to see her?"

Did I?

If I did, I would know if the image in my mind of the thin old woman with faded red hair was the same as reality. Taking a deep breath, I nodded. "I do."

REID

"Do you want to go see her now?" I asked.

I tried to assess what my wife was thinking behind her green-eyed stare as she looked up at me. If there had ever been a question regarding Lorna's strength, it had been put to rest in these recent trials. Truly with her recurring willingness to meet each hurdle, she'd shattered any illusion that she was the weaker sex. While she had ups and downs since it all ensued, I found myself in awe at her fortitude.

"You know what they say, why put off until tomorrow...?" She looked around the room at all of us. "I assume you've all seen her."

Laurel nodded.

"She was with you when the capos found you," Mason said. "Seeing her was unavoidable." He forced a grin. "Of course, you could avoid it."

"Do we...?" Lorna walked closer to her brother and

shrugged. "Should we...do something? Some sort of memorial?"

"I'd say a party is appropriate, but we should wait a bit before getting shit-faced. There are a few irons in the fire."

"There are always irons in the fire," Lorna replied.

"Do you think if you see her, you'll have difficulty sleeping?" Laurel asked. "You said that the sleeping pills have been helping. I don't want to see you regress."

Lorna turned my way, a blush of pink filling her healing cheeks as she undoubtedly had the same thoughts as me. Our recent routine assuring her tiredness before closing her eyes involved more than the sleeping pills. Sex wasn't unusual for us. It never had been. However, since her rescue, the physical reaffirmation of our love eased her mind, allowing her to slumber.

And being an accommodating husband, I have been willing to oblige.

Truthfully, I'd be remiss to not admit that it also helped me. The more dead ends we hit regarding her and Araneae's abductors and the more winding trails that led nowhere, the darker the world felt. Lorna was my lifeline keeping me from fully submerging into the black-hole abyss.

Lorna replied to Laurel. "I believe if I don't see her, it would be more detrimental to my sleep." Her head tilted. "You have confirmed her identity? This is Nancy Pierce."

I reached for her hand. "We have determined that the woman on 1 has statistically significant genetic markers to both you and Mason. We wouldn't have told you about her if we had doubts."

Mason's gaze caught mine.

I shook my head. "One thing at a time."

"What?" Lorna asked, her arms crossing over her chest. "I'm sick of lies."

"It's not lies," Mason said.

"It's omission and that's not a gift."

My nostrils flared as I exhaled. "Genetically, she's Nancy Pierce. We have no reason to doubt that. The thing is that any footprint of Nancy Pierce basically disappeared from the world not long after you graduated high school."

"Lorna," Mason said, "we assumed she was dead because everything pointed that direction."

"I never looked for her," Lorna said.

"Neither did I," Mason admitted. "I didn't give a fuck. When I joined the army, I listed you as my only family." He looked at Reid. "Which means that organization wouldn't have known about her."

"Then why?" We would think about that another day. "I looked for her," I admitted.

"What?" my wife questioned. "You never said a word."

"What was I supposed to say, 'Hey, sweetheart, still no sign that your mother is alive'? I looked for her after Mason's accident and before we married. I thought if she were alive she'd want..."

"She never wanted anything except to not have three kids," Mason said.

That faraway look glazed over Lorna's expression. "Maybe she wanted us."

"What?" Mason asked.

"Having kids made her checks bigger."

Mason exhaled.

Shaking away whatever she was thinking, Lorna's expression was resolute. "I want to see her. I think that knowing she's here and not seeing her would keep me awake with more questions. I want to put an end to questions." She looked up at me and then to Mason and Laurel. "Would you come with me?"

Mason's head tilted left and he stood taller. "If that's what you want."

"You don't want to?"

"You're right."

Lorna turned to me. "What about you?"

There was a list a mile long of work I needed to do on 2. I had programs running on recent crimes with Jettison's DNA. We had searches going for any information on Nancy Pierce. Where had she been? Was the answer the same as where Araneae's adoptive parents had gone for years?

One dead end after another.

There were other loose ends waiting for us to investigate. And now with what Laurel said, we needed to get in contact with Walters. Securing the institute was another thing. Of course it was safe. Araneae wouldn't be able to work there if it weren't, but like Mason's ranch, with time comes complacency.

Nevertheless, I answered Lorna with my heart instead of my mind. "Sweetheart, if you want me beside you, I wouldn't even consider being anywhere else."

As the four of us left our apartment, I wrapped Lorna's

hand in mine. It was as we entered the common area that Mason acquiesced. "We'll go down with you, too."

No one uttered a word as the four of us entered the elevator, the doors closed, and we were carted downward. I'd been the one to hit the button. Neither of the ladies had the access ability to make the elevator stop on 1.

When the doors opened, we all stepped out. Mason moved forward and turned back toward us. The area behind him appeared much like an office complex. In many ways it was. "Stay here with them," he said to me. "I'll do a sweep of the floor."

Pulling my phone from my pocket, I accessed an app and evaluated our security screens of this floor. With thermal imaging, I was able to see the entire floor and identify where people were located. Being later at night, the floor wouldn't be as busy as it was during the day.

This was where other members of the Sparrow outfit met for various reasons.

A floor plan became visible on my screen. "It looks like there are meetings happening in conference rooms 3 and 7." I looked up. "Patrick is in 3. Do you know who's in 7?"

"Yeah, Garrett is getting the weekly reports from the street."

"Oh shit. I've lost track of days."

Garrett met with different leaders on the street throughout and after each Friday, Saturday, and Sunday. Especially in the summertime, weekends were when the most street violence occurred. Sparrow was determined to clamp down on the general sense of unrest. Calling out as well as listening to the players involved was key to getting a hold on the disruptions. As the responsibilities the four of us have assumed have increased over the years, we were relying more and more on Garrett. He was getting the reputation as one of the highest members of the Sparrow trusted team.

"I'm still doing a physical sweep. Just a minute," Mason said as he walked toward the hallway where the conference rooms were located. There were more than conference rooms. This floor was a living, breathing business space for the Sparrow outfit.

Much as everything in our world, security was tight. Not anyone could make it up to this floor from the street. Not everyone on the street or even inhabitants of this building knew what happened up here. That said, we kept our wives away from this floor for a reason.

It often contained men and women who weren't well known for their charity work. In other words, we dealt with the dregs of the underground because they dealt with us. There was no reason for any of them to know that we lived with our loved ones only two stories away.

Lorna and Laurel talked quietly as we waited, and I continued watching the thermal imaging, even watching Mason's image move throughout the floor. A text message came across my screen from Patrick.

I clicked.

"NEED YOU BACK ON 2."

                                    .   .   .

Before I could respond, Mason appeared from the hallway. "We're clear."

I held up my phone, wordlessly asking if he also received the text message. A simple nod of his head let me know the answer.

"Follow me," he said.

Without answering Patrick, I placed my phone back in my pocket and took my wife's hand. There would always be fires, but right now, next to Lorna was where I belonged. As I watched the back of Mason's head, I knew he'd made the same decision.

"It feels odd to be here, on this floor," Lorna said. "In nine years, I've probably only stepped foot on this floor less than ten times." She looked around as we passed by more office space. "Who takes care of this floor?"

"Sparrow employs a regular cleaning crew," I offered. "If that's what you're asking."

One side of her lips curled. "It was. He told me once that he could have done that for upstairs, but he didn't want strangers in our private spaces."

I lifted her knuckles to my lips and brushed them with a light kiss. "He trusted you, sweetheart, even back then." She smiled as we fell a few paces behind Mason and Laurel.

They came to a stop by a door. From the hallway, one couldn't tell what was within. Two weeks ago, it was empty. Today it was a makeshift morgue. The refrigeration unit we'd had on hand was portable. It had been in storage across town. This wasn't its first use. Over the years, keeping a corpse undercover or available for possible other uses was always a possibility.

Mason turned back to us. "Are you sure about this, sis?"

Lorna nodded.

Leaning forward, a sensor near the door scanned Mason's eye. Milliseconds later, the locking mechanism clicked and the door unlocked. Reaching for the knob, he opened the door and turned on the overhead lights.

The room appeared clinical, cold, and sterile.

There was a mobile gurney, the top being a silver shelf rather than a mattress. There were mobile cabinets containing tools that were needed for the extraction of information. In a nutshell, a complete autopsy could be performed in here, the surfaces sterilized and wheeled away for another day.

Lorna let go of my hand and wrapped her arms around herself.

Instinctively, my arm went around her. She trembled in my grasp. "You don't have to do it."

"I'm fine. I'm cold. Why is the room so cold? Doesn't it just need to be cold in there?" she asked, tilting her head toward the mobile refrigeration unit.

"When the body is brought out to..." Laurel hesitated to give too many details. "It's better for the room to be cool to maintain the body's core temperature. Raising and lowering the internal temperature repeatedly affects and accelerates decomposition."

Lorna nodded. "That makes sense."

We'd been here before with Laurel and all seen the woman

Mason was about to remove from the unit. The slab she was on pulled out, much like a shelf from an oven.

I looked at Mason and nodded.

My wife leaned into me as Mason unlatched the door, lowered it on its hinge, and pulled out the slab. Lorna's hand went to her nose as the odor of chemicals and death infiltrated the air. One sheet was tucked around Nancy's body, covering from her breasts to her feet, and a second sheet covered her face and most of her head. A fine combination of gray, white, and red hair was all we could see.

Lorna stepped closer and reached for the sheet, slowly revealing the woman beneath.

REID

"I texted Patrick after we got Lorna back up here" — we were on the floor with the apartments— "to let him know we were on our way."

Mason nodded. "I can't fucking tell with my sister sometimes. Is she really handling seeing Nancy that well or is it an act?"

We stepped into the elevator and I hit 2 as I contemplated my answer. "I'd say, in general, Lorna doesn't act. She's honest to a fault." I hesitated. "It seems, though, when it comes to things about her childhood, she's more reserved."

"It sucked. There's no reason to relive any of that."

Our personal conversation ended the moment we stepped into the cement hallway and Mason scanned his eye to enter the command center.

Patrick's gaze met ours as the steel door opened and closed behind us.

"Do we have any more answers on the kidnappers?" I asked.

"I'm not sure."

"What does that mean?" Mason prompted as we both approached Patrick.

"Garrett and I have been in meetings earlier tonight. We learned something interesting."

While Mason reached for his chair and spun it around, I simply sat in mine and leaned back, wondering what possibly could be interesting on the streets of Chicago.

"Word is getting around," Patrick began as he brought up footage from various street cameras around the city. "...that Sparrow has had enough of the petty fighting. The constant warfare is making the city look like it's out of control, and that perception is bad for Chicago businesses as well as for Sparrow. He's even getting shit through his mother from the aldermen. They want to know if taming the streets needs to be taken to another level. A few of the aldermen have been pushing the mayor for a stronger response in the form of law enforcement, local as well as National Guard."

I crossed my arms over my chest. "It is their job."

"No," Mason said. "It's our job."

"Opening the door to law enforcement beyond Sparrow's reach," Patrick said, "will infringe on lucrative aspects of Sparrow. It will also end up backfiring. The gangs will lose merchandise, customers, and ultimately income. That will decrease our income. The incident last weekend, where eight people were shot at that club in North Lawndale was broadcast on all the major news outlets around the country and beyond. It's like violence doesn't happen in other cities too."

While I listened, I had a hard time keeping my mind off of Lorna. Hell, she'd just seen her mother for the first time in almost two decades. What was she thinking?

"Do you have any proof of the shipments?" Mason asked.

My thoughts returned to now as I looked up at the screen overhead. "What did you say? What shipments?"

Patrick stood. "Garrett and I both received reports of gun shipments mysteriously finding their way to some of the smaller factions in the city." He nodded toward the screen and a picture of various guns. "As you can see, we're talking high-quality assault rifles as well as rapid-fire pistols. These are the half a dozen that Garrett confiscated this afternoon. We've got them downstairs and he has capos running serial numbers on the ones that have them. He also has ballistics running, to see if any of these were used in recent crimes."

"Smaller factions? Subsets?" Mason asked. "Someone is supplying the little guys." There were literally hundreds of smaller factions and exponentially more subsets of the fifty-five primary gangs who operated within our jurisdiction.

"How many of the top leaders have been contacted?" I asked.

"They all have to report," Patrick answered. "If they don't, they're in danger of losing their real estate."

Mason stood and walked to the coffee machine, inserted a pod, and hit the button. It didn't matter that it was near ten o'clock at night; we had a long night ahead. After running his hand through his hair, he turned toward us. "Why the small factions?"

"Because they don't report," I answered.

"To us or anyone," Mason added.

"And because," Patrick began, "they're disgruntled in the first place. That state of mind combined with high-quality firepower is the perfect mixture to elicit street fighting."

That was true. A subset may be three guys. Three guys who for whatever reason decided that they were done being a piece of a bigger unit. They wanted more. They wanted to make their own rules and run their own show. Or they want retaliation.

"So someone is purposely supplying these groups to make Chicago look bad," I said.

"Who is supplying the firepower?" Mason asked.

"We don't know," Patrick answered. "We also don't know how these factions are being identified. It's not like they have help-wanted ads on the internet." He looked to Mason. "I could use your help to see if you can find anything on the dark web."

Mason shook his head. "I'll do it, but I guarantee if there is anything out there, it's buried. The feds are getting too good at monitoring the dark web."

"Another reason to stop this shit," Patrick said. "The last thing we need is the feds infiltrating Chicago's gang wars."

"If it's not on the internet, it has to come from someone on the street."

"That fucking narrows it down," Mason said, returning to

his chair with his coffee. "Chicago has four thousand miles of streets and nearly two thousand miles of alleyways."

"I was informed," Patrick began, sitting back at the keyboard, "about the location where the guns downstairs were acquired." He typed and brought together street cam and satellite images. "Remember the funeral home shootout last summer near Englewood?"

Mason and I nodded before I spoke, "Wait, this supply chain has been established in our city for months?"

Patrick nodded. "This is grainy as shit, but take a look at this image from behind Dino's Liquor on South Parnell Avenue."

He enlarged the image.

"Black Ford truck. Are you fucking kidding me?" I asked as I began hitting keys, retrieving the images from Montana.

"We already know that make and model isn't unique," Mason said.

"No," Patrick responded, "but look. There's no front plate."

"Illinois requires front plates," I said, pulling up the other images.

"If we look only at neighboring states," Patrick said, "Indiana doesn't."

Leaving his warm mug on the desk, Mason stared up at that picture. "Laurel lived in Indiana."

"When she was working on the compound," I said. "Here, look at the two trucks side by side."

"Can we get an image of the rear license plate?" Mason asked.

"What about the liquor store? I think we should make a visit to ask some questions."

"We've got capos on that. I'm waiting on a report." Patrick changed the image on the screen overhead. "I can locate this truck at the same liquor store multiple times over the last few months. I would be surprised if this is an outlet for only one subset. More likely, this is a supply location for many. And look at this image." He enlarged it even more.

"I see a man with a hat," I said. "He could be the same man from the truck in Montana."

"I was thinking the same thing," Patrick said. "Now look here."

"He's not alone," Mason said, looking up. "I fucking hate how grainy this is."

"Does the liquor store have security?" I asked. "If it's online, I can find it."

As my fingers flew across the keys, it was the most energized I'd felt since we went to Washington DC. There was a chance this was another dead end, but at least it felt like it had a possibility.

Lost in our work, time passed without notice.

"Fuck," I said, "I'm not finding online security for Dino's. From the street cams I see other cameras. They're either dummies or it's an in-house system." I turned to Patrick. "Have the capos reported back from there yet?"

"No. They're waiting until closer to closing. Fewer witnesses."

Liquor stores in Illinois were required by law to close by two in the morning.

"Have the capos retrieve any security tapes from the last three months," I said.

"If they have any," Patrick replied, looking at his watch.

His movement prompted me to do the same. "Shit." The clock told me it was nearly one in the morning. I stood, stretching my neck and shoulders as I contemplated all the work I could be doing. "I need to head upstairs for a bit."

"I was just noticing the time," Patrick said. "I'm sure Maddie and Ruby are asleep."

I didn't want to sound like the man who answered to his wife, but if we were all honest with one another, we all fit in that category. "I'd told Lorna I wouldn't be long and promised that I'd be back to our apartment by midnight."

"You should go," Mason said. "We can text if there's anything." He looked up from his phone. "I was wondering where Sparrow was."

Though I'd begun to walk away, I stopped. "Is everything all right with Araneae?"

Slowly, Mason nodded, his gesture turning into more of a shrug.

"What is it?" Patrick asked.

"Araneae is having memories. Laurel is with them."

My pulse raced within my veins, the beat sounding within my ears. "If Araneae is, then Lorna..." I didn't finish the sentence as I scanned the sensor and left the command center.

LORNA

*"Y*ou look real pretty, Lorna. You look like your momma.*"

The words circled in my head. From the moment I pulled back the sheet and stared at Nancy Pierce, taking in her gaunt body and graying red hair, I heard the sentences. The voice was gruff and unfamiliar, yet the sentences were there, making their way out of the shadows, taunting me.

Staring at Nancy Pierce in death wasn't much different than seeing her alive. I believed I had—seen her in life. Not only nearly twenty years ago, but also recently.

It seemed real.

I recalled the rain falling in large drops and a storm brewing in the distance.

The hard-packed dirt quickly covered with the simmering flood-like waters, turning the earth's surface from hard to slippery muck. She was there, leaning against a large rock. I didn't recognize her, but she said I knew who she was.

She knew me.

She'd told someone all she knew about me.

For a moment—only one, only a second, smaller than that, only a millisecond—I thought I was seeing myself, a reflection distorted by time, a glimpse into the future of what would be. Before I could stop myself, I'd said the question, the one that to the rational mind was irrational, yet I asked, *"Are you me?"*

Standing over her deceased body, witnessing the havoc her life choices caused, didn't give me satisfaction. I never wished for her to die. I never wished for harm to come to her. Truly as a young girl, I wanted the opposite.

It wasn't longing for a Carol Brady from the *Brady Bunch* to welcome us home every day. No, it was much simpler. Young Lorna wanted to be in Nancy's good graces, for her to look at me as our grandmother had looked at me, with love in her green stare.

The insatiable need I now recalled physically hurt. I berated myself for ever setting my worth on the actions of someone who never deserved that level of significance. And yet I had. I'd stood for hours, waiting and hoping she'd return home with food for our empty stomachs or clothes she'd promised would come for school.

The yearning to be important to the woman who was supposed to love me through everything was so intense that there was nothing I wouldn't do to earn it.

Even lie.

Was it wrong to do a bad thing for a good reason?

That was a difficult question for a thirty-five-year-old. It was impossible for a ten-year-old.

A few hours ago-

My trembling stilled as I stepped from Reid's embrace and pulled back the sheet revealing her face. The pervasive stench seemed to lessen, or my concentration was elsewhere. Her thin flesh was stitched together in a wide V beneath her collarbone. The sewn incision then went lower, beneath the second sheet.

I should be satisfied with a quick look and the test results.

I wasn't.

My curiosity pulled me closer to the woman I was supposed to mourn.

Nancy Pierce wasn't the woman from my childhood. She was barely her own skeleton. My fingertips roamed over her cheeks, feeling the bones beneath. Without embalming, her flesh was cold and tough, without elasticity. I didn't know if that was caused by death or if she'd been that way before her heart finally stopped pumping.

I pulled back the second sheet, the one covering her body, not all the way, but to her waist and the end of the incision.

"Lorna." It was Mason's warning to stop there.

I couldn't uncover anything that hadn't been seen by hundreds if not thousands. Did customers see the prostitute they purchased or simply use her or him? This was among the questions I truly didn't seek to answer.

My head tilted as my gaze scanned from the sheet upward.

I'd never gone on to college.

Was this what it was like to see a dead body in a science lab?

Could I insert a scalpel and identify what was within her heart if it still remained or ever had existed?

Was there ever a place within it for Missy, Mason, or me?

I ran my fingers over her ribs, feeling the peaks and valleys. Mine were healing and hers were on display. Her stomach area sank as if she didn't have enough of anything to fill the void. Maybe she didn't. Had her insides been removed during the autopsy?

My line of vision moved upward. I couldn't recall if her breasts had always been so small and nonexistent or if this too was a byproduct of her withering away. I touched a small white circle and then another. "What are these?"

"Scars," Laurel replied.

Scars?

"There are a lot more on her ass," Mason said.

My stomach twisted as I turned to my sister-in-law. "Cigarette burns?"

"Mostly, we can only assume. A few are larger. They might be from cigars."

My neck straightened as I refused to feel bad for her. She made life choices. They were hers and the rest of us were left to deal. She didn't feel bad about leaving us. I wouldn't feel bad about the consequences she faced. I focused again on her body as a whole. My memories of my mother resembled my own reflection more than the woman lying in front of me.

Her hands lay at her sides, palms toward her body. I lifted one as the arm sagged.

"Rigor mortis disappears over time. The refrigeration helps," Laurel said.

"Hmm." I studied her fingernails. When we were young, she always wore fingernail polish.

Why would I recall that?

The tips of her fingers were scarred. Her nails were unpolished, brittle, with ragged ends. It was as if she'd clawed at something, maybe beginning long before her death.

"You found her with me?" I knew the answer, but there were others I couldn't fit in the equation.

"Yes," Reid said, his deep voice strong and supportive as he stepped forward, coming to a stop at my side.

I didn't need to look up to see his love and adoration; it surrounded us such as a warm blanket in this cold room. His presence radiated more than heat at my side. It was support. In stepping forward he—without words—told me he was with me, no matter what.

"Was she kept where Araneae and I were kept?"

"Forensics says yes." Reid silenced for a moment before continuing. I would later believe it was because he and Mason were wordlessly discussing my *need to know* more. Thankfully, my husband prevailed. "There were two cells—like jail cells— in the bunker. Your DNA was found in one. Hers was found in the other."

"Was there blood in hers too?"

"Nothing recent. It was mostly hairs and dead skin cells."

I sucked in a breath before exhaling. "I wonder how long she was there."

"They're working on that."

"Why?" I asked everyone. "Why would the people who took us take her? It doesn't make sense. We haven't seen her for years."

Mason came up to my other side. "Have you seen enough?"

My hand went out to our mother's sparse hair. In my memory it was bright and red. I pinched a few white, gray, and faded red strands between my fingers. Each one was coarse beneath my touch.

"Her hair used to be like yours," Mason said with his most compassionate tone yet.

Taking a deep breath, I turned to Laurel. "Have you learned anything from the autopsy?"

She cleared her throat. "A few things." She gestured toward the door. "May we talk somewhere else?"

I turned back to what remained of our mother as I searched for words or even emotions.

Shouldn't they be pouring out of me?

Why was I at a crossroads when faced with her demise?

Reid kissed the top of my head. "Do you want to be alone to say goodbye?"

"That's kind of morbid, isn't it? I mean, this is her body. It's not her."

"I never got the chance to say goodbye to so many people I cared about."

"Did they care about you?" I asked.

When I looked up, his Adam's apple bobbed. "I believe they did."

"Then you were blessed." I turned away from the body. "Thank you for showing me." My gaze met Mace's. "I've seen enough." After Mason pushed the body back into the refrigeration unit and secured the latch, I asked, "What are you going to do with her?"

"I've always been partial to barrels of acid down at the docks."

My lips opened as I tried to assess if that was my brother's warped dark humor or if he was being truthful. Before I could respond, he shook his head. "Cremation." He reached out to me. "Don't fight that, Lorna. How do we explain the presence of a woman who has been virtually dead for nearly twenty years? Cremation will rid us of any explanation."

Reaching for Reid's arm, I complied without speaking— compliance by acquiescing.

As we stepped into the hallway, Reid reached for my shoulders. "I hate to leave you."

My gaze went to the phone he was also holding. "But there's a fire."

"Or an iron in it," Laurel said.

"Let us get you two back up to the apartments," Reid said.

Once we were in the common area, both Reid's and Mason's phones vibrated.

"Go," I said. "I'm fine."

"I can come over," Laurel offered. "I'll tell you anything you want to know about the autopsy."

I shook my head. "Not tonight. I'm reading a good book. I'll get lost in there for a while and be ready for sleep by midnight." As my gaze met Reid's, he grinned.

Present time-

"You look real pretty, Lorna. You look like your momma."

I woke from a scene, a nightmare. It wasn't my mother in a Montana autumn storm. It was different.

What time was it?

The clock read twelve thirty and yet I was alone. I knew I was.

Throwing back the covers, I walked naked into our bathroom.

The incomplete puzzle of thoughts waged in my head. There were ones that seemed to be more recent and others that didn't. My eyes met my reflection as I reached for the bottle of sleeping pills. I hadn't taken one earlier, expecting Reid to join me.

My gaze went again to my reflection as I sprinkled three tablets into the palm of my hand. Hesitating, I retrieved one and put it back. The prescription said one an hour before bed. If I didn't want to wait an hour, maybe two would do the trick. Popping them into my mouth and swallowing, I caught my own gaze.

Green to green.

At least I hadn't seen her eyes.

"I don't look like you. You're old and dead. I'm not you." My hand went to my hair. "I'll never look like you again."

Turning away from myself, I opened the shower door and turned the water to somewhere over warm to below scalding. Yes, I'd showered to rinse out the hair color, but now it was a need to feel the water over my skin, to let the spray wash away the dream.

Maybe if I soaked under the assault of the sizzling downpour long enough, the dreams would stop.

REID

*A*raneae was having memories.
What memories?
How was she?
How was Lorna?
Was she too having memories?

Those were thoughts and questions that cycloned through my mind as I willed the elevator to move faster. It was only one damn floor. As the doors closed and the mechanisms activated, I cursed myself for not being back at her side an hour ago as I'd promised.

As soon as the elevator came to a stop, I squeezed my way through the opening doors and hurried to our apartment. Without hesitation, I threw open the door.

Our living room was dark except for the glow coming from the streets and buildings of Chicago. Such as a pillow of light lingering below us, we were suspended high into the murky night. Without illuminating the familiar obstacles, my shoes clipped upon the tile as I made my way to our bedroom.

Pushing open the door, I stared. The bed was messed. Lorna's side of the covers was thrown back and her pillows held the indentation, yet she was missing. My heart sank as the sound of our shower filled my ears.

There was nothing wrong with showering or bathing, but in the last two weeks, she'd done it excessively.

Steam slithered from under the bathroom door as I opened it.

My eyes widened at who I saw beyond the glass under the spray.

"Lorna. What the hell?"

Quickly, she reached for the handles and turned off the water.

"Reid. I woke. I guess I..." She wrapped her arms around her breasts. "Can you get me a towel?"

Taking a large plush bath towel to the shower door, I opened the glass, still speechless over the woman before me. A mental battle ensued as the right words to say fought for their place on my tongue.

She smiled up at me as she reached for the towel. "Thank you."

As she stepped onto the bath mat, water drizzled down her legs as she began to wrap the towel around her. I knew every inch of this woman inside and out. If I were a sculptor, I could knead and mold clay into her likeness. My lips had explored her soft cream skin. My fingers had found each crevice. My ears had heard her fill our home with sounds of pleasure. My body had molded with hers, taken and been taken. I knew what it was like to be buried deep inside her, to feel her body hug mine and the way it convulsed as she let herself go, riding the wave of climax. Over the years we'd laughed and cried. We'd celebrated and mourned. She was my other half and without her I was incomplete.

My gaze went to between her legs seconds before the towel obstructed my view. It didn't help me. Lorna was obsessive about keeping herself shaved. Even there I couldn't confirm the redhead I'd fallen in love with.

"Do you like it?" she asked with too much glee.

What could I say?

Lorna walked to the mirror and tilted her face from side to side as water dribbled from the ends of her now-short hair.

I stood behind her, wrapping my arms gently around her. With the top of her head below my chin, I feigned a smile. "Sweetheart, you're always beautiful."

She reached up and teased the ends again. "I think it will curl more now that it's short."

"Did you do it yourself?"

She spun in my arms. "Well, there aren't a lot of salons open at midnight and besides, lockdown. Remember?"

"And the dye?" Beyond comprehension, I was trying to make sense of her dark brown locks.

"Oh, I texted the other women, and Madeline had a box of color. She said she won't use it while she's pregnant. Chemicals and everything." Her tone was light and uncharacteristically, singsong.

"Lorna, have you been drinking?"

She waved her hand. "You know I hardly drink."

"Hardly is some."

"No," she said, shaking her head, her short bob swinging near her cheeks. "Nothing but hair dye. I didn't drink it. I put it on my hair."

"Madeline let you have it without questioning why?"

"I told her it was for a project."

"And she believed you?"

Lorna stepped back, her smile fading. "You don't like it?"

"I-I..." Words failed me.

Pulling her arm away from my grasp, Lorna walked past me and out to the bedroom.

"Lorna."

"What, Reid?" She was in our closet. When she came out, she was wearing a long nightshirt. It was her way of saying sex was off the table. When we'd first found her after being taken, that had been my stance. Now it was hers.

"Lorna, shit. I'm shocked. Why would you cut and change the color of your hair?"

"Does it really matter? Are redheads your thing? You can't get it up for a brunette?"

"Fuck," I said, the one word filled with all the exasperation I felt. "No. Redheads aren't my thing. *You* are my thing. Getting it up isn't the issue."

She was now sitting on the edge of the bed and moving her legs to the mattress. "You're right. I'm tired. The pills are working, and I'm going to sleep."

"Lorna, talk to me."

"And say what? I'm still me, Reid. I wanted a change. So

what? Hell, if I could have gotten other colors, I might have tried purple or teal." Her smile returned. "There are great ideas online." She pulled the covers over her.

Taking a deep breath, I followed her until I too was sitting on her edge of our bed. I reached out to her wet brown hair and tugged on a strand. "You're probably right about the curl."

She pushed back against the pillow and stared at my hand. Holding her breath, her eyes were on only my hand. "Please don't touch my hair."

"Sweetheart, it's pretty. You're pretty."

Lorna scooted up to the headboard, shaking her head. "I don't look like her."

My lips came together as Lorna repeated her declaration, each time louder than the last. It wasn't only her raised voice. There was something unfamiliar in her eyes, as if she weren't seeing me.

"I don't...I don't," she repeated.

Unsure what to say, I leaned forward, wrapping my arms around her. Beneath my embrace her body stilled. Cold. Statuesque. A mannequin in my grasp. And then the arms I had captive bent as she pushed against me.

"Stop. I don't look like her. I'm not her."

Hell, I held a great deal of knowledge on many things. Understanding Lorna's outburst and change in hair color was beyond my comprehension. "Her? Who?"

"I'm not Anna."

Anna? Who the fuck was Anna?

Lorna's pushes turned to punches as her fingers formed

fists, and she pounded against my chest. "Stop. I won't tell. Please stop."

Each plea took a sliver of my heart. Instead of releasing the trembling petite body in my grasp, I held tighter. "Lorna, it's all right. You're safe."

Sobs overtook her as cries and gulps of air silenced her pleas. Finally, she lost her fight, her punches losing strength. She curled, her shoulders bending forward and her chin down, clinging to my chest. With her arms tucked in front of her, she continued to curl inward, as if she were trying to disappear within my hold.

I ran my hand over her short brown hair, soothing her as I spoke. "You're absolutely beautiful, Lorna. If you want purple or teal hair, I may decide to join you. How do you think I'll look with purple hair?"

When her crying calmed, she looked up at me. The stunning green eyes were the ones I loved. "I get so tired, but I can't sleep alone. I don't know what's real."

"You're real," I said. "I'm real. We're real."

"My thoughts and dreams—where do they come from?"

"Do you want to talk about them?"

"No," she said, encouraging me to join her in the bed by patting the space beside her.

Still clothed with lights still on around our room, I kicked off my shoes and climbed under the blankets on her side. As I did, she cuddled close, laying her head on my chest and curling next to my side.

"Why?" I asked. "Why don't you want to talk about them?"

"Because what if they're not real?"

I resumed stroking her hair, and as I looked down, I smiled. "You're a beautiful brunette."

She reached up and twisted a strand. "I can probably go back to red, but I can't glue the length back."

"Then keep it short, or let it grow." I rolled until my wife was on her back and I was over her. Her emerald eyes stared up at me, her face framed in chestnut. "If you think for one minute the color and length of your hair have anything to do with my love for you, you're wrong."

Looking into the depth of her stare, her orbs were so clear, open, and honest, it hurt. I wanted to look away, still fearful she'd see my dark thoughts. Yet I couldn't. My wife was my light, and I needed her in my life in the same way that I needed food or air. Without her, life wouldn't matter.

I'd failed her, let her down by not keeping her safe. Letting her down again wasn't an option. "I'm sorry I wasn't here sooner."

"It's okay."

I ran my finger over her cheek, pleased at the way the dark bruise had faded to green. "I want to be honest with you. We're getting clues, but I can't tell you more."

Her lips came together as a tear trickled from her eye.

"Talk to me," I pleaded before gently brushing my lips over hers.

"I don't know what to say."

"Answer my questions. Why did you color and cut your hair? Who is Anna?"

She sucked in a breath. "Why would you mention her?"

"Because you did."

Her head shook. "No, I didn't. I wouldn't."

"Who is she?"

Lorna's heart beat in double time within her chest, the vibration coming from her to me as simultaneously, her complexion paled. "Tell me why you'd say that name?"

"I told you. *You* said it. You said you weren't her, you weren't Anna."

Both of Lorna's eyes closed, long lashes batting away more tears.

My mind scrambled. Lorna was having memories, but of what? "Sweetheart, if you mentioned her before, I'm sorry. I'm drawing a blank." And then I recalled something from a long time ago. "Didn't you work with an Anna when we met?"

Lorna nodded as she closed her eyes tighter and lifted her hands to her ears. It was as if she were a child trying to block out the world. "No more. I can't. I promised."

I sat taller, looking down at my wife.

What should I do?

I could call Laurel, but last I heard she was with Araneae.

Gently, I tugged Lorna's hands away from her ears.

As I did, her body lost a bit of its tension. "Don't." Her eyes opened, glistening emerald shining my way. "Please don't make me."

Make her?

"Lorna, you do what you want. Don't tell me anything if it's upsetting. I'm sorry again that I let him take you."

"Him?"

I inhaled. "We have evidence that a man was with you."

Her head shook. "No, I wasn't raped."

"Not *with you* like that. With you—in the same room. Blood was found, his blood and yours. And his DNA matches the hair in the report Dr. Dixon gave us."

Slowly, the tips of Lorna's lips curled. "I fought."

"Yes, sweetheart, you fought."

"I didn't freeze."

Laying a kiss on her nose, I said, "You're a fighter. My fighter."

"And he didn't rape me."

"That's what the test said."

Sighing, she brought her lips to mine. "Reid, I'm sorry if I've lied to you."

"About what?"

"I don't know. There's something I need to know. It's right here, and I don't want to know it and I do. Laurel said there could be memories and flashes. In those flashes, he's dirty and smells. He says I am pretty like my mother, but she is no longer pretty."

A few minutes later, I'd stripped off my clothes and turned off the lights. Getting into bed on my side, I reached for my wife, half assuming she'd fallen asleep. I was wrong. Her voice was calm and cool. The earlier emotion was gone, replaced by a dream-like voice.

"Rape is only when there's forced sex. That's what my mother said."

The small hairs at the back of my neck stood to attention. "Why would your mother tell you that?"

"Because as long as a man doesn't put his penis inside you

—there—nothing happened." She sat up. "Your mouth doesn't count."

What the fuck?

"Your mother said that?"

Lorna nodded, again curling against my side. "I wasn't raped."

The temperature of my blood rose as I tried to connect the pieces of the puzzle. "Lorna, who is Anna?"

"Mom said it isn't bad if you are okay with it. Anna was okay. So I wasn't supposed to tell anyone about her either."

"Fucking Christ." I sat up. "Lorna, how old were you when your mother told you that?"

"Ten." In the darkness, her eyes glowed with a hint of fear. "Don't tell Mason. I promised I wouldn't."

A million images I couldn't stomach came to mind, yet the woman in my arms was no longer distressed. She'd shared her concern with me and moved on. Her muscles relaxed and her lips parted as she slipped into slumber.

Time ticked away as the numbers on the clock moved.

"Reid?"

I startled as I wrapped my arm around her. "I'm here."

"Good. Please don't leave."

"Never, Lorna. Never."

REID

*S*leep was difficult to come by. My thoughts were dominated by the beautiful woman in my arms. Psychology wasn't my thing. Give me numbers, codes, and computer programs. Give me a trail, just a small piece, and let me work on finding where it goes.

This was different.

I tried to recall Dr. Dixon's warning. It completely contradicted what Lorna said she'd been told. Dr. Dixon said, "It's a misconception that only the act of penetration is psychologically harmful. One day, she may remember. On that day, that minute, that second, she will need to know that even if it wasn't what most refer to as rape, her trauma is real and she may express it any way that will help her deal."

As Lorna lay in my arms, I struggled with what was happening in her head. It was as if once she made the connection that only penetration was rape, she was fine, unaffected, and asleep.

Why would I want to tell her otherwise and risk the opposite?

My eyes closed for a moment, only to open with an earlier thought.

Give me a trail, a small byte of information.

Easing my way out of bed, I messaged Mason.

"SLEEPING?"

As I stepped into my blue jeans and slipped my feet into canvas loafers, my phone vibrated.

"Reid?" Lorna's sleep-filled voice called through the near darkness.

I knelt on the bed. "I'm here, sweetheart. I'm going to go down to 2. Will you be okay?"

She nodded. "Yeah, I-I...still tired."

"That's all right. You sleep."

"Those pills...worked..."

"I love you."

Her words were mumbled. "Come back."

My lips brushed the top of her head. Even in the dim light of our bedroom, I saw her new hairdo, the way her shorter locks framed her face in dark brown ringlets. Unable to resist, I smoothed a stray strand between my fingers and watched as it sprang back to a curlicue. "Who hurt you, Lorna?" The question wasn't voiced loud enough for her to hear or disrupt her sleep.

My gut told me that this new hairdo wasn't about Andrew Jettison. If I could make an undereducated psychological jump, what happened with him, combined with seeing her mother's body, brought back something she'd hidden away from Mason, and if it was possible, even from herself.

I needed a small bit of information to figure this out. Whether my goal was revenge or something different, I needed a scattered crumb. With that, I'd find another and another until I'd created a trail. There was one person who could give me that crumb.

I picked up my phone. The message was a response from Mason.

"NOT ANYMORE. LORNA?"

I texted back.

"MEET ME ON 2."

I hadn't considered the time of night until after my second text. It wouldn't matter. This was what we did, all of us. When the calls or text messages came, we answered. It wasn't as unique as a bat signal or some other form of communication, and yet it was secure. Our phones and means of communication were secured by the best firewalls and virtual networks on the planet.

The clock on the bedside stand read 3:17 in large red numbers.

Two hours of sleep should be enough.

It would have to be.

I let out a sigh as I covered Lorna with the blanket, laid another kiss to her head, and walked quietly through our apartment. The canvas soles aided in my quiet escape as I walked down our tiled hallway. In the living room, I stopped for a moment to peer out the giant walls of windows.

Beyond our view was Chicago.

A dark red hue colored the skyline.

While we were getting closer to Andrew Jettison, my need to avenge could have a much closer target. Ten fucking years old. "Who are you? Are you still in my city? If you are, you won't be for long."

As I opened the door to our apartment, the elevator doors across the common room began to close. Just before they did, a hand reached for one, reversing their direction.

"You woke me," Mason said. "Get your ass in here."

Getting closer to my brother-in-law, last night's scene with Lorna replayed in my mind. I didn't give a fuck what she chose to do with her hair. It's *her* hair. I did care about why.

As the doors shut, Mason's green gaze narrowed. "What the hell happened? Is Lorna remembering too?"

For a split second, my single-minded focus had a wider

lens. There were others in our tower dealing with similar shit. "Did Laurel get home?"

"Yeah, about two."

"How is Araneae? What does she remember?"

Mason shrugged as the elevator descended. "A lot. Laurel was a bit freaked out. I think we may have a lead I never imagined. I need to hear back from Top."

"Good." The doors opened to our cement hallway. I lifted my hand to the scanner before the steel door opened.

"Really, Reid? I just told you about a lead and you say good?"

The door shut behind us.

I wasn't surprised no one else was on 2. It sounded as if Sparrow was dealing with his own wife's memories, and Patrick was no doubt with Madeline who was getting closer and closer to delivering. If I had been paying attention to time, I would say she had a little less than five weeks to go before what little sleep Patrick got was blown to hell.

My mind went back to the crumb I needed. "Where was that one-room apartment Lorna talks about, the one you moved to with your mom after your grandmother died?"

Mason lifted his chin and inhaled. "Fuck, South Side. It was an old house that was subdivided into too many units. Why?"

I sat at my desk and brought my screens to life. "I need to know where it was. Were there men who lived there?"

"Yeah. Singles, families, there were always people coming and going."

"Do you recall an address?"

"Hell, we moved a lot."

"But Lorna talks about that place. It's where she always mentions. Maybe it's because it was where Missy also lived." Mason visibly bristled at the sound of his sister's name. "Or because it was where you first lived with your mother."

"What the hell is this about?" Mason asked, bringing the coffee maker to life.

I inhaled, running my palm over my hair. "When I got upstairs last night, Lorna had..." I debated how to say what she had done.

Was it really a big deal or was I blowing it out of proportion?

Mason's lips came together as he stared my direction. "If you woke me from a warm bed where I was sleeping beside my wife to give me hints, I think I'll go back to bed."

Letting my chair roll back, I stood. "She cut her hair." When he didn't respond, I went on, "It's shorter than I've ever seen it."

"So? Laurel—"

"She also dyed it, dark brown."

His eyes narrowed. "Lorna dyed her hair?"

"And she said that she doesn't look like *her* anymore."

"Her?" Mason questioned. "Does she mean our mother?"

"I thought that, but then she mentioned the name Anna. Didn't she work with someone named Anna before you brought her here?"

His green stare widened. "What the fuck?"

"Lorna also told me something and made me promise not to tell you. She said she promised your mother she wouldn't tell because it never happened."

Mason set his coffee on his desk and interlocking his fingers, brought them behind his head. "What never happened? You're fucking making me nervous."

"Who is Anna?" I asked.

"First, that one-room studio wasn't the first place we lived with the bitch downstairs on ice. After DCFS took us from our grandmother's house, they found Nancy. She was living in a house in Englewood."

"A house? Lorna's never talked about a house."

"It wasn't fucking much to talk about. Nancy was living with an asshole named Gordon Maples. I hated that son of a bitch." Mason let out a long breath. "He had two daughters. One was named Anna, and as fate would have it, years later, the same Anna ran that run-down hotel where Lorna worked. The four of us lived there for about six months before one night when Nancy gathered us up and took us away."

"What happened?"

"Fuck, I didn't care. It was the middle of the night. She told us to be quiet and gather all we could carry. Then she took us to an old couple, friends of our grandparents. They let us stay for a few nights until we moved into that one-room apartment."

"Just left—in the middle of the night. Wasn't that weird?"

Mason shook his head. "Man, nothing was weird when it came to Nancy, or everything was. Hell, I didn't give a fuck why we left. We were away from the sadistic fucker."

My pulse pumped faster. "What did he do to you?"

"Maples was a fan of abuse in general. Screaming and hitting, usually accentuated with copious amounts of his drugs of choice—alcohol and tobacco. When Nancy wasn't passed out, she was his target. I was his second. I remember purposely pissing him off to keep him from hurting Lorna and..." He debated about saying her name. "...Missy."

"And you were how old?" I asked.

"About eleven. Yeah, eleven, because after we moved, that same year...is when she disappeared."

I began typing.

Gordon Maples.

"Can you give me more?"

"Englewood. South Carpenter Street. I don't remember the number."

I entered the information. As I did, Mason came behind me and gripped the back of my chair. "What does this have to do with Lorna's hair?"

Slowly, I turned my chair until he let go and we were facing one another. "She was talking oddly. I even thought she might have been drinking, but besides a few glasses of wine, she doesn't drink."

Mason spun a nearby chair and straddling the back, sat down. "She wasn't drinking."

"No, but she had taken sleeping pills. One, I hope."

"I told you I thought her reaction to seeing Nancy was too...even."

Collecting my thoughts, I went on, "I thought Lorna was talking about what happened when she was taken recently. I thought she meant the fight she gave Jettison, but then she said something that didn't feel right. You know, I think it's all of it, not one piece. Everything has come together in her head. She said more than once that she's not her, she doesn't look like her, and she's not Anna." I tried to remember. "Anna wanted it, so it was okay."

"What the fuck?"

"Your mother told Lorna that as long as a man doesn't put his dick inside her, it's not rape. She even fucking specified that in her mouth was okay, and never to talk about it."

"Why would she...?" Mason bolted from his chair. "No. I fucking...watched. I..." He spun in place before making his way to the coffee maker. In one broad sweep of his arm, the three mugs on the counter's surface flew, shattering on the concrete floor as ceramic splinters spewed in all directions.

In no time, I was up and in front of him.

My brother-in-law was a large man—not heavy, not an ounce of fat. He was made of muscle and even taller than me. Before his transformation, he was intimidating. After, he could be considered terrifying. It worked for him when he made his living on the dark web. A wolf in sheep's clothing. His face could be considered handsome. It was what was beneath the facade that kept him gainfully employed. It also didn't hurt in his current role as a Sparrow leader either. A fucking phoenix who rose from the literal ashes, if death couldn't stop him, nothing could.

"You were eleven years old. It wasn't your job."

Rage roared, glowing like a warning siren in his green stare. "What did that motherfucker do?"

I shook my head. "I don't know. I gather, he didn't penetrate."

"That leaves a lot open to the imagination that I don't

want to think about." Mason's cowboy boots crunched shards of broken mugs as he stepped, and his chest inflated and deflated with each breath. "She never told me. I would have killed the bastard."

"That's probably why she never said anything. I'm no expert at what she's going through, but I think what happened with Jettison and seeing your mother's body brought back the earlier memories." I shook my head. "Man, I've been married to her for nine years, and I never got the feeling she had...someone had..." I took a deep breath, suddenly questioning everything over the past nine years. I looked at Mason. "I mean, is it fucking possible to bury a memory so deep that even you forget it?"

His gaze met mine. "Yeah, it's possible." He looked to my keyboard. "Find out if that piece of shit is alive. I'm fucking twenty-five years late, but I'm paying him a visit."

"Not alone you're not."

LORNA

*T*he bed dipped, pulling me from my slumber. Unlike nights before, I didn't recall dreaming. It was as if once I finally closed my eyes, I simply faded into the dark abyss.

"Lorna."

Reid's call floated through my consciousness.

Without opening my eyes, I turned toward him and inhaled. The aroma of my husband's cologne mixed with his bodywash was clean and fresh. But that wasn't what I inhaled.

Trepidation infiltrated my serenity. Backing away from an unfamiliar stench, I held my breath as my mind sought to identify the rank odors.

Cigarettes and liquor.

"You're a pretty girl. Open your eyes and mouth, Lorna."

The increase in my pulse sounded a warning siren.

"No," I screamed as I scrambled across the big bed,

moving as if it were covered with the thousands of ants from my captivity. My heart raced as I fought the blankets and sheets tangled around my body. "Let go."

Still bound by the bedding, I slipped, falling and landing with a thud to the rug below. My feet kicked as I fought the restraint. "No."

I will fuck you in the ass.

I continued to kick as the bindings slipped away.

My eyes sprang open as with shaking hands I pulled the fallen sheet to my breast. Trembling from head to toe, I searched my surroundings. There was no cell and no man. I'd heard the dark-haired man, and yet...as I took ragged breaths, he was gone. I searched the corners of our room, the shadows, for that was where dark hid.

The door to our bathroom flew open, flooding our room with artificial light.

Standing in the doorframe, in his most Adonis-like form, was my husband. A cloud of fresh bodywash filtered into the bedroom, taking away unfamiliar scents as water dripped from his hair and handsome face and down his toned torso and muscular legs. Each drop glistened from the bright bathroom lights, creating sparkling diamonds on his skin. His wide chest expanded and contracted as he took deep breaths in rushed gulps. His arms were spread as he held tightly to the door and frame.

With his dark brown eyes staring my way, he asked, "Lorna, what the fuck?"

My chin sunk to my chest, as confusion settled over me.

His footsteps came closer as he squatted down in front of me.

I lifted my eyes from his toes on the soft rug. The way the water droplets clung to his skin had me mesmerized. My gaze moved higher to his bent legs and stalled as I took in what was between those legs—his cock, impressive even in rest.

Reid cupped my chin and lifted my face toward his. "Hey, sweetheart, my eyes are up here."

My eyes closed as I leaned into his hand. Pulling me to his chest, Reid's arms surrounded me. The trembling that had accompanied my waking ceased at the sound of his voice as I relished the comfort of his embrace. When he pushed me to arm's length, my eyes were glassy. "I'm sorry." I sniffled at my weakness. "You must think I'm a basket case."

Reid stood and offered me his hand. "I think you're remarkable, Lorna. Never doubt that."

Once on my feet, I straightened the nightshirt I'd worn to bed, trying to remember what had caused me to fright. As I slowly turned, taking in our bedroom, I couldn't recall exactly what had happened.

"Will you talk to me?" he asked as I sat on the edge of our bed.

"I wish I could." I sighed, laying my hands in my lap. "I feel like I slept well and then as I was waking...it was you, but it wasn't you."

"I was in the shower."

A grin came to my lips as my cheeks rose. "I figured that out from the water." I ran my hand over his arm, smearing the diamonds. It was as I stood again and stared into his dark orbs that I saw the dark that was threatening me from the shadows clouding his eyes.

Disappointment.

Sadness.

Unease.

I couldn't pinpoint the emotions, but I knew what caused them. Not what. Who.

It was me.

"Reid, I'm sorry. I don't want you to worry about me."

His large palm came gently to my cheek. "Remember that day I asked you to marry me?"

As I lifted my left hand, seeing the diamond ring he later gave me, the scene came back. Despite what had recently happened to Mason, Reid was my Prince Charming. As I was about to leave Chicago for what may have been forever, he charged in. Not on a white horse or wearing a crown. He didn't need props. Even now, unclothed, he was my prince.

I nodded.

"Remember when we said our vows?"

I nodded again.

"I'd already begun worrying about you, Lorna, before either of those events. Worry is part of loving someone. And I love you, Lorna Murray. I have since I saw you at that huge-ass house in New York. The first time I laid eyes on you." He teased a strand of my hair. "I knew you were too good for me. I suspected you were an heiress or royalty."

"I thought the same thing about you."

"An heiress?" he said as a grin curled his full lips. "Really? Was it my dress?"

"Royalty," I clarified, recalling how handsome he was in his tuxedo.

"And then you were here," he went on, "and I knew that even though I wasn't looking for my forever, it had found me. I've never stopped loving you. I never will and hell, yes, I will worry. And I will do whatever I can to not only keep you safe, but more importantly, so that once again, you can feel safe."

"I should. I mean, this tower is a fortress."

He ran the pad of his finger over my cheek. "Even in a fortress, I'll worry."

"I know what you mean. I worry about you too. I know what you do is dangerous, and I don't want to add to that. I'm fine. I'm still working through flashes." A cold chill came to my skin. "I-I think I remember a cell-like room and a dark-haired man. I was fighting him." My head shook as I closed my eyes. "I just don't know."

"How about we eat breakfast here alone?"

"Are you embarrassed by my hair?"

Reid's smile bloomed. "Hell no. I can't wait to fuck a brunette."

Something so crass shouldn't make me smile, really smile, but it did. And as I did, the dark shadows slithered away. I knew they weren't gone. They would linger out of sight, not leaving me until they pulled me in, but for now, my husband was my lifeline and I was holding on with all my might.

I lifted my arms to his wide shoulders. "I'm free right now."

"I guess that invitation depends on your answer about breakfast. If we're going upstairs—"

My lips covered his before I reached for the hem of my nightshirt and pulled it over my head. The cooler air beaded my nipples as Reid scanned me from head to toe.

"Panties," he said with a smirk. "Either they go or I rip them off."

My fingers snagged the waistband, and I pushed them down, over my thighs, my knees, and to my ankles until I kicked them away.

Reid reached for my hand, lifting it and spinning me as if I were the dancer in a child's jewelry box or we were dancing at that ball so many years ago. Instead of a gown and tuxedo, we were both completely nude. As I came to a stop, he ran his long finger along my collarbone, sending shivers scampering over my skin. "You're stunningly beautiful no matter the color of your hair."

I couldn't be sure if I led our dance or Reid was in the lead. We'd completed this waltz too many times not to anticipate each other's steps. As his fingers wove through my hair, tilting my head and deepening our kiss, we moved from the floor to our large bed. Once there, his kisses continued, not only on my lips, but peppering my skin as more words of adoration filled my ears.

I ran my hands over his muscles, feeling the indentations and the way they bulged as he moved. In between his loving words, his talented mouth sucked and nipped my nipples until each hardened and my breasts throbbed with rerouted circulation.

They weren't alone.

By the time Reid made his way to my core, I was slick with anticipation and needy for more of what he could give.

Now fully in the lead—the choreographer of our dance—Reid rolled me to my stomach, up onto my knees, and directed my hands to the headboard. Slowly, he teased, as his freshly showered body enveloped mine. His front to my back, my flesh tingled as I was lost in the fog of his fresh scent and his muscular body. Even before we became one, we were melded together.

I whimpered and moaned as he skillfully teased my core, assuring himself of my readiness. It was bliss and torture. Finally, I could no longer contain my wanton desire. "Please, Reid."

Bracing myself, I held to the headboard as his cock plunged between my folds. I called out as he found my entrance and thrust deep within. My back arched and my core clenched as we became one. Gripping tighter, my fingers blanched as I held on and with increased rhythm, he probed in and out. The friction within me built as his large hands held securely to my hips. Each movement was heaven as I became lost in the sensations within me.

My pleasure built. Such as bringing heat to water, the growing temperature radiated through my body until the once-still water rolled. No longer simmering, radiant heat burst like mini explosions within my veins. The heated contents rapidly flowed throughout my circulation until no part of me was left untouched.

Unable to maintain my grasp, my fingers loosened, and my

forehead fell to the pillows below. As my body continued to convulse, Reid too found his release, filling me in every way.

When we were no longer one, I rolled to my back, nose to nose with the man I loved and adored. He teased a strand of my new shorter hair away from my face. "I'm sorry someone hurt you."

I lifted my palm to his freshly shaved cheek. "It wasn't you."

"I never want to remind you...if I ever..." His Adam's apple bobbed.

"I wasn't raped."

He nodded as his forehead fell to mine. "You're always safe with me."

"I know that. I always have."

He rolled to my side.

"I've never thought about it," I began, "I guess I" —my head shook— "I had a flash of a man, a white man with jet-black hair. The room was cold like a jail cell."

Reid lifted his head. "Recent memory or old?"

"Recent," I replied, not completely sure what he meant by old. I reached for his hand and intertwined our fingers. "You." I swallowed and looked from our hands to his face. "I fell in love with you for so many reasons. I think part of it was how different you are."

"More than this?" he said lifting our hands, their total dissimilarity on display. One light and the other dark. One large and the other small.

"I never knew a good man," I said, moving my gaze back to Reid's. "I knew my brother, but he will always be my brother. But men, they..." I refused to fall into a rabbit hole I couldn't navigate. I smiled up at Reid. "You, Reid Murray, were nothing like any man I ever knew. Yes, you were much handsomer."

He grinned.

"But it wasn't just your appearance. You have never treated me...assumed or insisted. You've been patient and kind. It's not just with me. I watch you with everyone. You're quiet, deliberate, and thoughtful. You're so smart, but you don't make me feel inferior. You listen when I speak—when anyone does. I never knew anyone like you."

Lying back on the pillow, my husband reached for my arms and pulled me to his chest. "Lorna, I love you." A grin came to my lips at the way his chest vibrated under my cheek.

"I love you, too."

REID

*a*fter Lorna's shower, I had breakfast ready for her in our own apartment. My cooking skills were minimal, but I could handle scrambled eggs, toast, fruit, and coffee. As I began to cook, I sent Madeline a text message, asking if she would mind cooking for everyone in the penthouse this morning without Lorna. Of course, she responded she'd be happy to, followed by questions about Lorna. I told her Lorna had overslept. It wasn't completely inaccurate, perhaps misleading.

My wife had awakened. We'd just spent a little more time in bed than on a normal morning.

Cleaning up our dishes, I smiled at seeing my wife's hair.

"What?" she asked, running her fingers through the chin-length ends.

"I think you're beautiful."

"How was it fucking a brunette?" she asked, lifting her coffee cup to hide her seductive grin.

"Much better than the last time."

"Wait. What?" She set her cup down on the breakfast bar. "Oh no. If this hair color reminds you of someone else, I'll be a redhead before you get back from downstairs for dinner."

Going around the counter, I reached for her waist, spun the tall stool, and brought our noses together. "I'm teasing you."

"I like you teasing. You haven't been in much of a jovial mood lately."

"Oh, sweetheart, I'm not, but I'm closer. Your comment about the dark-haired man and the cold room—Araneae remembered the same. And it matches what the forensics team found as well as the man we had on satellite. Mason and I are working on something else too. My mood will improve after a few other people's worsen."

Lorna reached for my hand. "I don't need or want a head."

"How about a finger?"

She let go. "Gross. No."

"Are you going upstairs to the penthouse?" I asked.

"Yeah, I want to see everyone. I'm not sure how I'll explain this." She again fluffed the sides of her hair.

"Don't."

"Oh, you don't know them like I do. They'll want answers."

"Tell them you were fulfilling my fantasy." That wasn't a lie. "Tell them I was dying to fuck a brunette." That part was an exaggeration.

Lorna playfully swatted my chest. "I think I can come up with something better. And I'll probably talk to Araneae about what she remembers."

"We'd rather you don't."

"Why?" she asked.

"We don't want her memories to confuse yours or vice versa."

Lorna sighed and reached again for her coffee mug. "Can I talk with Laurel about them?"

I nodded. The phone in my pocket vibrated again. It had been vibrating on and off since we started eating.

"Go," Lorna said. "I'm fine. Do what you do and come back. Maybe I'll be blonde tonight."

After giving her a kiss, I told her what I promised would never change. "I love you."

"I love you too. Come back."

"You can't keep me away."

Leaving our apartment, I took my phone from my pocket and walked toward the elevator. From the number on the screen, I'd missed six text messages and a call from Mason. Before I'd come back to the apartment to shower, Mason and I had located Gordon Maples. We planned to pay him a visit.

I hit the call button, returning his call.

Mason answered right away. "We were getting worried. Is Lorna all right?"

"She seems better."

"It's weird for her not to be at breakfast."

My cheeks rose. "We decided to take the morning slow."

"Good."

"Are you ready to go?" I asked.

"Come to 2 first. Everyone is here."

Fuck.

I would concentrate on everyone and everything better after we paid Maples a visit.

However, experience told me that there was no fighting my near future. If Sparrow, Patrick, and Mason were assembled on 2, mine was the empty chair. I would fill it.

Entering the elevator, I hit 2.

Nearly a minute later, I scanned my hand and the steel door moved.

Three sets of eyes met mine. Patrick and Sparrow were dressed in their usual Michigan Avenue finest. Mason's attire was improved over our middle-of-the-night work session. It appeared we were all showered and ready for the day. My glance went toward the coffee machine. The earlier mess was gone. Mason and I had cleaned it and replaced the mugs.

I stopped and looked at Sparrow. "Sorry, Lorna—"

He lifted his hand, stopping my apology. "I get it. I wasn't here last night when you were all working. I'm not thrilled about going downtown today."

"How is Araneae?"

"Better since she's talked about things."

"You?" I asked.

"Still seeing fucking red. I want to locate Jettison yesterday, and I want to find out who the woman is."

"Woman?" I looked around.

Sparrow went on. "Araneae remembers a woman. Blonde

and petite. She said she was in charge. There was the man with dark black hair—"

"Lorna remembers him too."

"Araneae said she thinks there were other men, but she can't remember specifics."

"Did she see Nancy?" Mason asked.

"Not that she mentioned."

"I've got a call out to Top," Mason said. "It's the second one I've sent. When we met, he was confident this wasn't the Order. There have been very few soldiers to go rogue on the Order, but I knew one. So did Laurel."

Patrick stood. "Stephanie? What was her name...Moore?"

"Real name, Morehead," I said. "She was the one who tracked Laurel and her research."

"Yeah," Patrick said, "but she died in the fire at your house."

"I thought so, too."

"No," Sparrow said, "I remember Walters saying they recovered her body." He looked at Patrick. "Can you pull up the audio on that meeting a few years ago?"

"Yes."

Sparrow looked at his watch. "Listen, I'm booked until about three. Keep me informed, but if you have a lead, move on it. I'm tired of this shit. And if the same people who are supplying guns on my streets are the ones who took the women, they need to go down."

My gaze met Mason's. Just as quickly, Sparrow pointed our direction. "No rogue shit. Keep me informed. Keep Patrick informed."

"No rogue shit," Mason said.

I looked at Patrick. "Where are you headed?"

"I have a list and I'm taking Romero with me. Sparrow has Garrett. First, I'm headed downtown to Sinful Threads. Jana has prototypes for Araneae. Then, I'm following up with the capos who went to Dino's last night. Their report isn't as informative as I'd like. Either they'll give me more, or I'll go to the source."

"Take more backup," Sparrow said. When no one spoke, he went on. "If whoever they are figure out that we're on to them, things could get fucking crazy. No chances."

Patrick nodded. "I'll make calls." He looked at us. "Are you two following leads here? Mason, we need you to scour the dark web. My gut is telling me that's where the factions are connecting to this supplier."

"Mostly," he replied. "I have a few loose ends on the near South Side, and Reid is coming with me. We'll be back before lunch and work on leads."

"Take backup," Sparrow said as he walked toward the door looking at his phone and shaking his head. "I'd fucking fire my assistant if I—"

"Could get anyone else to put up with you?" Mason offered, finishing his sentence.

When Sparrow glared, Mason added, "I mean, you've found the only two women who can keep you in place. I'd say there aren't many more options."

"Keep *me* in place?"

"No, definitely the other way around," Patrick said as he smiled at Mason and me.

After Mason and I were alone, my brother-in-law exhaled. "Listen, I know we have other shit, but I am itching to meet up with that son of a bitch Maples."

"Let's go."

REID

"He still lives in the same house?" I asked as Mason drove us closer to our destination. Craning my neck, I looked back at the car behind us. "You didn't want those Sparrows in our car?"

"Yes, same house," he responded. "And no. I didn't want anyone hearing even a word that may be said about my sister."

"I wasn't planning on saying any."

"Wrong," he said, his grip tightening on the steering wheel. "You are. I want to know what I'm accusing this man of before I cut his fucking throat."

That's a messy way to kill someone.

"Did you call for a cleanup crew?"

"I did." His stare turned my way. "It seems too easy. Kader was his own crew. Either way, this fucker is going to pay for what he did."

"Well, fuck." I exhaled, leaning against the leather seat of the reinforced SUV and feeling the gun I had holstered near my side. "I have no issue with retaliation if it is due. Lorna hasn't said his name. She acted confused when I asked her if the memories were recent or older."

"You said that she said she wasn't *her*. She wasn't Anna."

I nodded as Mason pulled the SUV right toward an exit. Soon we were leaving I-94 onto city streets. The sign caught my attention. "Fuck, this is Englewood."

"Yeah."

"The same location as Dino's liquor store."

"How the fuck could this all be connected?"

"Maybe it isn't."

I stared out the windshield at the colorful, tree-lined roadway leading into an older neighborhood. Many of the houses appeared well maintained while others were more dilapidated. The GPS on our dashboard directed our way until we came to a stop on the side of a residential street.

"That one," Mason said, pointing to a less-maintained older white two-story house. "See that window up in the gable?"

"Above the second floor?"

"Yeah, that's where we slept. It's an attic. No fucking insulation. Hell, rarely a light. It was cold as a witch's tit in the winter. We moved in during the autumn. Thankfully, we'd left before summer hit."

"There weren't enough rooms in the house?"

"No, there were. Maples's room was on the first floor. We weren't allowed in there. The second floor had three or four others. I don't remember. He didn't want us using the rooms.

We slept in the attic like fucking mice, making beds out of discarded clothes and blankets. I'd cut his throat for that alone and sleep like a baby tonight."

The other Sparrow vehicle parked behind us.

Compared to the other cars on the street, our newer models stood out like sore thumbs.

"Let's do this," I said, reaching for the handle.

"Just a minute." Mason pulled out his phone and accessed an app we'd created. He could see the location of our men. We'd done as Sparrow said and secured backup. We had two Sparrows on foot in the alley behind the house and two others in another vehicle across the street.

Mason typed out a message.

"There, we're all on the same page." Mason turned to me. "I'm going to make him confess."

"I won't stop you."

"Just go with it. I promise, it's worked before."

Considering his life as Kader, my agreement could be for a wide range of plans.

The car doors slammed as we both stepped from the cab. I walked around the front of the SUV and met Mason on the street. For only a moment, we both stared up at that third-floor window. Seeing it tugged at my chest.

My Lorna deserved a castle, not a fucking attic.

"I used to climb out of there to get us food," Mason said.

Seeing the house caused the rage within me to simmer. Each consecutive bit of information added heat. The simmer was nearing the boiling point.

Together we stepped up onto the porch. A television

playing some sort of talk show sounded from behind the closed door. Mason stepped forward to knock.

We waited as I tried to assess the sounds from within.

"He lives alone?"

"Never saw where he married," Mason replied.

A woman not much older but more haggard than both of us came to the door. Her dirty oversized shirt hung from her thin frame. Her legs were covered with leggings with holes in the knees and runs. Despite the cool autumn morning, her feet were bare. On her hip was a baby in what my nose told me was a dirty diaper. I wasn't a good judge of age; the kid was maybe nine or ten months. The woman's gaze first came to me. Her lips made a straight line as she scanned me up and down.

That's right. There's a black man at your door, and if my fucking thoughts were confirmed, I'd bulldoze this dump—a little Forest Gump *on you.*

"What do you want?" she finally asked.

"I'm here for Gordon Maples," Mason said.

Her eyes went to him.

With his scars and tattoos covered, he could be almost handsome.

"Why?"

"He won a million dollars."

Without moving a muscle, I internally snickered. I'd never questioned Mason about his years as a mercenary, but I had a hard time imagining it was this easy. Then again, taking down an international terrorist wasn't the same as gutting a child predator.

"Dad," she called, yelling behind her. "Some men are here. You won something."

She opened the door wider as the volume of the TV grew louder, and an elderly man hobbled our direction. Much like his daughter, his clothes were dirty and stained. I tried to look away from his pants.

Shit, had he wet himself?

"What?" he asked, his voice raised over the television as he came closer.

His yellowed teeth, raspy voice, and shaking hands were clues that he was a contributor to the lingering stench of tobacco and alcohol that seemed to permeate from the paneling and carpet.

"I didn't enter no contest," he said, steadying himself by holding the door.

Mason looked at his phone. "Are you Gordon Maples?" He then rattled off his birth date.

"Yeah, but—"

"Your name," Mason interrupted, "was entered by a..." He paused, appearing thoughtful as he scrolled. "Oh, here it is. ...by a Nancy Pierce."

The man's gray eyes widened as he yelled, "Turn off that damned TV." He turned back to us, his tone now skeptical. "When did she do that?"

"Sir, our contest never expires. I can't see here when you were entered, but if you want to turn down your prize" — Mason reached for my arm— "we'll leave." My brother-in-law looked at me. "Tell them to rip up the check."

"I'll do—" I began.

"Wait." Mr. Maples opened the door wider. "What did I win?"

"May we come in?" Mason asked.

Maples didn't look at him, but his eyes were on me. "Both of you?"

"Yes, sir," Mason answered. "It's a condition of our company. We don't want any unsubstantiated claims."

Maples opened the door wider with a grunt.

The overpowering stench of the house hit my nose with more impact as we stepped through the threshold. As I looked around at the old paneling, the stairs headed up, and the worn furniture, it took every bit of self-control not to wrinkle my nose. Knowing Mason and Lorna had lived in this dump hurt my heart. My mother, grandmother, and I moved to a smaller home after my father died, but never had we lived in filth.

"We need to verify a few things," Mason began. He nodded toward a dining room table. Or I believed that was what it was somewhere below the mess. The surface was piled high with stacks of papers, newspapers, magazines.

Hey dude, the world has gone paperless. Try it.

Maples led us that direction.

As Mason pulled out a chair, he continued the farce. "So you confirm that you, Gordon Maples, are familiar with Nancy Pierce?"

"Yeah, I knew her."

"Knew her?" Mason asked as I cleared a chair and also sat.

"Yeah." Maples's eyes were on me as if I may steal a two-week-old newspaper. "Why is he here?"

"This is my associate," Mason answered. "And he's as invested in this visit as I am. Isn't that right?"

Oh, the question was to me. "Or more so."

"Now," Mason looked back to Maples, "back to the entry. It's invalid if you haven't had contact with Ms. Pierce in the last sixty months." Mason started to stand. "We're sorry to have inconvenienced you."

Maples stood. "No, wait. Yeah, I've seen her."

"In the last sixty months."

"Well...." He seemed puzzled at the time frame.

"Five years," I volunteered.

"Yeah. She lived here."

"In the last five years?" Mason confirmed.

"Off and on for fucking ever."

"You supported her?"

"Yeah. No. Mostly a place to crash. She was back on the street after the payments from some rich dude ended."

Mason's and my eyes met.

Rich dude.

Why was Nancy Pierce getting payments?

Maples waved. "Don't matter. I saw her in" —he looked my way— "the last five years. I'm sure."

Mason looked around. "Who besides your daughter and grandchild live here?"

"Ain't my grandkid; he's my son. It fucking took a while. Damn girls all over. But finally, I got me a boy."

Mason's stare came my way as my stomach rolled.

"Congratulations," Mason replied. "Who besides your daughter and son are here? Maybe the boy's mother?"

"That's her. It's just them."

Bile rose higher in my throat.

"Is that everyone?" Mason maintained his persona.

"No, my fucking butler is in the kitchen."

Maples laughed, looking behind him. From my vantage, what he referred to as the kitchen was overrun with trash and dirty dishes. No longer contained to the counter, there was a path through the debris.

"Just them," he said.

"What is your daughter's name?"

"Zella."

"Could you call her?" Mason asked.

"What about?"

"The contest."

"Zella," Maples yelled, "get your ass down here."

The sound of a crying baby grew louder as footsteps were heard over our head.

"Damn kid cries all the time."

"Congratulations on a son," I said.

When Zella appeared, the baby on her hip was stripped to the waist, wearing only a diaper. My nose told me it was now clean. "What, Dad?"

Mason reached into his pocket and pulled out a money clip. "Zella, we need confirmation of your father's identity to issue his prize. All I need you to do is to go to the bank and get a photocopy of his account information so we can transfer the money."

"Can't we do that online?" Maples asked. "Got me an iPad somewhere."

Of course he does.

Mason's head tilted. "You know, this contest has been around for so long the rules are archaic."

Maples looked at Zella. "Take him and go to the bank over by the beauty college. Marcy there will know me."

"If you have problems," Mason volunteered, "just call your dad." He handed her a one-hundred-dollar bill.

"What's this for?" she asked.

"For you, honey. For your trouble."

Her eyes opened wide. "Really?"

"Go," Maples instructed. "And before you walk there, ask Mrs. Stephens to watch little Gordy."

"Dad, I can—"

His tone was more insistent. "Take him to Mrs. Stephens. Maybe Darrell's home."

Tucking her chin, Zella nodded and hurried through the kitchen and out what I assumed was the back door.

Once the door slammed, Mason stood. "Let me introduce myself."

REID

"*I* haven't seen her," Maples repeated as Mason's knife cut another notch in his wrist.

"Next one will be deeper," Mason said. "Poor Zella, she's going to find you dead. If she can find anything in this shithole. I wonder if she'll be more distraught over your death or at not winning the million dollars."

Maples was now bound to the dining room chair where he'd sat nearly fifteen minutes earlier, his arms tethered to the chair's arms and his legs secured to the chair's legs.

"Who is the rich guy?" Mason asked.

"Hernádez, Garcia, Roríguez. Shit, some brown..." His beady eyes came my way. "Not like you, boy. You know...a Mexican. Not sure what we're supposed to call them or your kind now days."

As the small hairs on the back of my neck stood to attention, this asshole's poor choice of vocabulary added fuel to the flames of rage that began when I figured out what he'd done to my wife twenty-five years ago. I worked to keep my expression statuesque though it wasn't easy to suppress my enthusiasm for what was about to occur.

"Nancy was getting payments from" —Mason hesitated— "a—"

"Mexican," I said, finishing his sentence using Maples's words.

Missy was Latina. This had to be the connection. It was the only plausible explanation. "Why was Nancy getting payments from a Mexican?"

"He don't live there...he lives here. But she made some deal with him. He paid until...well, eighteen."

Mason's knife went to Maples's neck. "What is his name?"

Maples stretched his neck, backing away from the blade. "I can't—"

Mason pushed the blade against his sagging skin until a crimson drop of blood dribbled to his dirty, worn collar. "Wait. It was Garcia. Yeah, I'm sure."

Mason pushed the blade deeper. "Tell me what this has to do with my sister."

Maples's gray eyes narrowed. "The brown one or the pretty one with red hair?"

My fist landed in his stomach. "What did you do to Lorna?" I asked as his coughs turned to gagging.

Maples spat as blood dripped from his lip. "The payments were for the other one, but oh, that redheaded one was downright sweet. She had the softest little hands. And her lips—"

My next punch connected to his jaw.

He spat more blood and this time a front tooth. "Don't know why you're mad. She wanted it. We were friends and she liked my attention. All little girls like to hear they're special." He looked at me. "Oh shit. Are you fucking her now? Damn, I wanted that tight pussy. Is it still tight or saggy like her mother's?"

There was no conscious train of thought. I didn't consider the ramifications. For once, I wasn't thinking steps ahead. Taking Mason's knife from his grasp, I plunged it deep in Maples's upper arm.

It wouldn't kill him immediately.

"What did you do to her?" I asked again.

His words sputtered as blood mixed with his oxygen. "Nothing she didn't want. Just like her momma."

I looked at the blade in my hand, dripping with deep red blood. "This is for my wife," I said as I pushed the blade through his ratty shirt, above his belt and sliced laterally, as deep as the blade would go.

Maples's eyes widened as he watched organs and tissue roll from his wound.

There were moments of consciousness before death. It was his only time to make amends with a superior being or beg for his life, not that we could save it now, but he didn't. The vile creature stared at both of us.

Mason's eyes met mine before he took back the knife, and buried the blade into Maples's upper leg. Blood spouted as his body convulsed. We both stepped back as the asshole bled out before us.

His time for amends had expired.

"I would have been okay with him enjoying more of the experience," I said. "You know, since he was such a good friend to Lorna."

Mason took a deep breath before disappearing into the kitchen and returning with two towels. He handed one to me.

"Call the cleanup crew," I said as I wiped my hands on the towel. "After this is done, we're bulldozing this place. Too much shit happened here."

Mason nodded as he sent a text. Once he was done, he reached for the knife, wiped the blade on the towel, removed a leather sheath from his pocket, and reinserted the knife. Next, he put the knife back in his pocket. "What? It was a gift."

His casualness made me grin.

I took one last look at Gordon Maples. As grotesque as it sounded, the sight of him gave me my first glimmer of light. I would make this world safe again for Lorna. Killing this disgusting creature was only the first step.

Together Mason and I turned and walked toward the front door.

I'll bulldoze every last splinter.

The hinges creaked as Mason opened the front door inward and we stepped onto the porch. Scanning the scene, I saw our SUV across the street and one of our Sparrows nearby on the sidewalk.

It was as we proceeded toward the stairs to the walkway that the bang of a screen door hitting a house across the street caught my attention. I barely had time to register the chain of events that followed.

The first to step from the house across the street was Zella. She wasn't at the bank as she'd been told, but on that porch, her baby still on her hip. Next, a tall man came into view, exiting the house behind her.

Slow motion as in the movies was a cinematic illusion. In reality, the clock didn't slow, it accelerated. There wasn't time to register details. Things I'd been trained to recall such as the man's characteristics or identity were merely a blur.

"Watch out..." I began to shout as the man behind Zella lifted a long shotgun and pointed it in our direction. With my reflexes on high alert and without conscious thought, my hand moved, reaching for my gun, freeing it from the holster.

Out of the corner of my eye, I saw Mason crouched behind the porch's railing with his pistol already aimed. Our backup Sparrows flew into action. One on the street ducked behind a car and pointed his gun toward the man. Another stepped from the side of the porch, his firearm aimed.

Don't hit the baby.

That was one of my many thoughts as shots rang from different directions. The air filled with pops and bangs—multiple explosions—as if a pack of firecrackers left behind from an Independence Day celebration had been ignited.

And then...

It wasn't the impact of the bullet that I felt as much as it was the way its thrust propelled my body backward toward the open doorway. I reached for the doorframe. Crimson from my palm painted the jamb as my grip loosened, sliding down toward the floor as my knees gave way. Collapsing in the threshold of the home that had caused Lorna too much pain, light disappeared.

"Reid." Mason's voice came and went.

Dark claimed another victory.

Thank you for reading *DARK*...find out what happens next in the dramatic conclusion of Reid and Lorna's story, *DAWN*.

Pre-order your copy today by clicking on the link.

If you enjoyed *DARK* and want to know more about our other Sparrow men, *Web of Sin*, Sterling and Araneae's story is complete with *SECRETS* (FREE), *LIES*, and *PROMISES*.

Mason and Laurel's story is also complete in *Tangled Web*, with *TWISTED, OBSESSED*, and *BOUND*.

And Patrick and Madeline's story is complete in *Web of Desire*, with *SPARK, FLAME*, and *ASHES*.

It's time to binge Sparrow Webs!

ACKNOWLEDGMENTS

A special thank you to my beta readers: Sherry, Angie, Val, Ilona, and Mr.Jeff, my editor, Lisa Aurello, and my sensitivity readers, Renita McKinney and Yulanda Bolton for their dedication to my Sparrow Web world, the array of characters, and to making Reid and Lorna's story the best it can be.

You are all greatly appreciated. Please know I couldn't do this without you.

Thank you.

WHAT TO DO NOW

LEND IT: Did you enjoy DARK? Do you have a friend who'd enjoy DARK? DARK may be lent one time. Sharing is caring!

RECOMMEND IT: Do you have multiple friends who'd enjoy my dark romance with twists and turns and an all new sexy and infuriating anti-hero? Tell them about it! Call, text, post, tweet...your recommendation is the nicest gift you can give to an author!

REVIEW IT: Tell the world. Please go to the retailer where you purchased this book, as well as Goodreads, and write a review. Please share your thoughts about DARK on:

*Amazon, DARK Customer Reviews

*Barnes & Noble, DARK, Customer Reviews

*iBooks, DARK Customer Reviews

* BookBub, DARK Customer Reviews

*Goodreads.com/Aleatha Romig

BOOKS BY NEW YORK TIMES BESTSELLING AUTHOR ALEATHA ROMIG

NEW STORY COMING:

DEVIL'S DEAL

Coming May 2121

THE SPARROW WEBS:

DANGEROUS WEB:

DUSK

Releasing Nov, 2020

DARK

Releasing 2021

DAWN

Releasing 2021

WEB OF DESIRE:

SPARK

Released Jan. 14, 2020

FLAME

Released February 25, 2020

ASHES

Released April 7, 2020

TANGLED WEB:

TWISTED

Released May, 2019

OBSESSED

Released July, 2019

BOUND

Released August, 2019

WEB OF SIN:

SECRETS

Released October, 2018

LIES

Released December, 2018

PROMISES

Released January, 2019

THE INFIDELITY SERIES:

BETRAYAL

Book #1

Released October 2015

CUNNING

Book #2

Released January 2016

DECEPTION

Book #3

Released May 2016

ENTRAPMENT

Book #4

Released September 2016

FIDELITY

Book #5

Released January 2017

THE CONSEQUENCES SERIES:

CONSEQUENCES

(Book #1)

Released August 2011

TRUTH

(Book #2)

Released October 2012

CONVICTED

(Book #3)

Released October 2013

REVEALED

(Book #4)

Previously titled: Behind His Eyes Convicted: The Missing Years

Re-released June 2014

BEYOND THE CONSEQUENCES

(Book #5)

Released January 2015

RIPPLES

Released October 2017

CONSEQUENCES COMPANION READS:

BEHIND HIS EYES-CONSEQUENCES

Released January 2014

BEHIND HIS EYES-TRUTH

Released March 2014

~

STAND ALONE MAFIA THRILLER:

PRICE OF HONOR

Available Now

~

THE LIGHT DUET:

Published through Thomas and Mercer Amazon exclusive

INTO THE LIGHT

Released June, 2016

AWAY FROM THE DARK

Released October, 2016

~

TALES FROM THE DARK SIDE SERIES:

INSIDIOUS

(All books in this series are stand-alone erotic thrillers)

Released October 2014

~

ALEATHA'S LIGHTER ONES:

PLUS ONE

Stand-alone fun, sexy romance

May 2017

ANOTHER ONE

Stand-alone fun, sexy romance

May 2018

ONE NIGHT

Stand-alone, sexy contemporary romance

September 2017

A SECRET ONE

April 2018

INDULGENCE SERIES:

UNEXPECTED

Released August, 2018

UNCONVENTIONAL

Released January, 2018

UNFORGETTABLE

Released October, 2019

UNDENIABLE

Coming late summer 2020

ABOUT THE AUTHOR

Aleatha Romig is a New York Times, Wall Street Journal, and USA Today bestselling author who lives in Indiana, USA. She has raised three children with her high school sweetheart and husband of over thirty years. Before she became a full-time author, she worked days as a dental hygienist and spent her nights writing. Now, when she's not imagining mind-blowing twists and turns, she likes to spend her time with her family and friends. Her other pastimes include reading and creating heroes/anti-heroes who haunt your dreams!

Aleatha impresses with her versatility in writing. She released her first novel, CONSEQUENCES, in August of 2011. CONSEQUENCES, a dark romance, became a bestselling series with five novels and two companions released from 2011 through 2015. The compelling and epic story of Anthony and Claire Rawlings has graced more than half a million e-readers. Her first stand-alone smart, sexy thriller INSIDIOUS was next. Then Aleatha released the five-novel INFIDELITY series, a romantic suspense saga, that took the reading world by storm, the final book landing on three of the top bestseller lists. She ventured into traditional publishing with Thomas and Mercer. Her books INTO THE LIGHT and AWAY FROM THE DARK were published through this mystery/thriller publisher in 2016. In the spring of 2017, Aleatha again ventured into a different genre with her first fun and sexy stand-alone romantic comedy with the USA Today bestseller PLUS ONE. She continued with ONE NIGHT and ANOTHER ONE. If you like fun, sexy, novellas that make your heart pound, try her UNCONVENTIONAL and UNEXPECTED. In 2018 Aleatha returned to her dark romance roots with SPARROW WEBS.

Aleatha is a "Published Author's Network" member of the Romance Writers of America and PEN America. She is represented by Kevan Lyon of Marsal Lyon Literary Agency and Dani Sanchez with Wildfire Marketing.

facebook.com/aleatharomig

twitter.com/aleatharomig

instagram.com/aleatharomig

Made in the USA
Monee, IL
24 January 2021